JOHN DICKSON CARR
Available in Library of Crime Classics® editions.

Dr. Gideon Fell Novels:
BELOW SUSPICION
HAG'S NOOK
HE WHO WHISPERS
THE HOUSE AT SATAN'S ELBOW
THE PROBLEM OF THE GREEN CAPSULE
THE SLEEPING SPHINX
THE THREE COFFINS
TILL DEATH DO US PART

Non-series:
THE BURNING COURT
THE MURDER OF SIR EDMUND GODFREY

WRITING AS CARTER DICKSON
Sir Henry Merrivale Novels:
THE GILDED MAN
HE WOULDN'T KILL PATIENCE
THE JUDAS WINDOW
NINE–AND DEATH MAKES TEN
THE PEACOCK FEATHER MURDERS
THE PUNCH AND JUDY MURDERS
THE READER IS WARNED
THE RED WIDOW MURDERS
THE UNICORN MURDERS

Douglas G. Greene, series consultant

Carter Dickson

the reader is warned

INTERNATIONAL POLYGONICS, LTD.
NEW YORK CITY

THE READER IS WARNED

CONTENTS

Letter from Mr. Lawrence Chase to
Dr. John Sanders.

81 Soane Street,
Lincoln's Inn Fields,
April 26, 1938.

My dear Sanders:
What are you doing this week-end, the 30th? Whatever it
is, I hope I can persuade you to put it off. We should
very much like to have you with us at Fourways; and could
you manage to bring Sir Henry Merrivale as well?

Fourways, as you probably know, is Sam and Mina Constable's place. Sam is a sort of distant relative of mine, and
in any case you'll have heard of Mina. They ask me to ex-
tend the heartiest invitation to you both. The reason is this:
Mina has got hold of a mind-reader.

On my solemn word of honor, this is not a hoax or a joke.
And let not your scientific soul be shocked. The fellow isn't
a music-hall turn. He is a student of some kind. I don't
think he is a fake; at least (so far as my somewhat dazed
intelligence goes) I don't *see* how he can be a fake. Unassuming sort of chap, no fuss and feathers about him. But
he really does seem to read thoughts in a way that will
raise your hair. He's got some sort of theory that Thought is
a physical force, which might be used as a weapon.

It will be a very small party: just Sam and Mina; our
friend the thought-reader, whose name is Pennik; Hilary
Keen; and myself. Hilary Keen is a new gal, a great friend
of mine—so no funny business, see?

Now have I intrigued you, or not? We are making the
week-end from Friday, the 29th. Good train from Charing
Cross, 5.20 to Camberdene. A car will meet you at the sta-
tion. If you can manage it, drop me a line.
Yrs.,
Lawrence Chase

P.S. Is your fair lady, Marcia Blystone, still on that round-
the-world cruise with her parents? I hear all is not well;
hope nothing seriously wrong?

Letter from Dr. John Sanders to
Mr. Lawrence Chase.

Harris Institute,
Bloomsbury St., W.C. 1,
April 27, 1938.

My dear Chase:

Very glad to join you on Friday, but I am afraid it will be impossible for H.M. to be with us. He has to go north on some official business. But he is violently curious about your thought-reader, and promises to get back and at least look in by Sunday, if that will not be too late?

While reserving my own opinion until I have heard the evidence, I must say that if you have quoted him correctly your thought-reader appears to be talking scientific flapdoodle.

Many thanks to Mr. and Mrs. Constable. Charing Cross 5.20 Camberdene.

Yours,
John Sanders

P.S. I do not understand your reference to funny business. Nor to 'all not being well.' Yes, Marcia is still on the cruise. Her last letter was from Honolulu; they have gone on from there to Jamaica; back home in June.

Part I

TWILIGHT:

Concerning a Prophecy Made and Fulfilled

I

ON THE AFTERNOON of Friday, April 29th, Dr. John Sanders traveled down to Surrey by the recommended train.

He had no notion that he was on the eve of the criminal case which would turn the hair of the legal profession as gray as its wings, and upset precedents of both law and medicine. But Sanders was not easy in his mind. Not even the brilliant spring afternoon, with a soft wind and a clear-glowing sky, could allure him. The recommended train was crowded, so that he could not pull a certain letter out of his pocket and study it again as he might study a specimen through a microscope.

Of course, he had nothing to worry about. Marcia Bly-stone, though she might be six thousand miles away in Honolulu, was his fiancée. This world-cruise had been neces-sary because of a small scandal about her father arising out of the Haye murder case. She had not really been too keen to go, though Sanders could not blame her for her un-bounded delight at the prospect. And she wrote frequently. Her letters were informative and sprightly; sometimes, he thought, a little too sprightly. He would have preferred something more on the sentimental side, or even impassioned side. Once—when she was in a sentimental mood in Greece —he did get such a letter, and he walked about for days with his head in the air.

But it did not happen often. And what was actually be-ginning to gnaw at his imagination was the now persistent recurrence, in those letters, of the name of Kessler.

First the reference was casual. 'The passengers as a whole are a foul lot, but we have met one man who seems quite decent; Kessler, I think his name is.' Then presently: 'Mr. Kessler has made this cruise four times, and is able to help us a lot.' And: 'You should have heard Gerald Kessler's

11

description of his experiences with a camel in the Gobi.'
Damn the Gobi and the swank that went therewith. It was
always 'us,' but it became: 'Gerald Kessler was telling us,'
and finally, 'Jerry says.'

Sanders could trace the course of that acquaintanceship
through every sea, as clearly as a ship's officer pins flags
on a map to show the mileage from port to port. Kessler
had begun to haunt him. Kessler's features remained vague,
in spite of a snapshot of him with Marcia at Yokohama:
showing him tall and lounging in white flannels, with a pipe
in his mouth. He could not help endowing Kessler with
vast accomplishments. Back to chilly England, in the days
between December and March, came these tales of warm
waters and colored lanterns, where things seemed more
spacious for being under the almond-blossom. Sanders—examining the innards of a corpse for the Home Office pathologist—was at times badly depressed. Faceless Kessler. Now
they were at Honolulu. Sander's notions of Honolulu were
vague, being chiefly concerned with guitars and people
throwing wreaths round other people's necks. But he could
imagine that its effect on a girl like Marcia Blystone might
be sinister.

Kessler, Kessler, Kessler. Or what about that other fellow,
the one she barely mentioned? Mightn't Kessler be a screen?

Then again there were times when he wondered whether
he might not be losing interest in Marcia. The sight of a
letter beside his plate did not always produce the usual
symptoms. There were times, as he read Marcia's sprightly
and sophisticated descriptions, when he was almost tempted
to say sadly, 'Light of my life, come off it.' His conscience
pointed a stern finger at him for this; but there it was.

Such, then, was his state of mind when he went down to
Fourways, Sam Constable's country house, for the week-end.
It may have been partly responsible for what happened
afterwards—he could never be quite sure.

It was a quarter past six when the train left him at a
wayside station called Camberdene in the vast stillness of
evening. He liked that stillness; he liked the feeling of being
alone; for the first time he felt relaxed. The sky had that
darkening clearness, with something of the quality of polished
glass in it, by which everything seems large and fresh and
new-washed. And the countryside smelled of evening as dis-
tinctively as it smelled of spring. No car had been sent to
meet him, but he did not mind. A stationmaster, whose
voice rose with hollow loudness along the platform, informed
him that he could get no other conveyance there; and that

Fourways was half a mile up the road. He set out to walk it cheerfully, carrying a heavy suitcase.

Fourways, when he found it, could not be called a gem of architecture. The one thing you could say about it was that it managed to look at once massive and yet squeezed-together. It was Victorian Gothic: or, more properly, it started out in a smooth upward run of smooth dark-red brick, rose plainly to a narrow and massive height like the side of a ship, and then sprouted out into small pinnacle-towers, turrets, and gewgaw chimneys. Standing well back in the triangle formed by two sides of a cross-roads, its six or seven acres of ground were surrounded by a tall brick wall which itself must have cost somebody a fortune in the 'eighties.

Whoever built Fourways had wanted privacy, and had got it. Outside the walls at the cross-roads there was an A.A. box and an A.A. man directing traffic. But inside a turn of the path cut you off with trees, until you saw stained-glass windows and tiny balconies ahead.

Dr. Sanders—vastly interested—tramped up the sanded drive to the noise of his own footsteps. There was a flutter in a bird-bath before the door, and a heavy twittering of sparrows round the face of Fourways. Sanders knew nothing of Sam or Mina Constable except that they were great friends of Lawrence Chase; he had no idea why they should want to meet him. Chase, that amiable but sometimes confused young barrister, usually went on the assumption that you knew everything. But it must be confessed that Sanders rather liked their house.

He raised a large iron knocker on the door, and hammered it. The bird-bickering increased, but there was no reply.

After a pause he knocked again, without response. He could hear no footstep or stir of life inside. Coming on top of the absence of a car at the station, it disquieted him with several possibilities: the wrong date, a misunderstanding, a letter gone astray. He hesitated, put down his suitcase, and took a turn that carried him as far as the right-hand side of the house.

A wing, consisting of one large room, was built out from the middle of this side. It was a conservatory as the late nineteenth century knew conservatories: a spacious lounge built of wood, with tall stained-glass windows stretching to the ground, and rounded roof of glass. In this age it looked rich and archaic, stuffed and stuffy. One of the stained-glass windows was pushed halfway up; and to his relief, Sanders

13

heard a voice. It was a woman's voice, speaking above a faint musical noise like running water.

"He's got to go away," the voice said. "You've got to persuade Mina to send him away, Larry. Otherwise there'll be trouble: don't you know that?"

It spoke with such a note of urgency that Sanders stopped involuntarily. Someone else chuckled, and he heard Lawrence Chase's voice.

"What's the matter? Are you afraid he'll read *your* mind?"

"You know, in a way I am," the girl admitted.

Sanders coughed, scuffling his feet on the sanded driveway. Then he crossed the strip of lawn separating the conservatory from the driveway, tapped at the window, and ducked his head inside.

"Good Lord!" said Chase, turning round. A girl in a dark-colored frock got up quickly from her seat by a miniature fountain.

Inside it was even warmer and stuffier that Sanders had expected. Very little light penetrated through the glass dome of the roof, whose edges were heavily gilded. Large plants of a semi-tropical variety, interspersed with ferns and palms, thickened the dimness. The tiny fountain fell with such thin spray that it made only a kind of murmur in the center of a dull-tiled floor thick with rugs. Against this background of the outmoded, a modern portable electric fire made a glow which reflected orange-red in the floor, the spray of the fountain, and the glass roof.

"It's old Sanders," observed Chase, as though incredulous. "Good Lord, look here, I'm sorry about that car. We seem to have started the week-end badly already. By the way, let me present: Dr. Sanders, this is Miss Hilary Keen."

He gave Sanders a significant look, like one who repeats and-no-funny-business, understand? His face, already long, grew longer and more solemn. Lawrence Chase was a long lean young man with an unflurried manner and a genuine talent for the law. The words rolled from his tongue. At the time when this house was built, there was current a phrase which exactly described him: he looked as though he had just stepped out of a band-box. But solemnity was his keynote now.

"Everything is disorganized, I'm afraid," he explained. "That's why you weren't met. We've had an accident."

"An accident?"

"Yes. Mina and Hilary and Sam and I came down by train. So did our thought-reading friend Pennik. But the servants—all four of 'em—were driving down in Sam's car with

14

all the luggage. The luggage was sent on to us; but not the servants, I'm afraid."

"Not the servants? Why not?"

"Well, nobody seems to know. Hodges, that's Sam's chauffeur, evidently tried to take a curve on a hill too fast, and smacked into a lorry this side of Guildford. I don't understand it, because Hodges is the most careful driver I ever rode with."

"You mean they're seriously——"

"Oh, no, nobody is seriously hurt. But bruises and shock at the least of it, that'll keep them there all night anyway. In the meantime, we haven't even got anybody to fry an egg. It's inconvenient. Much more inconvenient for them, of course, poor devils," he added hastily.

"Much more," agreed Hilary Keen. "And *I* can fry an egg. How do you do, Dr. Sanders?"

Sanders had been waiting to acknowledge the introduction. In this semi-gloom it was difficult to see her distinctly. Though she must have been about his own age, in the early thirties, she seemed far younger by reason of a sort of smooth and warm aliveness: an aliveness of body and mind and even voice. It was not that she conveyed the impression of being fragile, but only of being young. She was not a beauty, for she had no personality of beauty. Her blue eyes and dark brown bobbed hair were of such a conventional type that you might not have looked twice at her if it had not been for that aliveness of personality. But, once having looked, you studied her. In addition to this vitality, Sanders had seldom seen a person with more poise, or less restlessness of gesture. She sat by the rim of the fountain, wearing a plain dark frock; and you did not forget her presence.

"Also, she had a very pleasant laugh.

"Odd," Chase was going on in a ruminating tone, "how lonely it seems in a house without servants. Odd—the six of us, shut up here over the week-end, with nobody to run the ship."

"Is it?" inquired Hilary. "What's odd about it?"

Though she took up the challenge instantly, Sanders could sense the same atmosphere which Chase could perhaps not define himself. In a room opening off the conservatory he could hear a clock strike; it was as though the curtains of Fourways muffled them off from the world. Chase hesitated.

"Oh, I don't know. Maybe I'm sharing the general tendency towards the psychic. And then poor old Sam will have a fit if the invaluable Parker isn't here to draw his bath or put in his cufflinks. —Hilary," he added, with a swift and fluent turn of the subject, "is in the same line of business

15

as we are, my lad. She works for the Department of Public Prosecutions. She charges 'em with the crime; you cut 'em up; I defend or prosecute 'em. With luck. We're a fine parcel of ghouls, aren't we?"

"I suppose we are, really," Hilary agreed with all seriousness. She appealed to Sanders. "But—you're the friend of Sir Henry Merrivale, aren't you?"

"I'm one of them, anyhow."

"And he *is* coming down here on Sunday, isn't he?"

"Oh, yes."

"Hilary expects trouble with our friend the mind-reader," said Chase. He spoke with a kind of expansive fondness, as though he were indulging a small girl.

"I am being accused of fads and fancies," said Hilary, examining her finger-nails. "Now let me ask you something; let me put a hypothetical case. Suppose this man is perfectly genuine. Suppose he has the power he says he has, and with the proper effort can read every thought in our heads like plain print. I don't necessarily admit he's genuine, though I never met a performance that made me feel quite so—so creepy. But, supposing him to be genuine, do you realize just what that would mean?"

Sanders must have looked dubious, for she caught his look with as imperceptible a turn as a fencer catches a thrust; there was in fact in her mind something of the quality of a swordsman. She smiled.

"Dr. Sanders doesn't believe in mind-readers."

"I don't know," Sanders admitted honestly. "But go on. Granting your hypothesis, what do we get?"

She stared at the fountain.

"I've been talking to Larry about a play called *Dangerous Corner*. The theme of the play, you may remember, is that in all conversations among friends or relatives there is a dangerous corner, where the most trivial word will turn the talk to disaster. Mostly we miss that corner; but sometimes the wheel skids by accident. Then a secret comes out— about somebody. But, once you've turned that corner, you've got to keep on down the road. The exposure of that secret will lead to the exposure of another secret about somebody else, until one by one the real inner life of everybody is shown up; and the sight isn't pretty."

"That corner is dangerous enough. But it is a corner; it is taken by accident or chance. On the other hand, suppose you had somebody who took it deliberately, because he knew where it was and what it would lead to? Suppose you had a person with a power to see into minds? To know every secret people were thinking about? The result doesn't

16

bear thinking about in itself. Life would become simply intolerable, that's all. Now wouldn't it?"

She had been speaking quietly, in an explanatory way
and without any emphasis on words. At the end she merely
raised her eyes. Lawrence Chase looked surprised and
doubtful (of her) and somewhat fretful.

"It's a bit too academic for me—"

"No, it isn't, Larry. You know that."

"And I also begin to suspect, my girl, that you have a
low mind."

"Perhaps I have. I honestly don't know. But I notice that
people always accuse you of having something wrong with
your mind whenever you ask them to exercise theirs."

"Of humanity in general, I mean," said Chase. Hitherto
he had been speaking with light good-humor, casting an
eye at Sanders as though bidding him to listen to the girl.
Now he drew himself up with such straightness that his sharp
shoulder-blades showed through the back of his coat. "Right
you are, then. We'll be desperately serious. Take the
play you're talking about: if I remember correctly, before
they finished digging out secrets they found that among them
the characters had committed nearly every crime in the
Decalogue. Hang it all! You don't seriously suggest that
would apply to any casual group of people, do you?"

"Oh, crime!" said Hilary, and smiled. "Let me ask you
something. Suppose every thought that came into your head
in the course of one day were written down, and the whole
thing read out to an assembled group of your friends."

"God forbid!"

"You wouldn't like it?"

"I rather think I should prefer to be boiled in oil,"
Chase declared reflectively.

"And yet you haven't committed any crime; any great
crime, that is?"

"No. None that worries me, anyhow."

There was a silence.

"Oh, and another thing," pursued Hilary, with a glow
of pure mischief in her blue eyes. "We can leave out crimes.
We can even leave out your feminine conquests, or attempted conquests. You don't have to own up to the
times you've seen a girl you rather liked, and invited her
away somewhere, and thought, 'That's nice; that'll be easy,'
when really you didn't know anything about her. People
talk about 'secrets,' but usually all they mean is secrets
about love-affairs or would-be love-affairs—"

"And usually they're quite right," said Chase with candor.

But even in the gloom you could see the blood come into his face.

"Well? Leaving out crime and all matters of sex, would you still—"

"No, look here!" interrupted Chase. "This is going too far. We're supposed to be having an academic argument; not a game of Truth. Besides, why have my shortcomings and stupidities got to be pitched on? Would you like *your* thoughts for the course of a day to be paraded out in front of everybody?"

"I should hope not," said Hilary fervently.

"Aha! Even aside from crime and sex, you've thought thoughts you wouldn't have known?"

"Yes."

"In fact, you've even thought thoughts about crime and sex?"

"Of course."

"Well, that's all right, then," said Chase, mollified. "So, before the party becomes rowdy, suppose we drop the subject."

"We can't drop it. That's just the point, don't you understand? You see how easy it is to start a thing like this going, just as we've been doing now. That's not because we're all criminals, but because we're all human. And it's why we've got to persuade Mina to get rid of this man Pennik."

Chase hesitated, and Hilary turned to Sanders.

"He's going to make trouble," Hilary said. "I don't mean that his intentions are evil or that he's a mischief-maker. No. On the contrary, his intentions are good and in that unassuming way of his he's rather charming—"

"Then what are you worried about?" inquired Chase; though he himself looked far from at ease.

"Because that's just the whole difficulty. Unless he's a bigger charlatan than seems possible, he really believes in this gift of his. Under that mild exterior of his he would do anything, anything, to convince people it was true. Particularly since Mr. Constable—"

"Sam."

"Sam, then. Particularly since Sam antagonizes him at every turn. You remember what happened when he gave that demonstration at their flat in town. Can't you imagine what he might do if he really chose to make trouble among a group like us? Or among any other group in the wide world? What do you say, Dr. Sanders?"

It was growing darker in the glass-roofed room, hollow with the faint echo of the fountain and full of plants

18

that had turned to shadows. The orange-red square of the electric fire glowed more brightly. Sanders had begun to understand his invitation to Fourways.

He looked at Chase.

"Tell me," he said. "Was it your idea that H.M. and I should investigate this fellow? Find out whether or not he's a fake?"

Chase looked hurt.

"Oh, don't put it like that. Not at all! Both Sam and Mina particularly wanted to invite you."

"Thanks. And, before we go into this, where are our hosts? I ought to present myself. Having barged in here—"

"That's all right. They're both out. They went over to Guildford to see how the servants were getting on, and to see whether they could dig up anybody to cook a scratch meal or attend to things generally. It's upset Mina, especially with another book on the way—"

"Another what on the way?"

"Book. You know." Chase broke off. His eyes opened wide, and he knocked his knuckles against his forehead. "Good Lord alive," he said; "you don't mean to say you don't know? I thought everybody knew."

"Not when you are entrusted with telling it."

"Mina Constable," explained Chase, "is really Mina Shields —the lady novelist, you know. And don't laugh."

"Why the devil should I laugh?"

"I don't know," Chase said gloomily, "except that for some reason all lady novelists are supposed to be funny. Sort of dogma. Anyhow, Mina is a modern Marie Corelli. By that I don't mean anything pompous or flighty or on the preaching side: Mina is the best of good scouts, as you'll see. She may write romances about reincarnation in Egypt or Satan in the suburbs, but she's sound. When she wanted to do a novel about a temple in the middle of French Indo-China, she didn't trust to the books; by George, she *went* to French Indo-China. That trip nearly killed Sam; and Mina too, for that matter. They both went down with malaria. Sam says he can't get warm even yet. Which is why they have these portable fires blazing in every room, and the place is like an oven. Don't open too many windows, or you'll have him on your neck."

Hilary spoke with a certain tensity, looking over her shoulder at the spray of the fountain.

"Yes. I dare say you will."

"Now, now!"

"Mrs. Constable is fine," said Hilary. "I like her enormously. But Mr. Constable—no, I am not going to call him Sam—ugh!"

"Nonsense! Sam's all right. It's only that he's the compleat British clubman, and he's a bit fussy."

"He is at least twenty years older than she is," Hilary said dispassionately, "and not attractive in any conceivable way that I can see. Yet the way he orders her about, ticks her off, calls attention to things in public—well, before I would let any man do that to me, I'd go off and take poison in a corner."

Chase spread out his hands. "She's fond of him, that's all. Like one of her heroes in the books. He was what used to be called a fine figger of a man before he retired."

"Which the rest of us can't afford to do," said Hilary rather bitterly.

"Oh, all right." Chase started to speak, and then seemed to change his mind. "Anyway, we might just as well stop talking about them in their own house." Again he hesitated. "Look here, Sanders, it's no good denying that bout of malaria changed him a bit, and Mina too. He snaps sometimes, though you can't help liking him. I don't know whether I want this mind-reading fellow to be proved a fake or the real thing. He's Mina's discovery, and she seems to think a lot of him; though I've sometimes wondered if it isn't her sense of humor working. Sam doesn't like him, and there's a kind of undeclared row hovering and darkening. The point is, will you and the notorious H.M. do your best for us?"

II

Sanders was almost himself again. He felt enormously flattered and, for the first time in weeks, cheered.

"Of course. But—"

"But what?"

"You seem to have got the wrong idea of me, I'm afraid. I'm not a detective. My work is forensic medicine. I don't see how anything I know or could investigate would apply to this man. At the same time—"

"Cautious blighter," Chase explained to Hilary.

"At the same time, it's hard to say what particular branch of science or pseudo-science *would* apply to him if he were genuine. What is his science? By what rule does he work, or pretend to work?"

"I don't think I understand, old boy."

"Well, most of the 'mind-readers' I ever encountered have

20

been of the music-hall variety. You know the sort of thing: working in pairs. The woman sits blindfolded, the man goes among the audience. 'What am I holding in my hand?' and so on. Then, of course, there's the fellow who works alone, makes you write questions on bits of paper, and reads them from a sealed envelope; but he is usually such an obvious fake that if you have an elementary knowledge of conjuring you can spot him. If he's like either of those two sorts, I can help you. Is he?"

"Good Lord, no!" said Chase, staring.

"Why the vehemence?"

Hilary Keen made a wry face. "What Larry means," she explained, "is that he's no end of an academic swell. Degrees from all over the place. I'm not necessarily impressed by that, but it's no good denying it carries some weight with regard to his sincerity. Besides, he's nothing like the sort you describe."

"Then what does he do? That is to say, he doesn't just look you in the eye and say, 'You are thinking of a bathing-hut on the beach at Southend,' does he?"

"I'm afraid he does," answered Hilary.

It was growing darker, a powdery twilight in which the palms of the conservatory became weights of shadow and the orange-red square of the fire stood out with fierce distinctness. Even so, they must have seen the expression on Sander's face.

"Aha!" said Chase, nodding with great profundity. "Shakes you up, does it? Why?"

"Because it's incredible. It's scientific gibberish." Sanders hesitated. "I won't deny that in the past there have been certain fairly successful experiments in telepathy. William James believed in it, for instance. So did Hegel and Schelling and Schopenhauer, though recently it has died down from sheer lack of investigation. The trouble is that nothing can be regarded as a scientific fact which won't work at will and all the time, on the same recurring principles; and more often than not telepathy hasn't worked at all. If the operator complains that he is not in the mood, or that 'conditions aren't right,' he may be honest, but he's not being scientific. Who is this man, by the way? What do you know about him?"

There was a brooding pause before Hilary replied.

"Nothing, really. Except that he's apparently quite well off and doesn't stand to gain a penny by any of this. Mina met him on her way back from this trip to Indo-China. He calls himself a student."

"A student of what?"

"Of thought as a force. You must get him to explain. And yet all the time," said Hilary, her soft voice tautening and sharpening, "I've got a feeling that there's something not quite right about him. I don't mean as regards his being a fake; but something at the back of his own mind. Worry? Self-consciousness? Inferiority complex? You have a feeling that he regards this thought-reading as only a kind of minor prelude to something—oh, *I* don't know! Talk to him; that is, if he will."

"*I should be only too pleased,*" said a new voice.

There was a rustle in the strip of grass outside the conservatory. Twilight touched the stained-glass above, and the long pale oblong of the open window below; and a man moved into that oblong.

The light was not strong enough to make out more than outlines. The newcomer was rather under middle height, with a broad chest, and legs very slightly bowed. You felt rather than saw a smile as he inclined his head. His voice was heavy, slow-speaking, and pleasant.

"Lights. We'd better get some lights on," Chase said hastily—and Sanders could have sworn that in the way he spoke there was a touch of panic.

Chase went over and pressed a switch. Under each corner of the glass dome, a cluster of electric globes bloomed like luminous fruit. They had the garish and snaky appearance of such fixtures popular at the end of the nineteenth century; they brought out the garishness of gilt and palms and colored glass.

"Dr. Sanders?"

"Thank you," said the newcomer.

"Yes. Mr.—?"

"Pennik," said the newcomer. "Herman Pennik."

He extended his hand. You would not have found a more unobtrusive or disarming figure than Mr. Herman Pennik, despite the curious momentary impression gained from his appearance at the window. He scraped the soles of his shoes carefully on the window-sill to avoid bringing mud into the room. Before shaking hands he even glanced over his shoulder, down at the soles of his shoes as he tilted them up, to make sure.

His age might have been the middle forties. He had a hard-looking head with homely looking sandy hair; a broad, homely face with leathery wrinkles round the jaw, darkish from hot suns; a broad nose, and light eyes under sandy brows. You saw no sign of strong intellect in that face. There was even a touch of heaviness or coarseness round the mouth.

22

But Herman Pennik had a habit of being inconspicuous in many things.

He spoke apologetically, with a slight ducking motion of the shoulders.

"How do you do, sir? I am sorry. I could not help overhearing what was said."

Sanders returned his formal courtesy.

"I hope I was not too frank, Mr. Pennik. You don't mind?"

"Not at all. You understand, I hardly know why I am here myself, not being much endowed with the social graces. But Mrs. Constable wished me to come, and here I am."

He smiled; and Sanders felt the pull of a curious psychological reaction. In spite of fighting against it, the very reputation Pennik had created for himself made Sanders uneasy. It surrounded Pennik like an aura; it had to be shaken off; it was formidable and disturbing. It prompted the insidious thought: What if this fellow can read *my* mind? For there was certainly a change in the atmosphere.

"Shall we sit down?" Pennik suggested suddenly. "Couldn't I get you a chair, Miss Keen? Wouldn't you be more comfortable than sitting on the rim of that fountain?"

"I'm quite comfortable, thanks."

"You're—er—quite sure?"

"Quite sure, thank you."

Though she smiled, Sanders felt that she also sensed another quality about Mr. Herman Pennik. His manner underwent a change when he spoke to her; his words were clumsy; he had an air of an embarrassed small boy; and afterwards he sat down hastily in a wicker chair.

Immediately he was easy again, though Sanders noticed that he took a deep breath.

"We were just telling the doctor," began Lawrence Chase, tall and lean and now revealed as going a trifle bald, "about some of the things you've done."

Pennik made a deprecating gesture.

"Thank you, Mr. Chase. And did he seem—responsive?"

"To tell you the truth, I think he was a little shocked."

"Indeed? May I ask, sir, why you should be shocked?"

Sanders had begun to feel dogged; it was as though he and not Pennik were on the defensive. At the same time, he wished the fellow would keep those damned eyes away from him. And curse all these undercurrents. All the time this was going on, Sanders found himself catching Hilary Keen's eye, being annoyed with himself, and looking away again.

"I should hardly call it shocked," he said dryly. "Startled,

23

if you like. Any person who deals with realities like anatomy—"

"Tut, tut," said Chase. "Keep it clean."

(Confound you, too.)

"Any scientist, then, is opposed to a claim which—" He paused. What he wanted to say was, 'a claim which upsets the uniformity of Nature,' but he realized that this would sound pompous and priggish enough to raise a grin. "To a claim like that."

"I see," said Pennik. "And therefore science refuses to investigate it because the results might prove inconvenient?"

"Not at all."

Pennik's homely brow was ruffled; but his eye had a twinkle.

"Yet you yourself acknowledge, sir, that successful experiments in telepathy have been carried out in the past?"

"To a certain extent. But to nowhere near the extent you claim to have carried them."

"You object to my making progress? Surely, sir, that is as unreasonable as saying that because the first experiments in wireless telegraphy were incomplete though successful the matter had better be dropped?"

(Be careful. He can give you points and a beating if you let him go on like that. The argument by false analogy is an old one.)

"That's what I was coming to, Mr. Pennik. Wireless telegraphy is based on principles which can be explained. Can you explain yours?"

"To the proper listener."

"Not to me?"

"Sir," answered Pennik, with a heavy, honest, disturbed look, "try to understand me. You think I am arguing falsely because I argue by comparisons. But when a thing is entirely new, how else can I argue except by comparisons? How else can I make my meaning clear? Suppose I tried to explain the principles of wireless telegraphy to a—a savage from Central Asia. I beg your pardon. Comparisons are invidious. Suppose I tried to explain the principles of wireless to a highly cultured Roman of the first century A.D. To him the principles would sound as mysterious as the result; the principles would even sound as incredible as the result. That is my unfortunate position when people demand blue-prints.

"Given time, I can explain it to you. The basis is roughly that thought, or what we call thought-waves, have a physical force not dissimilar to sound. But if it would take five weeks for an educated Roman to begin to understand wireless telegraphy, do not be surprised if you fail to understand wireless telepathy in five minutes."

24

Sanders disregarded this.

"You maintain," he insisted, "that thought-waves have a physical force like sound?"

"I do."

"But even sound, scientifically, can be measured and weighed."

"Of course. Notes in sound can shatter glass or even kill a man. The same, naturally, applies to thought."

He spoke with a kind of toiling lucidity. Sander's first notion—that the man was mad—he knew in his heart to be wrong.

"For the moment, Mr. Pennik," he said, "we will pass over the question of whether you might be able to kill a man by thinking about him, like a Bantu witch-doctor. Instead let's get down to plain words that even a person of my limited intelligence can understand. What exactly do you *do?*"

"I will give you an illustration," replied Pennik simply. "If you will concentrate your thoughts on something—anything at all, but particularly a person or idea that bulks large in your life—I will tell you what you are thinking about."

This was something like a challenge.

"You claim to be able to do that with everyone?"

"With nearly everyone. Of course, if you do not assist me, and try to hide what you are really thinking about, it is much more difficult. But it can be managed."

It was the complete simplicity of the man which shook Sanders's nerve. He found his own thoughts scattering wildly, bolting into corners, in case they should be seen.

"And you want me to test you?"

"If you will."

"All right; begin," said Sanders, and braced himself.

"Then since you have . . . no, no, no!" Pennik said rather pettishly. "That will not do."

"What will not do?"

"You were trying hard to sweep your mind clear of all genuine or important thoughts; mentally, you were rushing about to bolt and bar every door. Don't be afraid of me. I will not hurt you. For instance, you had decided to concentrate on the marble bust of some scientist (Lister, I believe) which stands on a mantelpiece in someone's library.'"

It was absolutely true.

There are some emotions whose effect is difficult to gauge because they are drawn from no source that we could ever have expected. To be "caught" in a thought is bad enough; to be caught by some friend who knows you and suddenly penetrates the defense with a guess. It rouses resentment and a certain helplessness. But to be instantly pinned to the

25

wall, the moment your mind has lighted on the smallest triviality, by a complete stranger who looks at you like a dog who has just retrieved a stick—

"No, no," urged Pennik lifting his forefinger and waggling it earnestly. "May I ask you to give me a broader opportunity than that? The bust of Lister means nothing to you. It might have been the Achilles Statue or the kitchen boiler. Will you try again?"

"Wait," interposed Hilary from her seat by the fountain. Her small hands were closed tightly round a handkerchief. "Was he right?"

"He was."

"Blimey," muttered Lawrence Chase. "Woman and children will now leave the courtroom. As I told you in my letter, Sanders, I didn't see *how* it could be a trick. It isn't as though he asked you to write on little bits of paper or anything like that."

"A trick. A trick, a trick," said Herman Pennik, only half humorously. For Sanders felt that under this dignified lightness Pennik was trying very hard; that deep inside him had been touched some huge inner spring of conceit. In short, he was showing off. And he might continue to show off. "A trick, a trick, a trick! That is all you—we English seem to think about. Well, Doctor, will you try again?"

"Yes. All right. Go on."

"Then I will try to ... ah, that is better," said Pennik. He had been shading his eyes with his hand, and now he peered through the fingers. "You have played fair and concentrated on an emotion."

Almost without hesitation, he proceeded to tell about Marcia Blystone on the round-the-world cruise with Kessler.

It was a curious sensation, Sanders felt; as though he were being physically pressed upon, as though facts were being pulled out of him like teeth.

"I—er—hope you don't mind this," Pennik broke off. "As a rule I should not have been so frank. My motto has always been that of Queen Elizabeth: *video et taceo:* I see and am silent. But you asked me to tell you what you were concentrating on. We could carry it further if we cared. There were, too, things you were trying very hard to conceal from me ..." He hesitated. "Shall I go on?"

"Go on," said Sanders through his teeth.

"I should prefer—"

"Go on."

"It is more recent," Pennik told him, with an abrupt and surprising satyr-like look. "Since you arrived at this house, you have been violently attracted to Miss Keen there, per-

26

haps on an emotional reaction. This attraction is the cause of your mood. You have been wondering whether Miss Keen may not be more suited to you than the other young lady."

"I knew it!" said Lawrence Chase, jumping to his feet.

Hilary did not speak; it was as though she had not heard. She continued to look incuriously over her shoulder at the glimmering spray of water in the fountain. The light shone on her rich dark-brown hair and the line of her neck as she turned her head. But her obvious start of astonishment was caused less by the words than the tone in which Pennik spoke them.

"Am I correct, Doctor?" Pennik asked, colorless again.

Sanders did not reply.

"So you admit it," said Chase. "All right, Mr. Pennik: what am *I* thinking about?"

"I'd rather not say."

"Oh? Now will someone just tell me why *I* am always accused of having a low mind? Why I am always supposed to be thinking—"

"Nobody said you were," Sanders pointed out mildly. "That would appear to be the trouble with this game. Our consciences are all over us."

"Well, then, what is Hilary thinking about?" Chase challenged. "What is the guilty secret she's been hiding all these weeks I've known her?"

Fortunately, they were interrupted. From the dark interior of the house, past an archway covered with velvet curtains, they heard hurrying footsteps and the sound of a rather breathless voice calling to them. The curtains were opened by a little, smiling, hurrying woman with her hat on crooked. This could be nobody but their hostess; and Sanders welcomed her presence with a surge of relief. He was beginning to realize that this game of thought-reading could not be carried too far, or it would end in a smash; yet, with ordinary human perversity, everybody insisted on carrying it too far. That was the trouble. And it occurred to him to wonder: Look here, just what is going to happen before this week-end is over?

III

"I'M SO SORRY to have left you alone," said Mina Constable. "And I'm afraid things are so disorganized I don't know which way to turn."

Sanders liked the look of her: she restored sane values.

27

Mina Constable had a friendliness and sincerity which seemed quite genuine. She was small and quick-moving, with a wiry strength insensible to fatigue. She had large imaginative eyes, dark brown in color; a dark complexion; and black hair cut close to her head. Sanders judged her to be very fashionably dressed, though her hat was put on anyhow. Speak to her, and she radiated charm. Yet he saw that traces of a bad attack of malaria were still present: in the pupils of the eyes, and in the difficulty she had in holding to her handbag.

Mina Constable glanced quickly over her shoulder.

"I—er—rushed on ahead to tell you," she went on in the same rather breathless voice. "I want to warn you, you mustn't mind Sam. That is, if he seems in a mood. He's had a filthy day, poor old boy; what with that wreck and now not being able to get anybody to do for us over the weekend. No, the servants are all right, thank goodness; chipper as you please, and it *is* rotten for them. You do understand, don't you? Oh!"

Catching sight of Sanders, she broke off. It was Chase who performed the introductions. And Chase, perhaps because he was off guard, showed an unusual lack of tact.

"You needn't flatter yourself, Mina," he said heartily, putting his arm round her shoulders. "Here's a fellow who never even heard of you. You're not as widely known as you think."

"I never supposed I was," said Mina composedly, and smiled at Sanders.

"He never heard," pursued Chase with relish, "of *My Lady Ishtar* or *Satan in the Suburbs* or even—by the way, our Mina even tried her hand at a detective story. But I still insist it wasn't very successful. I absolutely refuse to believe in that bloke who carted a corpse all over London and then convinced 'em it really died in Hyde Park. I also think the heroine was a chump, losing her head all the time. Still, if the heroine usually wasn't a chump I suppose there wouldn't be any story; so that's all right."

This touched Sanders where he lived.

"I beg your pardon: you wrote *The Double Alibi?* I certainly do know you. And I don't agree with Chase at all. You've probably been asked this till you're sick of it, but where did you get the idea for the poison you used there? It's new, and it's scientifically sound."

"Oh, I don't know," Mina said vaguely. "You pick people up. They tell you things." She seemed anxious to change the subject. "It's *so* nice of you to come down, but I'm afraid we've let you in for a most awful week-end. How

28

do you like Fourways? It's a lovely old house, isn't it?" she asked, with the candor of pure pride. "Ever since I was a child I've wanted a place like this. Oh, I know people are supposed to groan when you show it to them; but it suits me. I like the atmosphere. So does Sam; he's so understanding about things like that. Larry, do go and get us some drinks, that's a good fellow. I'm dying for a cocktail, and I know Sam will want a Gin-and-It. Er—won't you, my dear?"

She turned round cheerfully, and Sam Constable followed her into the conservatory.

Mr. Samuel Hobart Constable was about to speak, but checked himself abruptly when he saw a stranger. He also was breathing hard. Even the way he checked himself from speaking was ostentatious, as though he could speak but pointedly wouldn't out of good manners. He had been pictured as something of an ogre, but Sanders saw him as only fussy and touchy in the late fifties: over-fed, over-pampered, over-opinionated. Though not tall, he was still strikingly handsome in a gray-and-pink-and-white manner. And even in country tweeds he was so carefully dressed that the disarrangement of a crease would have been painful. After the impressiveness of his pointed silence, he caught sight of the open window. He looked at them again; he went over carefully, picking each step, and closed the window; he gave them a final look.

"How do you do?" he said—and devoted himself to Sanders to the pointed exclusion of everyone else.

"That's all right, my dear," said Mina, tapping his arm with great brightness. "Larry is going to get us some drinks (aren't you, Larry?) and then we shall all feel better. After all, Mrs. Chichester has promised to get us something to eat—"

Her husband ignored her. He kept his eye fixed on Sanders.

"You have probably heard what happened. Well, young man, you will be lucky to get anything to eat at all. In this house, at least. A certain Mrs. Chichester has at last graciously consented to preside: she can't do a proper dinner, but she promises us a 'bit of cold beef' and 'a nice salad.'" At the very words, his sallow color rose. "Well, that's no good to me. I don't want a bit of cold beef and a nice salad. I want a decent dinner, decently cooked. And since—"

"Sam, I really am terribly sorry," urged Mina, dragging off her hat and throwing it on a wicker settee. Her anxiety deepened as she plucked at his sleeve. "I do know how you feel. But this is early-closing day, and except for the cold things there simply isn't anything in the house."

Sam Constable turned to her with great courtesy, and a certain pompousness in his tubby figure.

"Is that my fault, my dear?"

"Well, with the servants not getting here—"

"That is no concern of mine. It's hardly my business to go about with a basket buying meat and whatever it is. Do try to be sensible, Mina. If you can make the minutest preparations to drag me through eight hundred miles of malarial swamp (and you should see your own eyes now, my dear), then surely it is not too much to hope for provisions in our own house. However, we must not quarrel before our guests."

"*I* will get you a meal, if you like," offered Herman Pennik.

It was so unexpected that they all turned to stare at him. Chase, who had started out to get the drinks, stuck his head back round the corner of a clump of ferns to get a better look.

And Sam Constable was surprised enough to speak to him.

"You are a cook, my friend?" he inquired, in the faintly contemptuous tone of one who says, 'I might have known it.' "That is, in addition to your other accomplishments?"

"I am a very good cook. I cannot do you a hot dinner, of course, but I can prepare dishes that will make you glad it is a cold one."

Hilary Keen laughed. It was a spontaneous laugh, a release from strain. She got up from the rim of the fountain.

"Oh, good! Well done! Please sit down, Mrs. Constable, and be comfortable," she urged. "Honestly, don't you think too much tragedy is being made over the question of getting a meal? If you were as poor as I am you wouldn't feel like that. Mr. Pennik shall get the dinner, I will serve it—"

"No, no, no," said Pennik, shocked. "You serve it? No, I could not allow that. Just leave it all to me."

"You have made a conquest, Miss Keen," said Sam Constable.

He spoke with ponderous gallantry. Whether he was tickled by the idea of Pennik as cook, or whether Hillary's words flattered him by implying fastidious tastes on his part, Sanders could not be sure; but Sam was suddenly in a gay good-humor. Mina—who had been looking round hopefully, as though to assure herself everybody thought her husband a devil of a fine fellow in spite of his little lapses—became dreamy again.

"Then that's settled," she declared. "Didn't Dumas cook a dinner for the gourmets of France? I wish I could. I think there's even a chef's cap in the kitchen somewhere: you know, one of those tall white things with the muffin tops. You can have that, Mr. Pennik."

"It will become him," said Sam gravely. "But you must give us your word not to poison us. Eh?"

It was Chase who intervened, swinging out a wicker table with a rasp of legs on the tiled floor which made Sam jump and his brow darken again. On this table Chase put down a tray full of bottles, glasses, and a bowl of cracked ice.

"Oh, he won't poison us," Chase assured them. "He won't do that whatever happens. He wouldn't need to."

"Wouldn't need to?"

"No. He would simply think about us, and—boppo! Gin-and-It, or shall I mix a cocktail?"

"Just what in blazes are you talking about?"

"True as gospel," said Chase, pouring out drinks rapidly. "Vote? No cocktail? Right. What about you, Mina? Didn't you want a cocktail?"

"Anything at all for me, please, Larry. Gin-and-It will be splendid."

"Mr. Pennik," pursued Chase, "says that thought-waves are a physical force. Of course we knew that; but now he says that properly used they could kill a man."

Over Sam Constable's face, as he accepted a glass, came a despairing expression. It was as though he said, 'Something. Al-ways something to pester and torment me. Why have all the nuisances got to be piled on me?' Pure pettishness and self-pity boiled up coldly under the surface.

"Indeed?" he said, swallowing noisily in the glass. "Then you have been playing thought-reading games again?"

"Well, ask Sanders here. Just ask him. Mr. Pennik told him to think of something, and got it first shot. He even got it when Sanders tried to hide what he was thinking, including—"

"Other things," interposed Hilary, with her eyes on the fountain.

"I wonder if I have got the right man for my money?" said Sam, looking at Sanders over the rim of his glass. "Young man, you *are* a medical man?"

"I am."

"And a consultant to the Home Office pathologist, they tell me?"

"Yes."

"And you hold with all this rubbish?"

"I don't necessarily hold with anything, Mr. Constable. I am willing to admit that Mr. Pennik gave a remarkable demonstration, which is a fair description of it."

Their host jumped to his feet.

"Mina, for God's *sake! Will* you stop twitching and jittering with that glass, like an old hag soaking up gin in a pub? If your hands are too shaky to hold the glass properly, put it on the table and drink over the rim. That at least would be more decent than the spectacle you are making of yourself now."

He stopped, and had himself the decency to look a little ashamed after this outburst. Probably he meant nothing. But there was a cruel scratch in it, for the trembling hands of a malaria aftermath are obvious enough by themselves.

Mina said nothing.

"All right, all right, I'm sorry," he grumbled. He drained the glass; took another pull at it when it was empty; and sat down again. "But you people make a fellow feel old. Have a little pity sometimes. I often say Mina will be the death of me yet, dropping things. Nerves. Can't stand it. All the same, what I say is that this thought-reading business is rubbish. It's wrong. It's"—the veins swelled in his forehead—"it's against everything we've ever been taught. It's against nature, that's all."

"You will work yourself up so, Sam," complained Mina. Her eyes shone. "Don't you see how fascinating it is? And you know perfectly well Mr. Pennik told you what *you* were thinking about when you tested him. Only you would interrupt and shout, 'Wrong!' before the words were even out of his mouth. And then afterwards you wouldn't test him at all. I'm sorry, my dear, but you know it's true."

Her husband looked at her.

"Shall we change the subject?" he suggested, with powerful courtesy. He took out his watch and studied it elaborately. "Ah, good, good! Nearly seven-thirty. Good time to bathe and dress before dinner—"

"But, Sam, surely we're not dressing for dinner tonight?"

He looked at her again.

"Of course we are dressing for dinner, my dear. Do you see any material reason for altering our custom? If I can dress for dinner among a lot of damned niggers, surely I can dress for dinner in my own house?"

"Of course, if you like."

32

"I do like, thank you. Parker would have to choose this night to be in hospital; only man I ever had who knew how to lay out my things properly. But there it is. That's the way things go. You will have to deputize for him, my dear, if you feel equal to the task. Er—" Tilting up his chin, he looked at Herman Pennik. "I must thank you, my friend, for your offer to get dinner for us. Shall we say, then, that you can have it ready as soon past eight o'clock as possible?"

"If you like," said Pennik. He reflected. "But I do not think, Mr. Constable, that you will get any dinner."

The other sat up. "Not get my dinner? Why the devil shouldn't I get my dinner?"

"Because I do not think you will be alive then," said Pennik.

It was perhaps ten seconds before the meaning of the words penetrated into the listeners' minds; before sense could be made out of sound. And it was longer than that before anyone spoke.

All through the previous conversation, through each word and jar and gesture, Pennik had been sitting so quietly that they were not even aware of him. Nor had they spoken to him. Now they were aware of him as an entity, perhaps a huge entity. He was sitting forward in his chair, wearing respectable blue serge, his feet crossed, his knees out at an angle, and his hands clasped together so tightly that bluish half-moons showed at the base of the nails. Each small sound was magnified in the bright conservatory: the murmur of the fountain growing to a splash, the scrape of a shoe on tile.

And the conservatory seemed much too cold for such a hot room.

Sam Constable broke the silence with hollow incredulity, like a child; the room came to life again.

"What are you talking about?"

"I said that I did not think you would be alive by the time dinner is served."

Lawrence Chase sprang to his feet.

"A seizure?" demanded their host, with sudden alarm.

"No."

"Then will you have the goodness to explain what you mean, my friend? Trying to frighten—" Sam Constable checked himself, peered round suspiciously, and held up his glass. "I hardly suppose you can mean that somebody has poisoned my drink?" he added with elaborate sarcasm.

"No, I do not mean that."

33

"I'll tell you what he means," said Hilary quietly. "Mr. Pennik, can you tell, or think you can tell, what each one of us is thinking about?"

"Perhaps."

And it's in someone's mind to kill Mr. Constable within a very short time?"

"Perhaps."

There was another silence.

"Of course," Pennik emphasized, gripping his hands together more tightly and nodding at each word as though to define his terms, "I do not say it is *certain* to happen. I— well, there are reasons. I will lay a place for you at the table, Mr. Constable. But you may not occupy it." He raised his eyes. "Since you set so much store by the quality you call sportsmanship, there is your warning."

"Oh, rot!" burst out Chase. "Look here—"

After an uncertain muttering, Sam glanced up. Then, surprisingly, his jaw came out and over his face crept an expression of fighting humor for which Sanders was compelled to admire him.

"Ah, well," said their host. "I thank you for the warning, sir. I shall keep an eye out. But who is going to murder me? My wife? And make it look like an accident, like that case in the paper? Be careful, Mina. Remember, after you have killed me, that you talk in your sleep. That will at least keep you virtuous during your widowhood." His elbow knocked over a glass, which broke with a crash on the tiled floor. "Lord, what utter blathering, driveling bilge! I'm going upstairs to dress. Coming, everybody?"

"Sam, he means it," said Mina.

"Are you sure you are quite yourself, my dear?"

"Sam, I tell you he means it!"

"I found somebody's suitcase standing outside the front door," said their host briskly. "Yours, Dr. Sanders? Good. It is in the front hall. If you will come with me, I will show you your room. Mina, take Miss Keen to hers. Larry, perhaps you will be good enough to show Mr. Pennik where the kitchen is, and the, er, rest of it, you know. Br, but it's cold!"

"Yes," said Pennik gravely. "I should like a word with Mr. Chase."

"Sam—" Mina almost screamed.

He closed his fingers firmly round her arm and led her out. The last glimpse Sanders had was of Pennik and Chase standing amid a tamed jungle by the wicker table; and Pennik had just said something which made Chase start and look round. Their shuffling footsteps sounded hollow under the glass dome. And a clock struck seven-thirty.

IV

IT WAS AT a quarter to eight that Sanders heard the faint cry from the next room.

Looking down from a window at Fourways, he had already decided, was like looking down over the side of a ship. You went through a series of padded lounges, into a main hall paved with tiny white unglazed tiles. You went up a main staircase built against a wall which consisted chiefly of tall stained-glass windows ascending like the treads of the stairs. All lights were in cutglass shades or in snaky bronze holders or in both. On the first floor up—there were four floors altogether—the six principal bedrooms opened out on a landing round three sides of a square.

It was a small landing, heavily carpeted and badly lighted, with a grandfather clock. Two bedrooms occupied each of three sides of a square, with the staircase-wall forming the fourth side. Sanders was given the room next to Hilary Keen. Sam and Mina Constable occupied the two rooms facing the staircase-wall. Chase and Pennik, he supposed, would be in the remaining two on the third side.

At the moment, what Sanders wanted was time to think. His bedroom fulfilled all predictions. The windows were heavily curtained in many overlays like oldfashioned petticoats; there was a big brass bed; and on a table by one window stood an unused china lamp. But, though not centrally heated, Fourways was well supplied with bathrooms, and Sanders had a private one.

To get this stifling atmosphere out of his brain, he turned off the heater and opened both windows. There seemed no way of fastening the curtains back, and he left them. Outside one window was one of those tiny and useless window-balconies cramped against the high pitch of the wall. After breathing deeply, he took a quick cold bath and dressed in some haste. Ready except for his coat and waistcoat, he lighted a cigarette and gave himself time to think.

Now, in spite of that demonstration of thought-reading, was Herman Pennik really—

Wait!

He could have sworn he heard a faint cry. He could also have sworn it came from the next room, though the walls were thick and it was difficult to trace the source of sounds. He waited, trying to follow what sounded like a mumbling or a creaking of windows. Then several things happened at once.

The heavy rep curtains belled out on the farther of the open windows. Someone seemed to be fighting them. The tiny table tilted up beside them; bumping, the china lamp slid on that smooth surface, whirled, and went to the floor with a crash that must have been audible downstairs. From under the curtains appeared first a black satin slipper; then flesh-colored stockings; then an arm and a dark blue gown; and then Hilary Keen, breathing hard, tumbled into the room. She was so frightened that the color seemed to have been drained from her eyes, and as near a faint as she had ever been in her life.

But even now she tried not to admit it.

"I'm s-sorry to break in like this," she said. "But I couldn't help it. There's somebody in my room."

"Somebody in your room? Who?"

"I came by the window," she explained, with the painstaking carefulness of the distraught. "There's a balcony. Please let me sit down for a minute; I don't want to disgrace myself."

For some time he had been trying to think of the quality which most distinguished her. And he saw it now, when it was upset. It was the quality of fastidiousness. About her smooth shoulders and arms, about her eyes and forehead, there was an almost shrinking fastidiousness which went with the cool look of her skin. One of the shoulder-straps of her dress had fallen down or come loose, and she pulled it up quickly. There was grime on her hands and arms from having come by way of the balcony; and, when she saw it, he thought her nerves were going to break down in tears. She sat down on the edge of the bed.

"Now, steady!" he insisted. "What is it? Just tell me what's wrong."

There was no time for a reply, for somebody knocked thunderously at Sanders's door.

Hilary sprang up.

"Don't open it!" she said. "Let it alone! Whatever you do, don't open——" But she broke off, with a breath of relief, when the door was opened without anybody's permission; and they saw that it was only Sam Constable, wearing slippers and with a dressing-gown pulled round him.

"What's the row?" he demanded. "Sounded like the house was falling. Can't a fellow finish dressing in peace?"

"Sorry," said Sanders. "It's all right; the lamp fell over."

But their host was not concerned with the lamp. He had

36

got a good look at them; his eyes opened; and he drew his own conclusions.

"Look here—" he began, raising his eyebrows.

Hilary was frozen into composure.

"No, Mr. Constable. Don't jump to conclusions. It really isn't what you're thinking."

"And may I ask, Miss Keen," said the other, becoming a complete stuffed-shirt again, "what conclusions I am presumed to be taking? Have I asked for any explanation?" He was quivering with outraged dignity; he lifted a hand and ran it through his heavy, silky gray hair. "I come to investigate a noise. I find a valuable heirloom smashed (look at it) and two of my guests in a position which in *my* day would have been called sufficiently curious. But have I asked any questions?"

"Miss Keen has been telling me—" Sanders began.

She cut him off.

"There was something in my room, and it frightened me. I ran in here by way of the balcony. Take a look at my hands, if you don't believe it. I'm awfully sorry about the lamp; I knocked it over when I climbed through the window."

"It is of no consequence," said Sam Constable, looking sly. "Only I regret that something in your room frightened you. Mice, perhaps?"

"I—I don't know."

"Not mice. If you remember, please tell me and I will have it seen to. Excuse me, then; I shall not intrude on you any longer."

Sanders, realizing that if he joined in the explanations it would only give their host the opportunity to look more sly, did not comment. Their host was evidently beginning to realize the possibilities of triumph in the situation.

"By the way, Mr. Constable," he said, "nobody has tried to murder you so far, I imagine?"

"Not as yet, Doctor. Not as yet, I am glad to say. The scrap-book remains on its shelf. Until dinner, then!"

Sanders stared at the closing door.

"Now just what did he mean by that?"

"By what?"

" 'The scrap-book remains on its shelf.' "

"I haven't the remotest idea," said Hilary. "And at the moment I don't know whether to laugh or cry. It does seem as though the whole affair so far has been to put you into one embarrassing position after another."

"Oh, that's all right. But the point is, what particular embarrassing position were you in a little while ago?"

She was quiet again, though the shock had left its aftermath and Sanders did not like the look of it. At times she would tremble, for no apparent reason.

"It's nothing. May I use your bathroom to wash up in? I don't want to go back to my own room for a while."

He gestured towards it, picking up the cigarette he had put down at her entrance. That sudden entrance, the look of her, had disturbed him in more ways than one. She was gone only a moment; and when she returned he noticed the strength of resolution about her chin.

"I really wanted time to think," she explained. "And I'm sorry, Dr. Sanders, but I can't tell you anything about it. Believe me, things are heading for a smash here; and I'm not going to add my unimportant mite to the total. It was nothing—"

"It was definitely something. In plain language, did somebody go for you?"

"I don't understand."

"Don't you?"

"Well, not in the way you mean. It was something else." She shivered. "I suppose, as they say, that I simply can't take it. Looks shouldn't break any bones, should they? May I have a cigarette?" She sat down in a padded chair; he gave her a cigarette and lighted it for her. For a time she blew smoke-rings. "Shall I tell you what's wrong with all of us here, and why it's going to end in a way we won't like?"

"Well?"

"When I was a little girl, I had a book of stories I was very fond of; though some of them were rather frightening. They did show you a world where you could have everything you wanted, provided only some witch or wizard took a fancy to you. One of them was about a magic carpet, the usual kind of magic carpet. The sorcerer said to the boy who had it that it would carry him anywhere—with one proviso. While he was traveling on the carpet, he must never think of a cow. If he thought of a cow, the carpet would go to earth again.

"Now, there was no earthly reason why he should think of a cow. But, once he had been told he mustn't, all he could think about was that cow. Once he got it into his head, it never left him when he saw the carpet. No, I haven't taken leave of my senses. I didn't understand the psychology of that story then; I disliked the story, rather. But it's true. Because somebody says, 'Here is a person who can read your thoughts,' all you can think about is what you don't want anybody to know. We're all practically concentrating on what we don't want known; it won't leave our minds however we try."

38

"But what of that?"

"Oh, don't be so—so virtuous!"

Sanders considered this.

"I'm not trying to be virtuous, Lord knows," he said. "And I still don't understand. Aren't you making too much of this? I'm inclined to agree with Larry Chase: it would be damned uncomfortable to have all our thoughts known, but, after all, we're not a bunch of criminals."

"Aren't we? Potentially? I have a step-mother. I hate her. I wish she'd die. What do you say to that?"

"Only that it's not a very terrible secret."

"I want her money," said Hilary relentlessly. "Or, rather, my father's money that she has a life-interest in. It's a real life-interest in it; she married him when he was about Mr. Constable's age. She isn't much older than I am, and hard as scrap-iron. I'm learning how to be hard too.... Tell me: what do you think of our mind-reader, Mr. Pennik?"

"I think he's a fake," answered Sanders.

Hilary, who had been staring hard at the cigarette, glanced up with surprise and something like alarm. There was relief in it, too, and a jumble of emotions he could not read. Yet he knew that in some superstitious corner of her soul she was being impelled into belief in the powers of Herman Pennik.

"Why do you say that? He read your thoughts."

"Apparently. I've been thinking about that. I haven't worked it out, but it's just possible that a good part of the answer may lie with Larry Chase."

"With Larry Chase?" cried Hilary. "How?"

"You know how he talks. He's interested in people. He will give you somebody's life history and afterwards tell you and quite sincerely believe himself that he hasn't said a word. I remember, now I come to think of it, that he knew or suspected something about—well, Marcia Blystone and things I'd rather not discuss. He mentioned it in a letter he wrote to me. If Pennik is an expert in pumping people and later making them forget they've been pumped ..."

"But that wouldn't explain how Pennik would know *when* you might be thinking about something."

"I'm not so sure. We'll grant that he is an expert psychologist. All successful fortune-tellers have to be."

"What about that statue of Lister, or whoever it was? And—" Hilary hesitated. She did not look up. "Excuse me for mentioning this, but what about the other thing he said? The last thing?"

"Lister I admit I don't understand. What you call the

39

last thing may be merely because I haven't got as good a poker-face as I should like to have."

Literally for minutes Hilary did not speak. Throwing her cigarette into the empty fireplace, she got up and measured out steps on the carpet.

"There's his prophecy about Mr. Constable."

"Mr. Constable," said Sanders politely, "is not dead yet, you know. And even if Pennik can read minds, I'm hanged if I'll believe he can read the future."

"But if the whole thing is a huge fraud—"

"I don't say it is. A certain degree of telephathic power may be quite possible. Pennik may merely be bolstering it up, as certain honest men have done in other things, by a little conscious fraud and a remarkable deductive ability."

"Then you don't believe in thought as a physical weapon?"

"I will go to my grave denying it."

From two rooms away, Mina Constable began to scream when the hands of Sanders's watch stood at one minute to eight.

There was an animal quality about those screams, one of almost physical pain rather than fright. Mina Constable seemed to be trying to scream and speak at the same time, so that all they could hear was the endless repetition of her husband's name. Hilary, her hand on the mantelpiece, turned round with a face of pure superstitious terror. But she could not stand the sound of those screams; and Sanders was afraid she would begin to cry out as well.

He had the door to the hall open while the noise was still going on. And he saw the scene he was so many times afterwards to describe.

Sam Constable, fully dressed for dinner, was leaning against the hand-rail round the well of the stairs—within one step of the descent. He was sagging forward across the hand-rail, one hand partly supporting him on the newel-post. He raised the other hand spasmodically, the fingers twitching; he heaved his back, and for a second Sanders thought he would pitch forward over the rail on to the stairs below. But he was already too inert. He slid down beside the banisters, his body curving against them, and one hand struck with a flat thud on the carpet. His face had been turned away, so that Sanders could not see it until he rolled over on his back.

The screams stopped.

Mina Constable, her teeth biting on a handkerchief, stood in the half open door of one of the two rooms facing the head of the stairs. She did not move. With that piercing

40

din gone, it was possible to think. Sanders ran over and knelt beside him. There was a faint flutter of pulse, which stopped as Sanders found it; and the man was dead.

Sanders, still kneeling, looked round. Three doors were open on that hall: the door of Mina Constable's room, his own room, and Hilary's room. From his position he could see across obliquely into Hilary's room. He could see under the chairs, under the bed, even under the dressing-table against the far wall. And his eye was caught by the outlines of an object which had rolled unnoticed or uncared-for under the dressing-table, but which he was to remember afterwards.

It was a tall white chef's cap, with a muffin top.

Ringing with fluid chimes, and then breaking off in dignity for official pronouncement, the grandfather clock on the landing struck eight.

V

AND NOW, he noticed out of the corner of his eye, there were three persons looking out into the hall besides himself. Mina Constable still stood by the half-open door, her jaws shaking. Hilary had taken two steps out towards them, and stopped. Across the hall Lawrence Chase had just opened another door, leading to his bedroom. None of them moved.

A dim little cluster of bulbs burned at a corner of the landing by the grandfather clock, which seemed to rustle rather than tick. That light threw shadows of the hand-rail's banisters across Sam Constable's face and body. Methodically, shutting his mind to everything else, Sanders made an examination of the body. What he found caused him no alarm, but a shattering sense of relief. And yet—

He felt rather than saw Chase tiptoeing over to his side, and making several ineffectual attempts to look past his shoulder. But he did not turn round until Chase, with a kind of pounce, seized his arm. Chase was coatless and collarless, his stiff shirt bulging out between striped braces, and his long neck looking even longer. He had his collar in the other hand.

"Look here," Chase began with hoarse thinness. "He's not dead, is he? You're not going to tell me he's dead?"

"Yes."

"Sam is dead?"

"See for yourself."

"But it can't be," said Chase, holding Sanders with one hand and shaking the collar in his face with the other. He

41

crowded still closer. "It's not true. He didn't mean any of it. He couldn't have."

"Who couldn't have what?"

"Never mind. How did he die? Just tell me that. What was it?"

"Steady! You'll have me over this rail in a minute. Get away, damn it!— Rupture of the heart, I should think."

"Rupture?"

"Yes. Or it may be plain heart failure, where the heart is weak and just conks out by itself. Get away, will you?" said Sanders, brushing the collar away from his face with a feeling that a hundred collars were being shaken at him. "You heard him talk about a seizure. How was his heart, do you know?"

"His heart?" repeated Chase, with a powerful gleam of hope or relief. "I don't know. Probably very bad. Must have been. Poor old Sam. Ask Mina; that's it, ask Mina!"

Hilary had come out quietly and joined them. Sanders touched an arm of each of them.

"Listen to me," he said, "and please do as I tell you. Stay here with him; don't touch him, either of you, and don't let anyone else touch him. I'll be back in just one moment."

And he went over to the half-open door where Mina Constable was waiting. Pushing her gently back before him, he went into the room and closed the door.

She did resist him, but her knees began to sag with an effect less like that of a fall than of a collapsing paper lantern. He put his hands under her arms and put her gently down in a chair. She had not finished dressing; she was wearing a large, padded pink dressing-gown, very untidy, with waxy-stains on the right sleeve. She showed a muddled face from which the black hair was brushed back. All her attractiveness was gone because her vivacity had gone. The lips were white, the pulse very rapid. But it was only when she seemed to realize he was keeping her away from her husband, was holding her back gently in the chair, that she began to fight.

"It's all right, Mrs. Constable. We can't do anything now."

"But he's not *really* dead! He's not! I saw—"

"I'm afraid he is."

"You would know? You're a doctor. You would know, wouldn't you?"

Sanders nodded.

After a long silence, during which she shuddered, she let herself fall back in the chair. It was as though fright were passing, to be replaced by something else. She seemed to be

42

bracing herself; then, slowly, the tears welled up in her large imaginative eyes.

"It was his heart, wasn't it, Mrs. Constable?"

"What did you say?"

"His heart was weak, wasn't it?"

"Yes, he always—no, no, no!" cried Mina, coming to herself and peering at him in a blurred way. "His heart was as strong as an ox's. Dr. Edge told him that only a week ago. Nobody had such a good heart as he had. I think. What does it matter anyway? I don't know. I didn't give him his two clean handkerchiefs. It was the last thing he asked me to do."

"But what happened, Mrs. Constable?"

"I don't know, I don't know, I don't know."

"That is, why did you scream?"

"Please let me alone."

Sanders braced himself, feeling the sympathy he must now allow to show.

"You know I hate to trouble you, Mrs. Constable. But, you see, there are certain things we've got to do. We've got to send for a doctor, his own doctor; and perhaps even for the police." He felt the muscles stiffen in her arm. "I'll take the responsibility off your shoulders if you'll just tell me what happened, so that I can attend to it."

"Yes, you're right," she said, trying to tighten her jaws; but the tears flowed faster for this very resolution. "I'll do it. You're very decent to me."

"Then what happened?"

"He was in there—"

They were in Mina Constable's bedroom, a frilled place which nevertheless had a certain austerity about the furniture. It communicated with her husband's bedroom by way of a small bathroom. All doors were open through the suite. Straightening up, passing the back of her hand across her forehead, she indicated the other bedroom.

"He was in there. He'd just finished dressing. I was in here, sitting over there at that dressing-table. I wasn't ready; I had to help him dress, and I was late. All the doors were open. He called out and said, 'I'm going downstairs.' (It was the last thing he ever said to me.) I said, 'All right, dear.'" This nearly brought on a new paroxysm of tears, though she held her eyes as steady as though the eyelids were fixed.

"Yes, Mrs. Constable?"

"I heard his door close, the one out into the hall."

Again she stopped.

"Yes?"

"Then I wondered whether I had put out the two clean

43

handkerchiefs he asked for. One for the breast pocket, you know, and one to use."

"Yes?"

"I wanted to ask him. So I got up and put on a robe," her shaky fingers touched it; she illustrated everything with gestures; "and went over—there—and opened my door to look out into the hall. I expected he'd already got downstairs. But he hadn't. He was standing out there with his back to me. Dancing or staggering, or both."

Again it was several seconds before she could go on. The efforts she made to control her face, tightening the jaws and pressing her tongue against her teeth, were of bitter stubbornness.

"Dancing and staggering?"

"It looked like that. He fell. Across that hand-rail. I thought he was going over. I started to call out to him. I knew he was dying."

"Why?"

"I can feel things."

"Yes?"

"That's all. You came out. I heard what you said to Larry Chase."

"Then that will be enough, Mrs. Constable. I'll attend to the rest of it. Come over here and lie down for a while. By the way, you didn't see anybody else in the hall?"

"No."

"How long was it between the time you last spoke to your husband and the time you saw him like that in the hall?"

"About a minute. Why do you want to know?"

"Just wondering about the length of time a seizure would take."

Yet he could sense a new, queer undercurrent in her voice. And more: a kind of self-contempt, a fierce hesitation on the edge of a decision, which sent her off again. "I can't lie down," she said. "I won't lie down. I want to go and sit with him. I want to think. 'The soul of Adonais, like a star.' Oh, God help me."

"This way, Mrs. Constable. You'll feel more comfortable."

"I won't."

"That's better," said Sanders, gently pulling the down coverlet over her as she sank down on the bed. "Just a moment."

By the long breath she drew, he was reassured. He wondered if he could find a sleeping-tablet or a bromide in the house. With a person whose vivid imagination made her such a bundle of nerves and secret fears as Mina Constable, there

44

would probably be some such thing. And he wanted to cloud her wits before she began thinking about Herman Pennik.

He went into the bathroom. It was dark except for the glow coming through from Sam Constable's bedroom, and he switched on the light. The bathroom was a tiny, damp-smelling cubicle, fitted only with a tub, a towel-rail, a wash-bowl with hot and cold, and a medicine-cabinet. In the medicine-cabinet (so packed with bottles and appliances that he had to move his wrist carefully to avoid a crash) he found a cardboard box containing quarter-grain morphia tablets under the prescription of a Dr. J. L. Edge.

Sanders tipped two out into his hand.

Then, closing the door of the medicine-cabinet, he stared at the reflection of his own face in the glass.

"No!" he said aloud. And he dropped the tablets back in the box, returned it to the cabinet, and went back to the bedroom. Mina Constable was lying very quietly, her eyes half open and little wrinkles slackening round them.

"I'll be within call," he assured her. "Can you give me the name of your husband's doctor?"

"No. Yes. Near here?" She was evidently trying to be sensible and cool. "Dr. Edge. You can telephone him. Grove-top 62."

"Grovetop 62. Shall I turn out this light by the bed?"

"No!"

It was not that she half started upright which made him draw back his hand. He had seen something, and it tightened his subconscious fear of giving anyone any medicine in this house. Beside the bed there was a night-table; and near the lamp was a writing-board, a row of sharpened pencils, and several writing-pads restlessly torn. All the tops of the pencils were frayed or bitten by sharp teeth. Under and just behind the table were a couple of very small book-shelves that could be reached from the bed. Thrust in among an Oxford dictionary, a book of synonyms, and fat notebooks or press-cutting books, he saw a taller, thin volume in imitation leather; across it had been pasted a label with the shaky printed words, *New Ways of Committing Murder*.

He went softly out into the hall. Hilary Keen and Law-rence Chase, their backs to what lay beside the banisters, were waiting with an air of composure.

"Well?" asked Chase. His collar was crumpled up in his left hand.

"You know where things are in this house. Get to the telephone, ring Grovetop 62, ask for Dr. Edge, and ask him if he can come over here at once. We won't ring the police just yet."

"The police, eh? Just exactly what are you thinking, old son?"

"Oh, you never know. But to know what I'm thinking you don't have to be a mind-reader like . . . where is Pennik, by the way?"

The three of them looked at each other. Pennik's absence was a tangible thing. In all that weighty house they could not hear a sound except the clock ticking, and the noise, sudden, soft and in-drawn, of an uncontrollable sob from Mina Constable's bedroom.

"I'll go to her," said Hilary quickly; but Sanders intervened.

"In a minute. We ought to have a council of war, because we all may have to answer some questions. You would have thought that screaming would have brought the dead up here. Where is Pennik?"

"Why look at me?" inquired Chase. "How the hell should I know where he is?"

"Only that we left you downstairs with him when we came up to dress."

"Oh, that? I was only down there a couple of minutes, and that was well over half an hour ago. I simply showed him the kitchen, and said get on with it. Then I came up to my room; I've been there ever since. What was that number? Grovetop what? Six-two. Right. Dr. Edge. I'll phone him."

He turned round, almost stumbled over Sam Constable's body, and then pulled himself together before he went at long strides down the stairs. All this time it had been impossible to read Hilary Keen's expression. Again she took a step forward, and again Sanders stood in her way.

"Don't you think it would be better to let me go?" she asked. "That poor woman is crying her heart out in there."

"Listen," he said. "I'm not trying to order you about. But, believe me, I've been tangled up in criminal cases before"—one solitary instance, he admitted to himself, yet the force of that still remained with him—"and things can get pretty unpleasant unless the whole truth is told at the start. Will you answer me one straight question?"

"No."

"But—"

"No, I will not! I'm going in there to her." Then Hilary stopped, the blue eyes half smiling at his expression. "Oh, all right! What is it?"

46

"Something or somebody scared you half to death to-night. Was it Pennik? Was he in your room?"

"Good heavens, no!"

"Ah," said Sanders, with a breath of relief. "Then that's all right."

"Why on earth should you think Mr. Pennik was in my room?"

"It doesn't matter. It was only an idea."

Hilary's color was higher. "Oh, but it does matter. Despite what you may happen to think, it does matter a good deal, you know. Why should you think Mr. Pennik was in my room? For some curious reason, I, *I* of all people, seem to excite the worst suspicions in everybody. First Larry Chase, then Mr. Constable, and now you."

"We're not suspicious of you. We're only suspicious of ourselves."

"Explain that, please."

"I'm sorry I brought this up. Under the circumstances—"

"Oh, *he* won't hear you. He's dead."

"I can only say—"

"I'm sorry too," said Hilary, abruptly changing her tone. She lifted her closed fist to her mouth; she bit nervously at the forefinger; and then, in the emotional reaction after all that had happened, she was on the edge of tears. Sanders's attitude changed instantly.

"It's only that I damn well want to know what scared you. Because it probably has some bearing on that," he nodded towards the stairs, "that that's dead. And can't hear us, as you say."

"You think I'm a tough bit of goods, don't you?" asked Hilary quietly, and raised her eyes. "You're forgetting where I work. You're forgetting I probably know as much about violent death as you do. Oh, you wouldn't know me; I'm only one of the umpteen umpteen little assistants who help the real lawyers prepare the cases. But I don't want to know anything about it. I don't *want* to."

She touched his hand.

"Why did you say that about Mr. Pennik?"

"Come here," requested Sanders. He took her to the open door of her room. "Lean down and look under the dressing-table across there. You see what's on the floor? That white cap like a chef's cap?"

"Well?"

"Mrs. Constable offered one to Pennik early tonight, and said he ought to have it. I was only wondering . . ." Seeing the concentrated and yet bewildered expression of her face, he paused. "It's probably nothing. Only a wool-gathering

47

idea. If you say it wasn't Pennik, that's all there is to it."

"That unassuming, rather charming little man?"

"If you think so. Then where is that unassuming little man now?"

Almost soundless on the heavy carpet, Lawrence Chase bounded up the stairs. He took the treads two at a time, which may have been why he was out of breath.

"It's all right," he assured them. "Dr. Edge is coming over straightaway." He took hold of the newel-post with long, powerful fingers. "And look here, Sanders: it may merely be a pre-prandial case of the jitters, but I'm not sure we oughtn't to ring the police after all."

"No good being in a hurry. But why?"

"For one thing, Dr. Edge says there was nothing wrong with Sam's heart. For another, Pennik——"

"Did you see Pennik?"

"As a matter of strict fact," answered Chase, gripping the newel-post more tightly, "I didn't. Don't worry; he's down there right enough. We mustn't take it too seriously if he begins talking nonsense. But he's down there. I heard him, and so I didn't exactly relish the prospect of seeing him. I looked into the dining-room. He's got the kitchen door partly propped open with a wedge. He's in the kitchen, because I could hear him whistling, and a sound like salad being stirred in a wooden bowl. Er—he's got the dining-room all done out: every light on, best china and cutlery, Mina's Irish linen that she's so keen on, and flowers in a bowl on the table. But the table is only laid for five."

Part II

DARKNESS:

Concerning Death in the Air

PRESS

East Surrey Morning Messenger

April 30, 1938

DEATH OF MR. S. H. CONSTABLE

The many friends of Mr. Samuel Hobard Constable, of Fourways, nr. Grovetop, will learn with regret of Mr. Constable's sudden death early last night. Mr. Constable is conjectured to have suffered a heart attack while on his way down to dinner.

Mr. Constable, who was only 56, was the son of Sir Lawrence C. Constable, the textile manufacturer. He was educated at Hartonby and Simon Magus College, Cambridge. At the end of his first year at Cambridge he elected to enter the Civil Service, where his career, though unspectacular, was sound, constructive, and in keeping with the best traditions of empire. He retired at the death of his father in 1921. In 1928 he married Miss Wilhelmina Wright, better known to her many readers under the pen-name of Mina Shields. He leaves no children.

London Evening Griddle

(SATURDAY NIGHT FINAL)

April 30, 1938

THRILL-NOVELIST'S HUSBAND DIES BY MYSTERY STROKE!

WHAT CAUSED DEATH?
Police 'Puzzled.'

By Ray Dodsworth, *Evening Griddle* Crime Reporter.

Samuel Constable, wealthy husband of romantic novelist Mina Shields, collapsed and died before the eyes of friends last night in his Surrey home.

What killed him?

Heart-failure, it was stated. But a post-mortem was ordered by the coroner, Dr. J. L. Edge having refused a death-certificate. This post-mortem was performed this morning by Dr. Edge, with the assistance of none other than Dr. John Sanders, famous pathologist. Afterwards the doctors were in consulation nearly seven hours.

Why?

The reason is believed to be that no possible cause of death could be found. Every organ of the deceased's body was sound.

"Have the doctors any theory to account for this?" was the question put to Colonel F. G. Willow, Chief Constable for Surrey.

"It is certainly puzzling," replied Colonel Willow. "I have no further statement to make at this time."

"But can a man die from no cause whatever?"

"I have no further statement to make at this time," said Colonel Willow.

Questions to the guests assembled for a week-end party at Fourways, gloom-wrapped country house where the mysterious death took place, were not permitted.

London Evening Griddle

(SAME ISSUE)

STOP-PRESS

Chief Inspector Humphrey Masters, of
Scotland Yard, will leave tomorrow for
Grovetop, Surrey, in connection with the
mysterious death of Samuel H. Constable.

VI

ON SUNDAY MORNING, when even the grass and hedgerows
seem to wake up late, drowsy sunlight poured through every
open door of the Black Swan Hotel between Guildford and
Grovetop. Dr. Sanders sat by the open windows of the parlor, drinking coffee and blinking out against the sun. It was
so quiet that he could even hear fowls scrabbling in the yard
behind the hotel. Then a car drew up noisily; and he
felt a vast relief to see the large, bland face of Chief Inspector Masters looking up at him from the road.

"Ah, sir!" said Masters, coming into the parlor with the
air of a galleon under full sail, and shaking hands with a
great bustle of cheerfulness. "Good morning, good morning,
good morning! Beautiful morning, isn't it?"

"I suppose it is."

The chief inspector refused to have his spirits damped. But
he was more subdued when he sat down.

"Coffee? Don't mind if I do. Lummy, sir, *you* look a bit
done in!"

"I suppose I am, a little."

"Well, I expect we shall be able to put that right. Eh?"
said Masters heartily. The coffee arrived, and he stirred it
with vigor. "And how are things with you, sir? Any news
from Miss Blystone? She's well, I hope?"

"So far as I know, she is perfectly well," snapped Sanders,
turning on him such a feezing look that the other stared.
Master's forehead grew more ruddy. Then, coming to a de-

51

cision after a shrewd look at his companion, the chief inspector hitched his chair close to the table with a conspiratorial air.

"Now, sir, what's all this about?" he asked, low-voiced and hearty. "I don't know why you should snap my head off for asking after Miss Blystone; but it's no ruddy business of mine anyway, so *that's* all right."

"Sorry. I didn't mean that."

Masters looked at him keenly. "The main thing is, what about that message you sent me? You said to come here, and here I am. But you know, Doctor, you know as well as anybody else, that I've got a duty to do. My duty's to drive straight on to Grovetop and report to the Superintendent there. Just so!" He was very persuasive. "Why should you want me to see you and get the facts from you first?"

"Because you'll blow up," said Sanders simply. "You'll go straight up and hit the ceiling. I thought you had better have warning."

Masters sat up.

"Bad as that?"

"Yes."

"Lummy, we're in it again," said Masters, after a pause. "Well, sir, I don't mind. I tell you straight, I don't. I've seen too much in the past six or seven years, and you don't know your man if you think anything could surprise me now." Nevertheless, his worry grew. "Besides, what's all the row? From what I could hear, it's nothing to be alarmed about. This old gentleman, Mr. Constable, was seen by his wife to walk out of his bedroom towards the stairs. In the middle of the landing he suddenly threw a fit, fell down, and died in a couple of minutes. Right?"

"Right as far as it goes."

"Oh?" said Masters, giving him a quick look. "Can you help me out further than that?"

"A little. It's not in the least complicated, if that's what you mean. On Friday night six persons were staying at Fourways: Mr. and Mrs. Constable, Miss Hilary Keen, Mr. Lawrence Chase, Mr. Herman Pennik, and myself. Our respective positions just before Constable died were as follows. Constable himself was dressing in his bedroom, which adjoins his wife's bedroom by way of a bath. Mrs. Constable was dressing in her bedroom. Mr. Chase was also dressing in his bedroom. Miss Keen was talking to me in my bedroom. All these rooms are on the same floor, set round three sides of a square. The only other guest, Mr. Pennik, was downstairs in the kitchen getting us a scratch meal.

"At about two minutes to eight Constable called out to his

wife, through open doors between, that he had finished dressing and was going downstairs. Just as she heard his door close into the hall, she remembered that she had forgotten to ask whether she had given him two clean handkerchiefs. She went over and opened her door into the hall.

"Both their rooms face across towards the third side of the square—formed by the side of the staircase, with a handrail. Mrs. Constable saw her husband standing in the hall with his back to her. Not standing, exactly. She described him as 'dancing and staggering.' "

Masters had taken out his notebook, which he spread flat on the table. His hard eye was speculative. He seemed to sense that something was going on under the surface, but could not quite catch what.

" 'Dancing and staggering?' Oh, ah. Just what did she mean by that?"

"She couldn't or wouldn't be clearer."

"Yes, sir. Go on."

"He pitched forward across the hand-rail guarding the stairs, and she began to scream. I was out in the hall within a couple of seconds after she started to scream. Constable was writhing across the hand-rail; he was twitching his left hand in the air—so—and seemed to be trying to push himself over. He fell down beside the rail instead, and died a few seconds after I reached him."

"Oh what, sir?" asked the chief inspector sharply.

"I thought at first it was rupture of the heart. Everything was characteristic: sudden pain, collapse, cramps, extremities cool and damp. And earlier in the evening he had mentioned a 'seizure' as though he were afraid of one. But I didn't like the dilation of the eye-pupils. I tried to question Mrs. Constable about his heart. But she was in no condition to be questioned about anything. That was the situation—a simple situation, you'll admit—until I talked to Dr. Edge, Mr. Constable's own doctor."

"Just so. Well?"

His heart was as sound as yours or mine. The man was a hypochondriac, that's all. And worse. At the postmortem we found every organ healthy: there was nothing whatever to show what had caused his death."

"But you *will* find it? Eh, Doctor?"

"I don't understand you."

"We-el, now!" said Masters, pursing up his lips and making noises of broad skepticism. He was indulgent. "It may look bad, I admit; but I don't see much to get the wind up about. Doctors are always going on like that. Arguments about what caused death——"

53

"I am telling you that there was nothing to show what caused his death. When the house falls on your head you'll understand why that is so important. And doctors do not 'go on like that.'"

"What would you say to poison, now?" suggested Masters, with the air of one making a fair business-proposition.

"No."

"Oh, ah? Sure?"

"Yes. Unless you're giving me 'mysterious poisons unknown to science,' which I won't swallow." In spite of himself Sanders grinned. "Inspector, I'll stake my reputation (such as it is) that Constable didn't die of any kind of poison, solid, liquid, or gaseous. Dr. Edge and I have been at it until we're half blind, and if there's any test we've omitted I should be interested to hear about it. It won't do."

The chief inspector scratched the side of his jaw. He had begun to look suspicious, a sign that he was disturbed.

"Then there's something wrong," he declared. "Eh? After all, you know, something killed the chap. That's to say, a man can't just drop over dead without there being *any* sign of what killed him."

"Oh, yes, he can," said Sanders.

"Sir?"

"On the contrary. I can tell you at least three ways in which a completely sound and healthy person can die without any sign, internal or external, to show what killed him."

"But that won't do!"

"Why not?"

"Because—well, lummy!" exploded Masters, making a broad gesture. He got up and stared out of the bright window, jingling coins in his pocket. "That'd put us in a bit of a hole, wouldn't it? I ask you, where would the police be if people started dying all over the place and not a blinking thing to show what polished 'em off?"

"Ah, now we're getting closer to the difficulty. We haven't quite hit it yet, but we're closer. I've copied out a statement here which you can hand over to the press if things get too hot. It isn't my statement, by the way, and it will carry a good deal of authority. It's a quotation from Taylor,[1]. so you can believe it."

He unfolded a sheet of paper covered with his own careful handwriting.

" *'Among non-professional persons a prejudice exists that*

[1] *Taylor's Principles and Practice of Medical Jurisprudence,* Seventh Edition, 1920. (London: J. & A. Churchill, 7 Great Marlborough St.)

54

no person can die from violence unless there be some distinctly mortal injury inflicted on the body—i.e., *a visible mechanical injury to some organ or blood-vessel important to life. This is an erroneous notion, since death may take place from the disturbance of the functions of an organ important to life without this being necessarily accompanied by a perceptible alteration of structure.'* "[2]

He pushed the paper across the table.

"There you have it, short and sweet. I repeat that I can tell you at least three ways in which a person can die by violence without any sign, internal or external, to show what killed him."

Masters was after this like a terrier.

"Oh, ah? You say 'violence.' You mean—murder?"

"Yes."

"I see," muttered the chief inspector, after a pause. He sat down and squared himself. "I don't mind admitting I'm learning things every minute. Only, whenever I talk to you or Sir Henry Merrivale, they're always things I wish weren't so. Three ways, eh? All right, Doctor: let's have 'em."

"First. People have been known to be killed very quickly as the result of an unexpected blow on the upper part of the abdomen or on the pit of the stomach. It acts on the nerves or nerve-ganglia. Yet there has been no mark of a bruise externally, or any physical injury internally, to account for death."

"Stop a bit," said Masters, sitting up. "You don't mean you could give somebody an unexpected wallop in the bread-basket and kill him?"

"Well, I shouldn't rely on it as a never-failing method of murder. You might kill him; and then again you mightn't. My point is that it has been known to happen. If you did that without witnesses, and the victim died, there would be nothing on earth to tell what had killed him."

"Is that so, now?" Masters ruminated. "Go on. What's the second way?"

"Second. People have died without mark from concussion of the brain. A man gets a severe blow on the head; he falls down dead on the spot or later dies unconscious. There may be a slight abrasion of the scalp. There may be no abrasion of the scalp at all; in the brain there may be no laceration or rupture of the blood-vessels, and all the other organs are healthy. Yet the man has died of violence."

"H'm. Third way?"

"Third. Nervous shock, caused by surprise or fright. Usually ascribed to vagus inhibition of the heart. Don't snort:

[2] *Taylor*, vol. I, p. 381.

it's a solid fact and a solid scientific force which can knock over a healthy man like a ninepin, with no external or internal mark on him.

"There are several other ways as well; though none of them will apply here.[3]. For instance, people have died without mark from electric shock, and you'd naturally think of that in a house so full of electric fittings. But he wasn't within yards of any such fitting; there isn't enough current to kill him if he were; and the whole point of electricity is that, if it kills, it kills on the split-second. Furthermore, there are certain drugs—like insulin—very difficult to spot if injected hypodermically; but I think we should have spotted anything of that sort. I don't want you to be under any misconceptions about it. That much at least I can do for you when your hour of great trouble rolls round."

For some moments Masters had been regarding him with a narrow and speculative eye, his forehead growing redder.

"Excuse me, Doctor," he said soothingly. "But are you feeling quite all right?"

"More or less."

"Glad to hear it. Because for the life of me I don't understand what ails you. Lummy, don't you see you've explained the whole thing? What more do you want? Let me see if I've got this straight. Mr. Constable could have died from a blow to the body with a fist. Or he could have died from a blow over the head with a blunt instrument. Or (hurrum!) somebody could have leaned out and said, 'Boo!' to him. If you don't mind," said Masters, with skeptical indulgence, "we'll just be dignified and call that last one vagus inhibition of the heart. Anyhow, there are three ways to account for his death?"

"Yes."

"Just so. And you believe he was deliberately murdered?"

"I do."

"Mind!" said the chief inspector, raising one finger. "No decisions yet. We'll wait for the facts, my lad. But let's argue this. The old gentleman, Mr. Constable, told his wife he was going down to dinner and walked out into the hall?"

"Yes."

"Between the time she spoke to him last, and the time she opened the door and saw him in a fit out in the hall —how long a time elapsed, now?"

"About a minute, she says."

[3] In looking over these notes of what I said, I think it only fair to add that Constable was not killed by any mechanical device which operated in the absence of the guilty person. The presence of the guilty person was necessary to make the method succeed. The reader is warned.—J.S.

"About a minute. Did anybody else look out into the hall up to the time the lady screamed?"

"No."

"So he was a whole minute alone in the hall?"

"Right."

"Suppose," pursued Masters, "there'd been a murderer waiting for him out there. Suppose the murderer got him as he came out. Eh? Caught him to the body or over the head. Wouldn't there have been ample time for the murderer to have slipped away—down the stairs, or back into one of the bedrooms—before Mrs. Constable looked out?"

"Ample time, I agree."

"Then—?"

"You see," Sanders explained, "we are now entering the narrows of the trouble. All this may be true. Take what theory you like. But even supposing it were true, *how could you prove it?*"

There was a silence. Masters started to get up, and started to speak; but he checked himself in both motions. His eyes grew fixed.

"Am I making myself clear?" inquired Sanders. "The point is that there is nothing whatever to show how he died. It is possible that he might have died from a blow to the body or head, which in itself might have been caused by an accidental fall when he was alone. In either case, you have no grounds for saying that he did die like that. It might just as well have been a pure accident of nervous shock, again when he was alone. There is no realm more mysterious, more incalculable, or less understood than that same nervous shock you were making such fun of a minute ago. People have died from seeing a railway-accident. From listening to a radio broadcast. From games and initiations. Even from thinking they were attacked when there wasn't a soul near. But, since we haven't the remotest notion of how Sam Constable did die, you will never be able to prove anything. Masters, if this is murder, the murderer is perfectly safe from the law."

Again there was a silence.

"But it's not reasonable!" protested Masters querulously.

"No. The only trouble is that it sometimes happens."

"Well, sir, we'll have to see what we can do about it," said Masters, with an attempt at cheerfulness. "All the same, I'm bound to admit I don't like that lack-of-proof thing—"

"Oh, that's the least of your worries."

Again the chief inspector started to speak; then he regarded his companion with some suspicion. "Just a minute,

Doctor. If I didn't know you so well, blow me if I wouldn't think there was something queer in all this! Are you sure you're not on a wild-goose chase? Murder? By everything you've told me, the whole thing could have been accidental death? Eh? Just so. Then why have you been stirring everybody up with the idea that Mr. Constable didn't die naturally?"

"Because a mind-reader named Herman Pennik said he would die round about eight o'clock on Friday night," answered Sanders. "And I don't believe in mind-readers."

Along the main road outside, where the sun was strengthening towards midday, a bus lumbered past at its Sunday gait. The bus stopped with a squealing of brakes, and Sanders glanced at his watch. Meantime, Chief Inspector Masters had been looking at him fixedly. After drawing a deep breath, the chief inspector got up and walked out of the room. Dr. Sanders heard him speaking in the dulcet tones of one who wishes to cajole an idiot.

"Miss," he was saying, "is the bar open here on Sundays?"

An indignant female voice replied that it was.

"Ah!" said Masters. "Two pints of bitter in here, miss, *if* you please."

Mr. Herman Pennik was at this moment getting down from the bus outside. Dr. Sanders could not have said why he seemed so incongruous in that homely road on Sunday. Yet Sanders was oppressed by the same feeling that had troubled him ever since the death of Sam Constable: a feeling that with every hour Pennik's character was growing and emerging like a mango-tree under a cloth, stirring the dull cloth, sending out tentacles.

Chief Inspector Masters returned carrying two tankards of bitter. His air was one of elaborate off-handedness.

"Now, Doctor!" he said. "By the way, seen anything of the old man recently? Sir Henry, I mean?"

"He's coming down here this afternoon."

"Is he, now? Does he know what you've just told me?"

"Not yet."

"Ah!" said Masters, with a sudden unholy relish which could not altogether have applied to the beer. "Knows nothing about it, then? Bit of a surprise for him, eh? Well, well, well! Well, here's all the best."

"All the best. And in the meantime there's someone else I'd like you to meet. He's here now. (Hoy! Mr. Pennik! This way!) This," Sanders went on, "is Mr. Masters, who is a chief inspector from Scotland Yard. Masters, this is

58

Mr. Pennik, the thought-reading phenomenon I was telling you about. I sent for him to come here too."

Masters's musing satisfaction had been short-lived. Putting down his tankard hastily, he gave Sanders a brief reproachful glare before he turned with his usual blandness to Pennik.

"Yes, sir? I didn't quite catch—?"

"I am what Dr. Sanders calls the thought-reader," said Pennik, his eyes never leaving the other's face. "Dr. Sanders told me you would be put in charge of the case."

Masters shook his head.

"I'm afraid I'm not as yet, sir. So there's not much I could know about it, is there? However," he became confidential, "if you wouldn't mind giving me your own views, strictly sub-ju-de-cay and among ourselves of course, I don't say it wouldn't help me a lot. Take this chair, sir. What'll you have to drink?"

(Watch out for him when he's in this mood.)

"Thank you," said Pennik. "I never drink. It is not that I have any objection to it; but it always upsets my stomach."

"Ah! Lot of people'd be better off without it, I daresay," declared Masters, surveying his tankard wisely. "However! The trouble is, you see, that some people would say we haven't a case anyway. Be a bit awkward, wouldn't it, if we cut up a row and then found Mr. Constable had died a natural death?"

Pennik frowned slightly, turning a pleasant but puzzled look towards Sanders. Yet again there was that suggestion of the mango-tree stirring under the dull cloth; and it was not pleasant.

"Dr. Sanders cannot have told you much about the case," he said. "Of course it was not a natural death."

"You believe that too?"

"Naturally. I know it."

Masters chuckled.

"You know it, sir?" he inquired. "Then perhaps you can even tell us who killed him?"

"Of course," answered Pennik, lifting one hand to touch himself lightly on the chest. "*I* killed him."

VII

IT WAS THE LIFTING of the hand that did it. Why, it might be wondered, was there a faint hint of the florid about Pennik this morning? His country tweeds were as solid and

59

unobtrusive as Sam Constable's. His soft hat and crooked stick lay across the table. His manner (perhaps fiercely) was so repressed as to seem wooden. But on the little finger of his left hand was a ring set with a bloodstone.

Nothing could have exceeded the grotesque contrast between that ring and his surroundings: the country pub, the Sunday countryside with fowls in it, the sunlight through fresh curtains on Pennik's bullet head. The ring changed him; it lit him up.

Sanders saw it to such an extent that he missed the expression on Master's face.

But he heard the tone of the chief inspector's voice.

"What's that you said?"

"I said *I* killed him. Didn't Dr. Sanders tell you?"

"No, sir, he did not. So that's why you're here, is it?" Masters drew himself up. "Herman Pennik: do you wish to make a statement about the death of Mr. Constable?"

"If you like."

"One moment! I must warn you that you are not obliged to make any statement; but that, if you do, anything—"

"That'll be quite all right, Inspector," Pennik assured him; and Sanders saw peeping out from behind those quiet features a huge amusement. But there was annoyance in it as well. "I cannot understand, though, why Dr. Sanders failed to tell you. Nor do I understand the cause of all the uproar. Dr. Sanders will bear me out when I say that I carefully warned Mr. Constable, in the presence of all the others, that I was going to try to kill him. I did not say it was *certain*, mind you, because I was not sure I could manage it. I only intimated that I meant to try. How there could have been any misunderstanding it is difficult to imagine. I certainly don't lay claim to supernatural powers; and nobody, so far as I know, has ever been able to read the future. I intimated that I would kill him, and I did kill him. Hence why all the fuss about it?"

"Goddelmighty," said Masters, getting his breath. "Let me get a word in edgeways, sir! I must warn you that you are not obliged to make any statement; but that, if you do—"

"And I repeat that it will be quite all right, Mr. Masters. I am told that I can make whatever statement I like without danger to myself."

"Who told you that?"

"My lawyer."

"Your—"

"Or, rather," Pennik corrected himself, "he was my lawyer. (I mean Mr. Chase.) He has since recoiled from me and said he thought I was joking. But I was not joking."

"No sir?"

"No. Before killing Mr. Constable, I asked Mr. Chase whether I could be charged with murder if I killed him under the conditions I described. Mr. Chase said I could not. Otherwise I should not have done it. I have a horror of being shut up; it unnerves me; and the experiment was not worth while if I ran the risk of being tried for it."

"I daresay not, sir. How do you feel about hanging, though?"

"Are you also under the impression that I am joking, Mr. Masters?"

Masters cleared his throat powerfully. "Now, now, sir! We've got to take it easy, you see. Excuse me, Doctor: but is this gentleman crazy?"

"Unfortunately, no," said Sanders briefly.

"Thank you, Doctor," said Pennik with great gravity; but behind that broad nose Sanders thought he detected a flash of malice, which was spreading to the whole face with the effect of flattening it.

"Well, why didn't you go to the local police with your story?"

"I did," said Pennik.

"When?"

"As soon as they were called in. I wished to make sure that nothing could be done to me, you see."

"And how did they feel about it?"

"They agreed that nothing could be done. . . . As regards how they felt about it, that is a different matter. Colonel Willow, I believe, kept a straight bat and a stiff upper lip; but Superintendent Belcher is made of less stern stuff and I understand that only the thought of a wife and four children prevented him from putting his head into the gas-oven."

Masters turned round with dangerous calm.

"Is this true, Doctor?"

"Quite true."

"Then why the blazes didn't you tell me?"

"That's what I'm doing," Sanders answered patiently. "That's why you're here. Like Mr. Pennik, I warned you. It didn't seem wise to—er—give you the works all at once."

"But, blast it all, the police can't be crazy too!"

"They are not," Pennik assured him. "Though at first they seemed to share your original view about me. However, I agree with you that Dr. Sanders should have told you. I told Dr. Sanders, and the other guests at Fourways, just as soon as the thing happened. For some curious reason they seem—all except the doctor here—to regard me with a kind of superstitious terror. They even refused to eat a meal which I was at some trouble to prepare. I tried to explain, but they would not listen. Of course I was proud to have succeeded"—again there was a curious flash across his face—"but I am a human being; I lay no claim to supernatural powers. Such ideas are nonsense."

Masters corked himself down. For a moment he breathed slowly and steadily, as though counting. Then he raised his head.

"If you don't mind, sir," he went on, with a kind of bursting suavity, "we'll just take this thing from the beginning. Eh? Do you mean to sit there and tell me you killed Mr. Constable?"

"I am afraid we can never get any further, Inspector, unless you at least try to consider that as a possibility and stop asking the same question. Yes. I killed him."

"Right you are. Right you are! *How* did you kill him?"

"Ah, that is my secret." Pennik grew thoughtful. "I am suddenly beginning to realize what an important secret it might be in this world. You cannot expect me to betray that."

"Can't I, by George!—No, wait, steady! Easy does it. Now. Why did you kill him?"

"There are you more easily answered. I regarded him as an ill-mannered imbecile, brutal to his wife, insulting to his guests, an obstruction to all mental or moral progress. Judged as a person, he had challenged me beyond all human patience. Judged as the subject of an experiment, he was a man whose loss would hardly be felt in the scheme of things. Even though Dr. Sanders disagrees with me in everything else, he will agree with me in that. And so I made him the subject of an experiment."

"An experiment," repeated Masters. "Come now, sir! About how you did it," he spoke with broad persuasiveness, "just what means did you use? Have you developed a new blow to the abdomen, now? One that always works? Or a new way of coshing, maybe? Or frightening the poor bloke?"

"So you have been hearing about the scientific possibilities," observed Pennik, turning his light eyes towards Sanders.

"Well, which one of those ways did you use?"

"That is what you will have to find out for yourself," smiled Pennik.

"Oh, ah? So you admit you used one of those ways?"

"On the contrary. I used none of them, except in a certain sense."

"Except in a certain sense? What do you mean by that?"

"That I certainly used a weapon which can strike and, if properly applied, kill. If you want a name for it, call it Tele-force—the power of drawing out or, conversely, crushing, from afar. I did not know"—again the white look came round his eyes and gills—"that it could be made quite so strong. Inspector, I am very tired. Do not try me too far now. But it is an extension of the same process which enables me to tell what you are thinking at the moment."

So you know what I'm thinking about, do you?" inquired Master, putting his head on one side.

Pennik smiled vaguely.

"Well, of my untimely demise, of course. That will be evident to anybody who looks at you. I was referring to your hidden thoughts, the thought you have been trying to banish out of your mind. You have been putting on an air of false and forced geniality today because you are hideously worried. You have a child (a daughter, I think) who goes into a nursing home tomorrow for an operation for appendicitis. She is not a strong child; and you did not sleep at all last night for worrying."

Masters went red, and then rather pale. His friend had never seen such an expression on his face.

"Did you tell him that?" the chief inspector demanded, whirling round.

"I didn't know it," said Sanders. "I'm sorry."

"But it is true?" asked Pennik. "Be persuaded, my friend. You will have to acknowledge it sooner or later."

"We'll just leave my affairs out of it, sir, *if* you please," said Masters. "Hurrum! Now I don't suppose you could prove what you were doing when Mr. Constable was killed?"

"I have been wondering when you would ask that question," replied Pennik, showing his teeth. "Let us clear it up once and for all. Dr. Sanders (and Miss Keen as well) will testify that Mr. Constable was alive and in very good health at a quarter to eight on Friday night. I believe he had gone to investigate some curious occurrences in Dr. Sander's room." Here a flash of malice passed towards Sanders; you could almost feel it like a vibration. "At this time I was downstairs. At about a quarter to eight the doorbell rang—the back doorbell, that is. I answered it. A certain Mrs. Chichester had promised to come and get the household a meal since all the servants were away. It was Mrs. Chichester, accompanied by her son Lewis: evidently as a chaperon. I was going to get the meal, but I told them they might help me if they liked. For some reason they seemed nervous—"

Here Sanders interposed. It was one of the parts he liked least about the whole affair.

"Why not tell the chief inspector why they were nervous, Mr. Pennik?"

"I don't understand."

"Mrs. Chichester and her son," Sanders explained "will tell you that when Mr. Pennik opened the door to them he breathed as though he had been running, and rolled his eyes round. From a quarter to eight until eight o'clock he was occasionally inflicted with a minor seizure. At eight o'clock, when Mrs. Constable began to scream upstairs, they couldn't stand it any longer. They bolted out of the house as though the devil were after them, and didn't come back."

"Yes, sir? What about it?" frowned Masters.

Sanders looked at Pennik.

"I was only wondering why he breathed hard when he opened the door. Had he been upstairs, for instance?"

"No, I had not," said Pennik. "But Dr. Sanders has very kindly," a slight pause, "has *very* kindly outlined my case for me. Mrs. Chichester and son will tell you that between a quarter to eight and eight o'clock I did not stir out of the kitchen or the dining-room: the door was propped open between those two rooms, and they can be sure of it. As a matter of medical fact, Dr. Sanders will tell you that Mr. Constable died at about eight o'clock. That takes care of everything, I think."

Masters put his fists on his hips.

"Oh? A perfect alibi, eh?"

"As you say, a perfect alibi," grinned Pennik.

There was a pause.

"Now, Inspector, I know the law of England. You dare not arrest me: you could not even get a warrant. You cannot try any such weapon as the third-degree. You cannot even shut me up under the mysterious term of a 'material witness'; as I say, I have a horror of being shut up. In any case I am not a witness. I merely killed the man. But I really do not see what you are going to do about it."

The chief inspector stared back at him, speechless. Pennik reached out for his hat and stick. The hot sunlight touched his shabby sandy hair; briefly, he expanded his chest and raised his eyes upward.

His voice suddenly deepened as though with inspiration.

" '*And it came to pass,*' " said Pennik, " '*at the seventh time, when the priests blew with the trumpets, Joshua said unto the people, Shout; for the Lord hath given you the city.*' " He closed his large fist and brought it down with a crash on the table.

"With my heart and body and brain I have made a new and great power, gentlemen. I have plundered the treasure-house of the unknown. Dr. Sanders will tell you that there is no realm more mysterious, more incalculable, or less understood than the force called nervous shock; but I have found its secret. Before I have finished I shall have made bats and owls of their scientists, and shown their logic for puerility. But the gift must be used sparingly. It must be used for good. Yes. Always for good. Always, always, always. Mr. Constable, however estimable you might have thought him, will hardly be missed—"

"It hadn't occurred to you," said Sanders, "that he might be missed by his wife?"

"His wife!" said Pennik, half-contemptuously.

"She is a useful and decent woman. Will you understand me if I say that, always providing you did do this, you broke her heart?"

" 'Always providing I did it?' " repeated Pennik, raising his sandy eyebrows slightly.

"That is what I said."

Pennick leaned across the table and spoke in a different voice.

"Are you challenging me, sir?" he inquired.

There was a silence. It was broken by Chief Inspector Masters.

"Steady!" he roared. "Steady, now. This can't go on. It can't, I tell you!"

"You are quite right," agreed Pennik, drawing a deep breath. "I beg your pardon, Doctor. I must keep in mind certain facts; I must do nothing foolish or hasty." He turned half-petulant. "Try to understand me, gentlemen. I claim no supernatural powers of any kind; I work by a natural force well known to myself. I do not say the force would *always* operate. No, no, no. I am more modest than that: I say it would perhaps succeed in seven cases out of ten. This I shall make quite clear to the gentlemen of the press—"

A new cause for worry presented itself to Masters.

"Now, now!" he said. "Half a tick! You don't mean you're going to talk to the newspapers?"

"And why not?"

"But you can't do that, sir!"

"Oh? And how do you propose to stop me, Inspector? ... There were quite a number of journalists at the Grovetop police-station. I told them I should issue a statement later in the day. I was first approached," he took a card out of his pocket and studied it, "by Mr. Dodsworth of the *Evening Griddle*. The *Griddle*, I am informed, is a 'scandal-sheet.' I do not object to it on those grounds: scandal is often stimulating and healthy. But there are others which are definitely not scandal-sheets. Let me see. Mr. Banks of the *News-Record*. Mr. MacBain of the *Daily Trumpeter*. Mr. Norris of the *Daily Non-Stop*. Mr. O'Brien of the *Evening Banner*. Mr. Westhouse of the *Daily Wireless*. And (yes, here we are) Mr. Kynaston of the *Times*."

Masters choked.

"So you want publicity, eh?"

"My dear sir, I neither court publicity nor do I coyly shrink from it. If these gentlemen have any questions to ask me, I shall be happy to answer them."

"Oh, ah? And you propose to tell them what you've just told me?"

"Naturally."

"You know they won't be allowed to print a word of it, don't you?"

"We must see what happens," said Pennik, uninterested. "It would be unfortunate if I were compelled to exercise my power again merely to prove it. Do not drive me to those lengths, my friend. I am a simple-minded soul and I wish to do the right thing by everybody. And now, if you have no further use for me at the moment, I will say good day. You will be able to find me at Fourways whenever you want me. True, Mrs. Constable has ordered me out; her dislike of me has begun to border on the maniacal; but the police have told me to stay and, as you notice, I am always happy to obey any reasonable request."

"Sir, I'm telling you straight! I forbid you to say a word about this to any news—"

"Don't be a fool, Inspector. Good day."

It was his last word. He adjusted his hat, picked up the crooked stick, and went out after a cool nod to Sanders. They saw him going rather self-consciously along the road towards the bus-stop. Sanders said one word.

"Well?"

"He's insane," declared the chief inspector.

"Do you really believe that?"

"What else can he be?" said Masters. He brooded. "And yet there's *something* about the man. I'll admit that. Lummy, I never had anybody talk to me quite like that before in all my born days. For the life of me I can't treat him like the usual crank who comes in and says he did a murder. I know that kind; met thousands of 'em; and, I tell you straight, he won't fit in."

"Suppose," muttered Sanders thoughtfully, "just suppose, and don't rise up in wrath: but suppose he says somebody else is going to die at a certain time—and the person does?"

"I shouldn't believe it, that's all."

"Well, that's very straightforward and sensible; but it's not much help, is it? Can you imagine what the popular press could do with a story like this? No wonder they think it's hot."

Masters shook his head skeptically. "I'm not much worried about that side of it, sir. Even off their own bats there isn't a paper in town that'd dare handle a yarn like that; and they certainly wouldn't when they get their orders. But what worries me—urr!—yes, I'll admit it. What worries me is that I think that chap *did* kill Mr. Constable after all."

"Are you being converted?"

"Not like you mean. Not me. But, Doctor, that chap was sincere. He meant it, or I'm a Dutchman. I can smell things like that. What I mean is that he's maybe got a new, simon-pure, fool-proof way of polishing people off, like a new kind of blow to the stomach..."

"Even when it can be proved absolutely that he was downstairs with Mrs. Chichester and her son?"

"What we want is facts," said Masters doggedly. He considered, and his expression had a far-away gleam. "So far as I can see, there's just one consolation so far. Lord, how it's going to get hold of a certain gentleman we both know!" And now round his eyelid there was the suggestion of a happy wink. "Just between ourselves, Doctor, what do you think Sir Henry Merrivale is going to say?"

VIII

Phooey!" said H.M.

At about the time Fourways was built, certain enterprising decorators made popular an article of furniture or decoration which was known as the "Turkish corner." In one corner of your drawing-room you built up a small nook or alcove hung with heavy Eastern curtains, tasseled and thick-draped. These framed a recess filled by a striped ottoman; dim scimitars hung crossed on the wall inside. Sometimes a tiny yellow glass lantern burned there, but not often. The effect was towards mysteriousness and romanticism at home; inevitably, the Turkish corner attracted courting couples and also all the dust in the house.

In the gloom of late afternoon, in the drawing-room at Fourways, H.M. sat on the edge of the ottoman and glared.

Even Masters had seldom seen a more malevolent expression on his face. Moving his glasses up and down his nose, he peered alternately between Dr. Sanders and the chief inspector. Occasionally, as he shifted his large bulk on the ottoman, dust would sift down on his bald head and make him look up and swear. But he was too concentrated or too dignified to move. Or perhaps he rather liked the Turkish corner.

"And that's the situation, Sir Henry," said Masters almost happily. "Just offhand, now, what would you say about it?"

H.M. sniffed.

"I'd say," he answered querulously, "what I've said before. I dunno why it is. But, Masters, you manage to get tangled up in some of the goddamndest cases I ever heard tell of. They won't let you alone, will they? You'd think that sooner or later they'd get tired of thinkin' up ingenious dirty tricks especially for your benefit, and go off and pester somebody else for a while. But, oh, no. No such luck. Will you tell me why it is?"

"I suppose it's because I get mad so easily," Masters admitted, with a certain candor. "Like you."

"Like me?"

"Yes, sir."

"What d'ye mean, like me?" said H.M., suddenly putting his head up. "Have you got the infernal, star-gazin' cheek to suggest that I, I of all people in the world—"

"Now, now, sir! I didn't mean anything like that."

"I'm glad to hear it, said H.M., brushing the lapels of his coat with immense dignity, and relaxing. "In all this world there's nothin' but misconceptions, misconceptions, misconceptions. Take me, for instance. Do they appreciate me? Haa! You bet they don't."

Sanders and the chief inspector stared at him. This was a new mood: not the plaint, of course, but the dreariness of the tone which seemed to suggest that flesh is but grass, and man traveleth a weary road but to die.

"Er—there's nothing wrong, is there?"

"What d'ye mean, wrong?"

"Well, sir—this reducing business hasn't affected your health, or anything like that?"

"I've been makin' a speech," said the chief of the Military Intelligence Department, inspecting his shoes gloomily. Then he fired up again. "After all, I was only tryin' to do somebody a good turn, wasn't I? I'm a member of the Government, ain't I? It was to help Squiffy out. Y'see, Squiffy was to make the speech officially declaring open a new branch railway-line up north. He had a touch of flu and couldn't go, so I offered to do it. It was a whoopin' big success, except for a spot of bother coming back. They had a special train. And I discovered the engine-driver was an old friend of mine. Well, so naturally I had to ride in the

68

cab with old Tom Porter, didn't I? Curse it all, what would you expect me to do? Then I said, 'Look here, Tom, move over and let *me* drive the thing.' He said, 'Do you know how?' I said, 'Sure I know how,'—because I've got a mechanical mind, haven't I? He said, 'All right; but take her dead slow.' "

Masters stared at him.

"You don't mean you wrecked the train, sir?"

"No, 'a' course I didn't wreck the train!" said H.M., as though this were the whole point of the grievance. "That's just it. Only I sort of hit a cow."

"You did what?"

"I hit a cow," explained H.M. "And they got pictures of me arguin' with the farmer afterwards. Squiffy was wild: which is gratitude for you. He said it lowered the tone of people in public life. He said I was always doing it, which is a lie. I haven't been at a public ceremony since I christened that new mine-sweeper at Portsmouth three years ago; and then was it my fault it they launched her down the slip too soon and the champagne-bottle conked the mayor instead? Burn me, why have they always got to pick on me?"

"Well, now, sir—" began Masters soothingly.

"I'll tell you what it is," growled H.M., suddenly coming to the root of the trouble. "You mightn't believe it. But I've heard rumors. And I've heard there's some low, evil-minded talk about puttin' me in the House of Lords. I say, Masters, they can't do that, can they?"

Masters looked doubtful.

"Hard to say, sir. But I don't see how they can put you in the House of Lords just because you hit a cow."

"I'm not so sure," said H.M., darkly suspicious of their capabilities in any direction. "They're never tired of telling me what a maunderin', cloth-headed old fossil I am. You mark my words, Masters: there's dirty work afoot, and if they can make use of any more accidents I'll wind up in the House of Lords. On top of that, what happens? I come down here expecting a quiet tag of the week-end after all my heavy labors, and what do you give me? Another murder. Cor!"

"Speaking of Mr. Constable's death—"

"I don't want to speak of it," said H.M., folding his arms. "In fact, I'm not goin' to. I'll make my excuses and I'll clear out. And by the way, son, where *is* Mrs. Constable? Where is everybody?"

Masters looked round inquiringly.

"Couldn't tell you, Sir Henry. I just came on from the

police-station myself. But Dr. Sanders came back here ahead of me...?"

"Mrs. Constable," Sanders told them, "is upstairs in her room, lying down. Miss Keen is with her. Chase is talking to the policeman they've left posted in the kitchen. Pennik seems to have disappeared."

H.M. looked uncomfortable.

"So," he said, "the lady isn't takin' her husband's death at all well?"

"No. Very badly. Hilary had to sleep in her room both Friday night and last night. But she's better now, and she particularly wants to see you."

"Me? Why me, curse it?"

"Because she thinks Pennik is both a fraud and a criminal lunatic, and she says you can expose him. She knows all about the Answell case and the Haye case and the rest of them; she's a great admirer of yours, H.M. And she's been looking forward to this; she hasn't talked of much else. Don't let her down."

H.M. stirred and glowered.

But his sharp little eye grew fixed; he pushed his glasses back up to their proper position, and then peered over them.

"So she says Pennik's a fraud, hey?" he inquired in a curious voice. "But that's rather rummy, ain't it, son? Wasn't she the one who found Pennik and swore he was genuine and backed up Pennik against her husband?"

"Yes."

"Then why the complete about-face? When did that happen?"

"When Pennik killed—or said he killed—Constable. When Pennik announced it, that is."

"Oh? Did she think somebody else ought to have the credit, then?"

Sanders spread out his hands. "She doesn't pretend its rational. At the moment she doesn't think; she only feels. She wants to hit out at Pennik in some way. That's why I hope you and Masters will take over and straighten this business out. I've been exposed to the *danse macabre* for two nights, and it isn't the pleasantest thing in the world."

H.M. muttered to himself. Then he looked up.

"Masters," he said, "this business is queerer than you think."

"It can't be any queerer than I think," said the chief inspector. "Of course, remember one thing. We can't say for certain it was murder—"

"Oh, Masters, my son! Of course it was murder."

"All the same—"

"Pennik says a man will die before eight o'clock. And a man does die before eight o'clock. Oh, my eye. Don't that nasty suspicious mind of yours, that wouldn't trust your own mother to fill the baby's bottle, at least have a twinge of curiosity about it?"

"All very well, sir," said Masters stubbornly. "That's what the doctor said, and to a certain extent I agree. The question is, how can we prove it when there isn't a thing to show how Mr. Constable died? Wouldn't you allow, now, that as far as proving anything at all goes we're landed in the worst mess of our natural-born lives?"

H.M. lowered his defences.

"Uh-huh," he admitted.

Getting to his feet, he began to lumber back and forth with his thumbs hooked in his waistcoat pockets and his corporation, ornamented with a large gold watch-chain, preceding him in splendor like the figure-head of a man-'o-war. If he had been reducing since Sanders saw him last, it was not apparent.

"All right, all right," he growled. "Let's argue this out, then. —Not that I'm takin' it up, mind!"

"Just as you like. But what," said Masters persuasively, "what would you say about our friend Pennik, now?"

H.M. stopped short.

"No," he said with some firmness. "I'm not goin' to tell you what I think, if anything. I'm too worried, Masters. The thought of me dressed up in a robe and coronet—son, it's enough to make my flesh creep. If those hyena-souled bounders are really skulkin' in ambush just waitin' for another excuse so they can stick me into the House of Lords, I got to think of a way to circumvent 'em. No. I don't mind listening to what you know about this case, but you've got to tell me what *you* think."

Masters nodded.

"Fair enough, sir. To begin with, I'm a plain man, and I don't believe in miracles. Except the Biblical kind, which don't count. Now, I've been all over the facts with Superintendent Belcher; and Herman Pennik didn't commit this crime (if it is a crime) because he couldn't have. That's the first step. Next, who else can we definitely eliminate on the ground of alibis? Who else didn't do it?"

His pause was rhetorical.

"I didn't," replied Sanders, as seemed to be expected of him. "And Hilary Keen didn't. We can confirm each other because we were together."

"That's established, son?" inquired H.M.

"Yes," agreed Masters, "that's all right. Very well, sir.

71

Stands to reason!—if Mr. Constable was murdered, he must have been murdered either by Mrs. Constable or Mr. Chase."

"That's nonsense," said Dr. Sanders curtly.

Masters held up his hand.

"Just a moment, sir. Ju-ust a moment." He turned to H.M. "There's opportunity, you see. A blow to the body. A crack over the head. Even something that gave the old gentleman a nervous turn and killed him. Any of them *could* have been done either by his wife or Mr. Chase. Neither of 'em has got an alibi. Eh?"

H.M. continued to pace.

"So far," pursued Masters, "we've accepted Mrs. Constable's story about the old gentleman walking out of his bedroom and throwing a fit in the hall. Belcher accepted it. Colonel Willow accepted it. But is it true? Dr. Sanders didn't see the old gentleman until he was in the last stages of the fit just before he died. The lady could have hit him. The lady could have scared him. Or, taking it the other way round, Mr. Chase could have hit him and nipped back to his room before anybody saw it."

Here Masters lifted his fingers weightily.

"What's next to be considered, sir? I'll tell you: motive. Who might have had a motive? Pennik hadn't a motive, not what I'd call a motive; this talk about 'scientific experiments' is hugaboo. Dr. Sanders didn't have a motive. Miss Keen didn't have a motive. But what about Mr. Chase and Mrs. Constable?

"Mind, I'm only suggesting here. Mr. Chase is a relative, they tell me. Also from what they tell me, he seems to have been uncommon attentive to a gent old enough to be his father, and not his lively type at all. Is it just possible he gets a good slice of Mr. Constable's money? As for Mrs. Constable—we-el," said Masters, with another broadly skeptical look, "I shouldn't want all night with a wet towel round my head thinking of several reasons why she might have wanted out of the way a wealthy husband twenty years older than herself. Eh?"

"May I say something?" asked Sanders.

H.M. nodded, still without speaking.

"It's this. I have never in my life seen a woman more genuinely knocked over with grief than Mrs. Constable was."

"Oh, ah?" said the chief inspector.

"I don't give that as an opinion. I state it as a medical fact. I will take my oath she did not, and never could have, killed her husband. That woman nearly died on Friday night."

72

"Of a broken heart?" inquired the chief inspector.

"If you want to put it like that. Masters, you can't fool a doctor with crocodile tears; and she didn't try. She was as genuinely shocked and scared by the death of her husband as Hilary Keen was genuinely shocked and scared by something in her room earlier on Friday night. It was a matter of physical symptoms with both of them."

Sanders paused.

"I tell you that before telling you something else, which you will probably find out anyway. It's better for you to hear it from me. On Friday night at about quarter to eight ---this part of it you know—something frightened Hilary in the next room. She ran over to me by way of the balcony outside both windows. When she came in at the window, she knocked over a lamp. Mr. Constable heard the row and came down to see what was the matter. As he was leaving us, I said to him something like, 'Nobody has tried to murder you so far, I imagine?' He said, 'Not as yet. The scrap-book remains on its shelf.'

"Wait! I didn't know what that remark made, and I still don't. I can only tell you one other fact. Under Mrs. Constable's bedside table, where she probably writes at night, there are a couple of bookshelves; and in among the works of reference there does happen to be a large scrap-book labeled, *New Ways of Committing Murder.*"

Again there was a silence.

Masters looked very thoughtful.

"New ways of committing murder," he mused, with rising excitement. "You know, Doctor, I shouldn't be surprised, I shouldn't be at all surprised, if this may not give us just what we want. Eh, Sir Henry?"

"I dunno," said H.M. "What frightened the gal?"

"Eh?"

"I said, what frightened the gal?" repeated H.M., pausing in his stumping walk and turning a face of exasperation. "This Hilary Keen you've been talkin' about. Everybody seems to know she got a fright; but nobody seems to know what did it. Or even care what did it. Didn't your friend Belcher ask her about that?"

Masters chuckled, leafing back through his notebook.

"Oh, yes, the superintendent asked her. *He's* got a nasty suspicious mind if you like. He wanted to know what she was doing in Dr. Sander's room. She said she'd suddenly got the wind up, about Pennik's prediction and everything; she couldn't stand being alone any longer, so she ran next door to the doctor's room." He hesitated. "Nothing in that, is there?"

73

"Oh, Masters, my son! Why go by way of the balcony?"

"Well, there's that, of course."

"There is. Balconies are messy and full of dirt. Climbin' through windows is messy and undignified. If you want company, why do that when all you've got to do is walk down a hall and open a door? Furthermore, she smashes a lamp and Sanders here says she was in a state borderin' on real collapse. It looks as though there must have been something or somebody between her and the door."

Outside the long windows of the drawing-room, the afternoon light had grown dull and chilly. It made the polished floor a pale lake across which their shadows moved. But it did not penetrate far among the curtains or the spidery furniture; and, under a white marble mantelpiece, the orange square of the electric heater deepened its glow. So, Sanders reflected, Hilary had refused to tell the police as well.

Then he felt H.M.'s eye on him.

"But she must 'a' told you, son? Or given you some hint?"

"No."

"You mean she refused?"

"Yes, in a way."

"Still, you were there on the spot. You must have had some idea what caused it?"

"No. That is, I thought I had, for a minute; but it turned out to be wrong, so we can forget about it."

"Hold on a bit, Masters!" urged H.M., waving his hand towards the chief inspector as he seemed about to interfere. H.M. spoke in a new voice. He moved his spectacles up and down his nose. Sitting down on the ottoman, which creaked wirily under his weight, he continued to move the spectacles up and down his nose. He added: "Y'know, son, you worry me."

"Worry you? Why?"

"Who is this gal?"

"Miss Keen? I don't know. I've only known her for a couple of days."

"I see. Fallin' for her, are you?"

"I hardly see why you should think that."

In his heart Sanders had always stood a good deal in awe of H.M. He thought H.M. was funny; he enjoyed H.M. most when the old man went quite soberly and seriously about foolishness; but even at the moments of grousing he never quite lost that original feeling. He had, therefore, to muster up his nerve to snarl back.

It made no impression.

"Ho ho," said H.M. "I'm a mind-reader, that's why. Now if Pennik had said that, merely by using his eyes and his intelligence like me, you'd have handed him the gold-plated wizard's cap. It's an old medieval custom."

His tone changed.

"Oh, I got no objection. And *I* can tell you who she is. Her father was old Joe Keen, who married that gold-digger out of the Holborn *Viaduct* chorus when his first wife died. A very intelligent gal, I hear: the daughter, that is. But that's not the point at issue, son. The only point at issue at the moment"—here he looked very hard at Sanders—"is, who or what did you think frightened her?"

"I thought it was Pennik," said Sanders; and he told them about the chef's cap under the dressing-table.

Masters was about to interrupt with fiery interest, but H.M. cut him short.

"So? Did you ask her about it, son?"

"Yes, and she denied it, so there's an end to that."

"Still—a chef's cap's not a very common thing to find under a dressing-table in a bedroom, is it? Did she tell you what it was doin' there?"

"We had other things to think about."

"You mean she wouldn't answer you?"

"I mean I did not carry the subject any further."

"Steady, son. Fair play. What else was there that made you think it might have been Pennik in her room?"

"All this week-end," said Sanders rather wearily, "we've been accustomed to having our thoughts stimulated up to a high old pitch before they were dragged out of us. This was merely the result of it. It was Pennik's attitude towards her, a sort of doglike devotion. He couldn't talk naturally to her, or be quite easy in her presence. He was on to anything that concerned her in a flash. He seemed on the edge of something. I had an uneasy feeling that that whole 'prophecy,' about Constable's death, came from a wish to show off in front of her. To be frank, when she climbed in my window her state didn't suggest a woman who had been given a merely mental fright."

H.M. stirred.

"So? Humble and unassumin' admirer suddenly goes off the rails." He hesitated. "I say, Masters, I don't like this." He hesitated again. "Still—she's not what you'd call the fainting type?"

"No."

"And that," the chief inspector intervened, "was why you asked Pennik this morning whether he'd been upstairs on Friday night, Doctor? Just so! Which he denied."

"Which he denied," agreed Sanders.

H.M. scowled.

"It still bothers me. You'd have thought she'd have been able to handle a situation like that a bit more firmly, wouldn't you? I'm not goin' to generalize. Women are apt to say they'd do one thing if somebody went berserk, and then do something else altogether when it happens. But it still bothers me like blazes. Supposin' it wasn't what you thought it was: what could Pennik have done to her that would have *scared* her as much as that?"

That had hit it.

It was, Sanders knew, what had been subconsciously worrying him since Friday night.

"But she says it wasn't Pennik," he pointed out, "and in that case I'm betting it wasn't. We don't know who or what it was. All we do know is that she was frightened."

"S-s-t!" said Masters quickly.

They all looked round, for there were footsteps on the unglazed tiles of the hall outside the door. Lawrence Chase, straight-backed and at ease, came in with his brisk walk which seemed to push the floor away behind him like a man climbing a ladder. He was smiling, and he eyed the newcomers with frank interest.

"Here we are," said Sanders. "Mr. Chase—Chief Inspector Masters. And Sir Henry Merrivale."

While Chase shook hands with subdued enthusiasm, his quick eye missed no detail.

"Hel-lo," he said. "So the mighty have arrived. I've never been better pleased. How do you do, Chief Inspector? And you, sir? I know a great deal about you both, you see." Then he turned round with a certain arrogance, and spoke casually to Sanders: "You'd lose your money, old man."

"Money?"

"Your bet."

"But what bet?"

"That Pennik wasn't in Hilary's room on Friday night," explained Chase, drawing a cigarette-case out of his inside pocket. "I can't imagine why it should be of any interest to the lords of Scotland Yard; but there it is. I certainly never thought anything of it until now, but he was there. I saw him."

Drawing out a chair of some discomfort, he sat down, adjusted his knees and his long legs, spun the cigarette-case into the air, caught it, and looked at them all with interest, as though he were awaiting applause for a conjuring-trick.

IX

IT WAS MASTERS who came into action now.

"Just one moment, sir!" he warned, getting out his note-book and giving Chase that perfunctorily sinister look which a statement of this kind warranted. "You say you saw Mr. Pennik in Miss Keen's room on Friday night?"

"Well, to be strictly accurate, I saw him come out of it." Chase corrected himself. He spun the cigarette-case again.

"And when was this, may I ask?"

"About a quarter to eight."

"Oh? And yet we're given to understand, sir, that at about a quarter to eight Mr. Pennik was downstairs opening the back door to Mrs. Chinchester and her son."

"Yes, that's all right," said Chase. He reflected. "I'm pretty sure I heard the back doorbell start to ring as Pennik was barging down the stairs."

Masters looked at him.

"Now, sir, you have already made a statement to Superintendent Belcher?"

"That's right. Good old Belcher. Cripes, what a name!" Evidently seeing that he had struck the wrong note, he suddenly became almost austere. His narrow shoulders went back. Behind everything you seemed to see curiosity twining; but, though he continued to spin the cigarette-case in the air, his voice grew curt and businesslike. "I gave the superintendent a statement, as you say. Yes?"

"Yet you didn't mention this to him."

"No; why should I? It had nothing to do with poor old Sam's death. Besides——"

"*If* you don't mind," said Masters, lifting a lordly hand. "Just let me read you a part of your statement. You say, '*At seven-thirty Mrs. Constable asked me to show Pennik where the kitchen was, while the others went on upstairs. I showed him the kitchen, and the refrigerator, and so on, and then I went upstairs. I was not with him longer than a couple of minutes. Afterwards I was in my room dressing, and I did not leave it until I heard Mrs. Constable scream at eight o'clock.*'"

"Yes, that's all right." After listening critically, he raised his head. "What of it? It's all true. I didn't leave my room. I wasn't with Pennik, and didn't speak to him. But I saw him."

"Will you explain that, sir?"

Chase relaxed.

"With pleasure. At about a quarter to eight my bath was running and I was getting out of my clothes. I heard one whacking great crash, like glass or china smashing. I opened the door of my room and looked out. I saw Pennik come out of Hilary's room, close the door behind him, and go downstairs. That's all."

"But didn't that strike you as odd?"

Chase frowned. He put up his head and studied Masters with a strange, broad look like a man trying to get a good view of a too-large picture.

"No, certainly not. Why should it? Hilary had offered to help him with the dinner; or to serve it, at least—Sanders will confirm that. That's why I supposed he was there."

"Is that right, Dr. Sanders?"

"Quite right."

"Hurrum! But didn't the smash of china strike you as odd, Mr. Chase?"

Chase hesitated.

"Yes, it did—for a second. Then I got an explanation of it; and I didn't think about Pennik afterwards." His look grew aloof. "No sooner had Pennik got downstairs, than the door of Sam's room opened and out came poor old Sam in a rush, pulling on a dressing-gown and stumbling all over the place in his bare feet to put them right in the slippers. He went straight down to Sander's room, and banged on the door, and opened it. I heard him ask what was going on. And I heard Sander's voice say, 'It's all right; the lamp fell over.' "

He paused.

"Yes, sir?" prompted Masters.

Chase lifted his shoulders. "I also heard Hilary's voice."

"Well?"

"So I closed my door," said Chase in an elaborately casual tone, and as though he were closing the subject. "It was no damned business of mine. But why should I think any more about Pennik? After all, Hilary hadn't been in her room."

He did not explain further; he did not need to.

So that, Sanders reflected, was the explanation of Chase's humors over the week-end. If ever a case existed in which everybody (perhaps naturally) misunderstood everybody else's motives, it was this one. But he not say anything, for the chief inspector's eye warned him. Masters suddenly grew bland and hearty—a sign which Chase recognized, for he unbent as well.

"I see," observed the chief inspector. "Quite understand-

78

able, as you might say. Quite! So we might as well clear up the point while we're on it, eh?"

Chase grinned at him. "Ask your questions, Chief Inspector, and no soft soap. Soft soap is always a sign that there's dirty water about. Remember that I'm not apt to trip over my own legal feet."

"Just so. Now, when you *did* see Mr. Pennik at that time, did you notice anything odd about him?"

"You keep on using that word 'odd.' What do you mean, odd?"

Masters merely made a gesture.

"No, I can't say I did. The light in the hall was too dim for me to make out his expression, if that's what you mean. Except that he went along at a kind of waddle, like a damned great ape. But then (and I am not afraid of slander here) I already suspected he was touched in the head."

"Touched in the head?"

"Look here, Chief Inspector," Chase spun the cigarette-case into the air and caught it. He seemed to come to a decision. "I've been in some degree of hot water over this already. It's quite true: he really did ask me, in the kitchen, whether he could be charged with murder if he killed a man under the conditions he described. I said that even in the present state of the law it still wasn't a crime to sit down and think as hard thoughts about a man as you liked. He was so infernally reasonable and academic about the whole thing; you can't help rather liking the fellow. —Don't you agree, Sanders?"

"Yes, I think I do."

"But to take him seriously: oi!"

From the Turkish corner, where H.M. sat with the corners of his broad mouth turned down, issued a chuckle of sour amusement.

"Ho, ho," said H.M. "So you were beginnin' to take him seriously, then, son?"

Chase pointed the cigarette-case.

"Well, a little thought-reading is one thing," he said, as though arguing that boys will be boys. "But to crack a man's bones and skull with thought, like a death-ray, is coming it too strong. Think! Think what it would mean if it were true. Hitler, for instance. Hitler suddenly claps his hands to his head and says, *'Mein Gott!'* or *'Mein Kampf!'* or whatever it is he's always saying, and falls over as dead as Bismarck. I argued. I said, 'Well, could you kill Hitler, for instance?' "

This evoked so much interest that Masters shut up his notebook.

H.M. pulled down his spectacles.

"And what'd he say to that, son?"

"He said, 'Who is Hitler?'"

"So?"

"Yes; just like that. All of a sudden it was like talking to the Man in the Moon. I asked him where he had been for the last five or six years. He said quite seriously, 'In various parts of Asia, where we do not get much news.' He then asked me—*me*—to be reasonable. He said, first, that he didn't claim to succeed with everybody; and, second, that he would have to meet the victim in question and 'fit a cap' on him, whatever that may mean, before he could succeed; finally, that he must have lived in conjunction with the victim, who must be of an intelligence inferior to his own."

Chief Inspector Masters turned a satirical eye towards H.M.

"Which," Masters pointed out, "which, for one reason or another, " 'ud seem to rule out bumping off Hitler or Stalin or any of the big pots. But you didn't get all this out of saying a word or two to him on Friday night?"

"Oh, no, I tackled him yesterday. He—where is he now, by the way?"

Masters was soothing.

"It's all right, sir. He won't hurt you."

"You bet he won't; not if I can help it. But where is he?"

"I expect the gentleman's off sulking somewhere. He wanted to talk to some reporters at the police-station; but I convinced 'em he was harmless," said Masters with rich satisfaction. "Come, now, sir! You're not impressed by all this rubbish, are you? Then why bother about where he is now?"

"No. It was only," said Chase, "that I thought I saw him outside the window just now."

Masters got up. Went over to the three full-length windows in their bay facing the front of the house, where the last light showed between curtains beaded at the edges like a Spanish hat. Setting his heavy shoulder under the frame, Masters pushed up on window with a screech; and then he ran it up smoothly.

"Bit too warm in here. I'll just take the liberty—" He indicated the liberty he had taken. Then he leaned out and sniffed the air, which stirred with a cool touch down the room.

Thin noises dropped into the hush: a flutter near the birdbath, a crackle as though of vines contracting at nightfall. But the path outside was empty.

"Probably somewhere about. Mr. Pennik likes wandering, they tell me," Masters went on. He became brisk. "Now,

Mr. Chase! There are some questions I'd like to ask you: not about Mr. Pennik, but about yourself. And while I do— I wonder, Doctor, whether you'd mind going up and asking Miss Keen to join us? Eh?"

Sanders went, closing the double doors of the drawing-room behind him.

He had not quite liked the way Masters had looked out of that window, like a marksman on a tower. But, when he went upstairs and knocked at the door of Mina Constable's room, nothing could have seemed more domestic. Hilary Keen, with a certain determination, was sitting near the window, knitting; and she bent close to the window to catch the light. Mina, wrapped in a rather gaudy silk robe, sat back in a padded chair by the bed. There was an ashtray full of cigarette-stubs beside her, and she was smoking still another cigarette: rolling it round and round in her mouth as though the lips were too smooth to hold it. Both women showed a kind of relief. The atmosphere was one of peace —but a dry and drained peace, as though they had exhausted each other's conversation, and merely waited.

Mina was struck to animation as you strike fire from a lighter.

"Who is it downstairs?" she asked, turning large eyes. "Is it that superintendent again? I heard you let him in."

"No, Mrs. Constable. It's Chief Inspector Masters and Sir Henry Merrivale. They want to see—"

"I knew it. I knew it. I'll get dressed and go down straight-away. But I haven't got anything black. Oh, dear, I haven't got *anything* black." For a moment he thought her eyes were going to fill with tears. "Never mind. What does it matter? It will have to do. You will tell him to wait, won't you, Doctor?"

Sanders hesitated.

"You needn't bother to get dressed, Mrs. Constable. Sit there and take it easy; they'll come up here. As a matter of fact, it is Miss K— Hilary they want to see first."

Hilary, who had been frowning hideously over the white wool, looked up.

"Me? Why me?"

"Some little mix-up in the testimony. Steady, Mrs. Constable!"

Mina, brushing past him, had hurried into the bath-room, turned on the light, pulled a towel off the rail, stumbled against the electric heater, and finally turned in the doorway with her eyes grown hard. It was easy to sense something hard and sinewy and supple in her character, something that was not at first sight apparent. But that was not what attracted his attention. The light from the bathroom fell across her bedside table and the two bookshelves under it; and the tall scrap-book labeled *New Ways of Committing Murder* was now missing.

"Some little mix-up in the testimony?" inquired Mina, massaging her hands on the towel. "What is it?"

"Nothing important. Honestly."

"Something to do with the toad Pennik, who wears a jewel in his head?"

"Yes."

"I knew it. I knew it!"

"Please sit down," Hilary urged her. She turned to Sanders. "And—Jack," the hesitation they had about pronouncing each other's Christian names showed a strong self-consciousness, "there is something that will have to be settled here and now. Must you be back at work in town tomorrow?"

"Yes, I'm supposed to be. There's the inquest, of course, but that will be adjourned."

"Couldn't you make some excuse and get leave to stay over?"

"Yes, of course. But why?"

"Because that lady," she nodded at Mina, who was still absently massaging her hands, "must not be allowed to stay here overnight alone. I mean it, Jack. The hospital phoned to say that two of the servants, the cook and the maid, will be out tomorrow; but not until tomorrow. Mrs. Constable has got the bee in her bonnet that she wants to stay alone, and she mustn't be allowed to. I'd stay myself like a shot, only we've got the Rice-Mason case coming up tomorrow and unless I go up tonight it quite plainly and simply means the sack. Can't you stay?"

(After all, Sanders was reflecting, with his eye on the gap in the bookshelf, where *New Ways of Committing Murder* had stood, I'm not a policeman. It is no business of mine. But I wish that book hadn't disappeared.)

"Please, aren't you listening?"

"Of course," he said, pulling his thoughts back. "I'd be only too glad to stay, if Mrs. Constable doesn't mind having me. And she could do with looking after for another night: she isn't as well as she thinks she is."

Mina's eyes puckered up; then her face grew gentle with a smile of great charm. Tossing the towel aside, she went over impulsively and put her hand on Hilary's arm.

"Whatever happens," she said, "thanks anyway. You've been very decent to me, both of you. And you, Hilary: I don't know what I'd have done without you. Cooking the meals! And even washing the dishes!"

"A terrible job," said Hilary dryly. "A perfectly back-breaking job. It quite wore me out. What on earth do you do when you're off on one of these heathenish trips of yours and there isn't anybody to wash the dishes?"

"Oh, I pay somebody to do it," said Mina with a certain vagueness. "Saves time and trouble, you see." Her tone changed. "But don't you worry about me, my dear. I shall be quite all right, too all right. I'm looking forward to it. That is, if I can persuade the toad Pennik to stay too."

"Pennik?"

"That's right."

"But I thought—"

"I want to talk to Sir Henry Merrivale," Mina went on. "Then we shall see what we shall see. Now get out of here, *please*, both of you; and let me dress. There!"

She impelled them out with the briskness of one who was again on the edge of a breakdown, and the door closed noisily. Sanders was not sorry to go. He had certain things to say to Hilary; and yet he found that he would have difficulty in saying them.

The hall was very dark except for the line of great pale-glowing colored-glass windows descending beside the staircase. They seemed even loftier, the curve of a shell; it was like being inside a warm kaleidoscope. 'And twilight saints and dim emblazonings,' was the thought that occurred to him while he and Hilary walked down the stairs side by side on the thick carpet. The other words still stuck in his throat; and Hilary talked.

"You can't speak to her frankly. That's the real trouble. You either can't get past her guard at all, into what she's really thinking—"

"Who?"

"Mina, of course! Or else she becomes almost theatrically literary. There's truth on both sides of it, maybe, but how I wish I knew what was really going on here!"

"Hilary."

"Yes?"

"Why didn't you tell me the truth about Pennik being in your room on Friday night?"

They both stopped. They had gone about ten steps down; above and behind them they could hear the grandfather clock ticking. He was afraid the people in the drawing-room below could hear them. "Come here," he said, and drew her farther back up the stairs. She did not resist; her arm felt flaccid under his grip.

Presently a quiet voice asked: "What makes you think I didn't tell you the truth?"

83

"Larry Chase saw him coming out, just before you got in through my window. Chase has told the police about it: that's what they want to see you about now. The point is, there's no harm in it. What they want to know is what frightened you so much. But he was there, wasn't he?"

He felt her draw a deep breath.

"Yes," said Hilary. "He was there."

X

THEN WHY didn't you tell me?

She was taking refuge: this time in an affected whimsicality which she sustained admirably but which was all wrong. He felt that. After a kind of Victorian curtsy she sat down on the tread of the stairs, clasped her arms round her knees, and looked up at him. In the dimness of colored glass her expression might have meant anything.

"'And why should I tell you, sir?' she said," inquired Hilary, wagging her head.

"Come off that."

"Perhaps there are things that a supremely innocent-minded young man ought not to know."

"Perhaps. But the supremely innocent-minded police are going to cut up rough if they don't know. That's what I'm getting at."

"Are you threatening me?"

"Look here, Hilary," he said, sitting down on the tread beside her. "You're talking exactly like the heroine of a bad thriller. Getting all up in arms and on your dignity; and concealing some trifle for no reason under the sun. The police are interested in Pennik and any movement he made. I'm interested for a different reason. What was it Pennik did to you that scared you so much?"

"What do you think?—Oh, there *you* go; like the hero of a bad thriller. Do you think I wanted it shouted all over the place? Do you think any woman wants a fuss made about a thing like that, setting everybody by the ears? That is, unless she's a certain kind of woman; and there is a word for them. Much better to go on and pretend nothing has happened. It—"

Then Hilary's mood changed. Sanders felt her shiver.

"As a matter of fact, you're quite right," she said. "There was something else. And the poor man didn't even touch me."

"'The poor man?'"

84

Hilary leaned back under the tall window, her head back against the ledge and her body relaxed "Tell me," she said suddenly. "This girl you're going to marry, this Miss Blystone. What is she like? Go on: tell me." There was almost a nagging in her voice.

"But—"

"Please tell me."

"Well . . . I think she's a little like you."

"How?"

In his mind there was a remembrance of a steamer's whistle blowing; the sun on the white castle-towers of a liner; a crowd in which Marcia Blystone bobbed about, confusedly trying to say good-by to everybody. Kessler must have been one of those on deck.

"I don't know; what brought this up? She's less mature than you are. More—sprightly," he said it because he hated the word. "Good fun on a party, and a good conversationalist. She's light where I'm stodgy."

"What does she look like?"

"She's smaller than you are, and more slender. Brown eyes. She's an artist."

"That must be very interesting."

"It is."

"Do you love her?"

At the back of his mind he had been expecting this.

"Yes, of course."

For a moment Hilary remained where she was. "Of course you do," she said, sitting up and speaking rather quickly. "And that's why we can be good friends, can't we?"

"We are good friends."

"Yes; I meant—" She stopped. All pretense of either Victorian coquetry or nagging seemed a mood; it was gone in a flash; she went on quietly, but with desperate seriousness. "Listen. A minute ago you accused me of talking like a heroine in a thriller. I used to laugh at such things too; but in a way that is exactly how I feel. Master-Mind Chases Girl. What happened two nights ago isn't worth twopence compared to Mr. Constable's death. But in its way it was horrible. Herman Pennik isn't really evil; he's only dangerous. I'm not going to tell them everything, because I don't want it bruited about that—well, never mind. The trouble is that if I do tell them everything I'll be accused of holding things back; and if I don't tell them everything I can't have any protection. For the first time in my life since I used to get put in a dark room when I was a child, I'm afraid; really and genuinely afraid; and I've *got* to have

85

someone to stand by me. You'll stand by me, won't you? You will stand by me?"

"You know I will. Hilary——"

He was interrupted.

In the gulf of the hall below a line of light slanted out. There was a scuffle and bump of feet, an oath, and the shaking thud of a potted palm toppling over in the hall.

"If you'd just take the trouble to look for the light-switch, sir!" said an exasperated voice. "Excuse me, but if you wouldn't go mucking about until you know where things are, then you wouldn't knock things over."

"What d'ye think I am, a goddam owl?" shouted a still more heated voice. "Burn me, Masters, if you think you can see in the dark you come and look for it. I know what I'm doin', don't I? Aha! Got it!"

There was a click; and, as Hilary and Sanders jumped guiltily to their feet, the whole hall was illuminated and showed them. It also illuminated their faces, which were revealing, to H.M. and Masters staring up from below.

"Oh," grunted H.M. without further comment. He lumbered up the stairs. "Evenin'," he went on. "Are you Joe Keen's daughter?"

Hilary nodded without speaking.

"I knew your father years ago. Good egg, old Joe was," said H.M. He sniffed. "I say, the chief inspector down there wants to ask you some questions. Mind goin' along? No, son." He touched Sanders's arm. "You come with me. I want to be introduced to Mrs. Constable."

Again Hilary nodded coolly.

"I'm quite ready," she answered, looking at her wrist-watch. "But I hope it won't be too long. I've got tonight's dinner to prepare."

She ran lightly down the stairs, while Masters assumed a stern and stuffed look. Lawrence Chase, who glanced out into the hall at that moment, began to whistle between his teeth. And Sanders went on upstairs with H.M. The latter did not say anything: he only looked.

Yet even in a state of discomfort Sanders knew that *all* this display could not have been for the benefit of Hilary and himself. There was something else in the wind. What it was he discovered almost as soon as H.M. was presented to Mina.

Mina met them wearing a brown dress and a certain cold poise.

"I was just coming downstairs," she told them, closing the door. "But perhaps it will do just as well here. Do sit down. Then we can get to business."

"Ma'am," began H.M., with the elephantine delicacy which could be as overpowering as his luridest rages, "ma'am: I'm not glad to be here."

"But I am delighted that you can be here," smiled Mina, dabbing powder off her neck. Her eyes brightened. "I only wish you could have come—earlier. You're not staying with us?"

It sounded grotesque, but H.M. only shook his head.

"No, ma'am. I told you I could only look in for the day. But"—he lowered himself very carefully into a chair, putting both hands on its arms; and he scowled over his spectacles—"but, d'ye see, they tell me you wanted to speak to me anyway. And so I sort of thought I could put some questions to you that'd come easier from me than from Masters. They're rather awkward questions, ma'am."

"Ask any questions you like, do."

"Well—now. Is it true your husband has thought for some time you were tryin' to kill him?"

"Who told you that? Larry Chase?"

H.M. made a gesture.

"He didn't exactly tell us. It sort of came bubblin' up out of the pure and undefiled well. Is is true?"

There was only one light on in the room, the lamp by the bedside, and this was behind her head. But she choked with something like laughter.

"No, no, no, no! It's so utterly absurd that I can't tell you how ridiculous it is. But why must Larry say that? He *knows* better. Still, he didn't actually say it, I suppose. It was only poor Sam's idea of a joke."

"That's a pretty serious subject to joke about, ma'am."

She was again all glitter and brightness. Sanders, watching, felt that she held (or thought she held) the other sword in a duel.

"Not really. You see," she half smiled, "I write things."

"I know."

"Oh, that's good. You see, I only once wrote a straight detective story, which was most unmercifully slated anyway; but in the other ones I nearly always put in some kind of mysterious or violent death. Sam," she kept her eyes steady, "Sam said I had a criminal mind. I said, on the contrary, it was a cheerful and healthy sign; I said it was the people who kept it bottled up that had the criminal minds. It was just his joke that I might want to murder him."

"And that worried you sometimes?"

"No; never." She looked surprised.

"I was just thinkin'—where do you get the material for all these reelin' mysterious deaths?"

"Oh, people tell you things. And there's a lot of material in the Egyptian and medieval records. And then, of course, I keep a scrap-book: I call it *New Ways of Committing Murder*."

Even H.M. blinked a little at this. Poker-players at the Diogenes Club have found any attempt to read his face a highly unprofitable occupation, but a very queer and fishy expression was on it now. He folded his hands over his stomach and twiddled the thumbs.

"So? A scrap-book, hey? It must make interestin' reading, Mrs. Constable."

"No. Not any more, please God," said Mina, gripping her own hands together. "I burnt it yesterday. I am through forever with thinking about all such things, even in books."

She bent forward.

"Sir Henry, I don't know whether they have told you why I was so anxious to see you. I do admire you. I really do; that's not a social compliment. I know all your cases, as far back as the Darworth business in '30 and that film star's murder at the Christmas of '31 and the poisoned room at Lord Mantling's. I don't think they appreciate you enough. I've often said they should have given you a peerage."

H.M. turned a rich, ripe purple.

"And what I like so much," Mina went on, oblivious, "is the way you can put your hand through brick walls and show that the bogles were only turnip-ghosts. We need that sort of thing; we need it! That's why I am appealing to you on grounds that I hope will make you help me. I want to expose Herman Pennik. I want you to nail him down and see that he gets what he deserves: hanging, if possible. Have you met Pennik?"

With an effort H.M. got his breath.

But he remained surprisingly quiet.

"Well—now," he said. "You're openin' out a large field, Mrs. Constable. Are you suggestin' that Pennik killed your husband in the way he said he did?"

"I don't know. I only know that the man is a fraud."

"But that's a bit inconsistent, isn't it, ma'am? First you suggest he might have killed your husband by a kind of super telepathy. Then you say he's a fraud. What exactly do you mean?"

"I don't know. I only know what I feel. Have you met Pennik?"

"No."

"You will find him wandering about," said Mina. Her eyes narrowed. "Sir Henry, I've been trying for days and days to think of what that man reminded me of. I know now. He's like Peter Quint in *The Turn of the Screw*. You remember that dreadful business, of the frightened governess in the house called Bly? Bly: even the name is narrow and secretive. Quint on the tower, Quint at the window, Quint on the staircase. And all in a kind of perpetual dusk. But that reminds me too. I can tell you how to handle Pennik."

She leaned forward still further.

"He's always wandering about outside, and walking up on you when it grows dark. Do you know why? He suffers from what they call claustrophobia. He can't endure being shut in. That's why he likes these high, big rooms here. So you see what to do, don't you? Take him, on some charge or other. Shut him up. Shut him up for a week or so in the smallest cell you can find. Then he'll talk! Then he'll tell you."

"I'm afraid we can't do that, ma'am."

"But why?' she demanded plaintively. "Nobody will ever know."

H.M. gave her a long look. He seemed a little disconcerted.

"Y'see, ma'am: we've got a law. Whether we like it or not, it's a fair law. You can't monkey with it. There's absolutely nothing we can do to Pennik, even if he yells blue thunder that he killed your husband. And also, y'see, that law draws the line at torture."

"Torture? You think *he* draws the line at torture?"

"Well—"

"So he would make Sam an 'experiment,' would he? Just like that, would he? Sam was no good to the world, wasn't he? He could be spared, could he? We must see. Then you decline to help me, Sir Henry?"

"Oh, for cat's sake!" roared H.M. "Take it easy, ma'am. I'm the old man. I'll help you as much as I can. But this is a slippery business; a greased pig of a business; so far there's no way to get a hold on it. And until we can get a proper hold on it, what are we goin' to do?" He stopped, for a shade had gone across Mina's face; a hardening of resolution; a drawing back to her shell, as though all touch were now lost with her. She was smiling vaguely.

"Listen to me!" said H.M., suddenly on the alert. "Are you listenin'?"

"Yes?"

"If I'm to do any good at all, ma'am, you got to help me. It's no good goin' into trances like that. I've got an idea; a sort of cloudy ghost of an idea; and what I want is the facts from you. Are you goin' to tell me what I want to know?"

"I am so sorry," said Mina, waking up and brightening. "Of course I will tell you anything."

(H.M. was really worried: Sanders knew that. He had flung the words at her as though they were a rope to draw her back. For a moment H.M. breathed asthmatically without speaking.)

"Right, then. Now!" He looked round the room. "I say, your husband didn't share this room with you, did he?"

"No, no. He complained that I talked in my sleep. His room is in there. Would you like to see it?"

She got up without interest, and led them through the bathroom into Sam Constable's bedroom, where she switched on the light. The room was little different from any other bedroom in the house, and with little more personality than the guest-rooms. It was high, square, and bluff. Its furnishings—bed, wardrobe, chest of drawers, table, a few chairs—were of dark walnut against bilious-looking greenish-papered walls picked out with panels in gilt. A number of heavy-framed pictures did not add to its attractiveness.

H.M. peered round it. Then he began to lumber and brush round its edges. A gun-case stood in one corner; the top of the wardrobe was piled with hat-boxes; and on the table lay an assortment of *Tatlers* and sporting magazines. Little more trace remained of its late occupant. One of the windows opened out on another cramped cup of a balcony, with stone stairs winding down to the ground. H.M. inspected this before he turned round to Mina in the doorway of the bathroom.

All this time Mina's yellowish-tinged eyes were watching him.

"Uh-huh. What room is on the floor under this, ma'am?"

"Under us? The dining-room."

"I see. Now, let's go back to Friday night. You and your husband came up here at seven-thirty, hey? What'd he do then?"

"He had his bath and started to dress."

"Where were you at that time?"

"In here."

"In here?"

"Yes. Parker (that's his man, you see) was in hospital; so I had to lay out his dinner things and put the studs and cufflinks in his shirt. It took rather a time. My hands—" She stopped.

"Go on, ma'am."

"He was about half-dressed, and I was tying his shoes for him—"

"So? Couldn't he tie his own shoes?"

90

"He had vertigo, poor old boy. He couldn't bear to lean over like that." She looked at the wardrobe and shut her jaws hard; it was evidently her worst moment so far. "I was just doing that when we heard that terrible crash. I said, 'That's in the next room.' He said, 'No, it isn't; that's my great-grandmother's lamp, and it's in that young fool doctor's room.' (Dr. Sanders isn't really, but Sam had hoped he would come down here and expose Pennik, and he was disappointed. I know how he felt now. But you needn't worry, Sam. It'll be taken care of)."

For a moment, looking at her, Sanders had a feeling that was not far removed from eerie.

"He said he was going to see what's what. He put on his dressing-gown and went out. In a minute or so he was back again. He said that Hilary Keen and Dr. Sanders were —" Then she seemed to wake up. "I beg your pardon, Doctor! I didn't notice. There was nothing to it anyhow. Well, anyway, when I had got him into his shirt he told me to go on, go on, get myself dressed; or I should be late. He would tie his own tie, because my hands weren't good for that." She smiled sadly. "I went to my room. In a few minutes I heard him brushing his coat. Then he said he was going downstairs. I said, 'All right, dear.' When I heard the door close I remembered about the two clean handkerchiefs. You must know what happened then. I've told it, told it, told it, over and over and over. Must I tell it again?"

"No," said H.M.

He stood broad and straddle-legged in the middle of the room, his fists on his hips. He had listened quietly; but there was a faintly sinister expression round the corners of his down-turned mouth, and it seemed even to shine from his bald head. He sniffed.

"Humph," said H.M. "I say, son." He turned to Sanders. "I don't like to bend over either, which is 'cause I'm fat." He pointed. "Down there on the floor, by the caster at the foot of the bed. And over near where Mrs. Constable is standin'. Scrooch down and get a good look and tell me what it is."

"It looks," answered Sanders, examining the carpet, "like spots of wax."

"Wax," said H.M., scratching the side of his nose. "So?"

Again he looked round. On the chest of drawers, at opposite ends, stood two china candlesticks each containing a purely ornamental greenish candle. H.M. lumbered over to them. He put his hand on the top of each.

"Cold," he said. "All the same, somebody has been burnin'

91

these candles. Both of 'em. Look at the tops. Have you been burnin' 'em, Mrs. Constable?"

"Good heavens, no!"

"Haven't been having any trouble with the lights, or anything?"

"No, certainly not."

"But somebody's been burnin' 'em," persisted H.M. "Wouldn't you know?"

"I'm afraid not. I haven't noticed anything, much." She pressed her hands over her face. "But does it tell you anything? Why does it matter?"

"Because it's rummy," said H.M. "It's the only rummy or out-of-place thing in a smooth, ordered room and a smooth, ordered bit of dirty work. Somebody walks about with a pair of lighted candles in a place where there're already enough lights to equip Piccadilly Circus. And just outside this door a bloke throws a fit with nobody near him, and dies. Oh, my eye! And besides—"

Mina Constable showed a pale face of resolution.

"Have you finished, Sir Henry?"

"I'm afraid so. For now, anyhow."

"I haven't finished," said Mina, smiling her nervous and sympathetic smile. "On the contrary, I am going to begin. I will show you. Will you come downstairs with me, please?"

Sanders had no idea what was on her mind. Neither, evidently, had H.M. In silence they went out and downstairs. Mina walked straight to the drawing-room, whose double doors were now wide open. Under a snake-glowing chandelier Masters sat with his notebook on his knee, writing laboriously. Lawrence Chase watched him. Both looked up in surprise when Mina stalked in, but she paid no attention to them. On a table near the bay-windows was a telephone.

Taking it off the rest, she put it down on the table. Then, steadying her right wrist with the grip of her left hand, she began to spin the dial. There was a certain expression about her face.

"T-O-L," spelled Mina with concentration. She picked up the 'phone again.

Masters jumped up from his chair.

"Excuse me," he said. "You're Mrs. Constable, aren't you? Just so! Would you mind telling me what you're doing?"

"What's that?" inquired Mina, turning a bright and pleasant but determined face over her shoulder. She looked back again. "Toll? I want to put through a call to London,

92

please. This is Grovetop three-one. I want Central nine-eight-seven-six. Yes, please. . . . What did you say?"

Masters was beside her with remarkable strides.

"I asked you what you were doing, Mrs. Constable."

"I'm ringing the *Daily Non-Stop*. I know the literary editor; I did some articles for them once. I don't know anybody else on the staff, but he can tell me who I should speak to. Excuse me.—Hello? *Daily Non-Stop?* May I speak to Mr. Burton, please?"

"Half a tick," said Masters grimly. He put down a large finger on the hook and cut off the connection with a click. "I'm sorry, Mrs. Constable."

Mina looked up.

"Do you mean to say," she asked, "that I can't put through a telephone call from my own house?"

"Of course you can, Mrs. Constable. Of co-ourse," beamed Masters, with windy heartiness and deprecation. "Only—well, you know, wouldn't you rather see us, first? Eh? We're old hands at this. Maybe we could advise you. What did you want to tell them?"

Mina did not flare out at him. She looked wizened and not altogether attractive under that harsh light; her manner was detached, but she kept tight hold of the receiver and pressed it against her breast.

"You must be Chief Inspector Masters," she said. "Tell me. What is the worse insult you know?"

"Ah! Hard to say, that," said Masters wisely. "If you're thinking of applying it to me—"

"I was thinking of applying it to Herman Pennik." She looked thoughtful. "My husband always used to make him jump, on a certain subject. I wonder why? But we can begin with Fake, capital F, and plain bounder."

"If you'd just let me have that phone, Mrs. Constable? —A-ah! Thank you. There we are! Eh?"

Mina let go. She looked round. There was perhaps nobody in that room who did not feel his heart contract with pity at the expression on her face.

"I've been through hell," she said. "For God's sake give me my little chance to hit back."

Then her eyes overflowed.

The phone clinked and jingled as Masters fitted back the receiver in a vast silence. Through the tall open window in the bay, cool air stirred and drifted.

"I know, ma'am, I know," said Masters with hearty sympathy. "But that's no way to do it, is it? I mean, you can't just ring up a newspaper and call a man names; now can you?"

"I don't propose to do that."

"No?"

"No. So," she went on in a very quiet voice, "Mr. Herman Pennik claims he can use thought as a weapon, does he? Silly little liar. You see, my husband was a fairly wealthy man. And I'm going to do what Sam would have wanted me to do. Sam, who was never afraid of anything or anybody in his life. All right: let the toad Pennik try out his weapon on me. I challenge him. That's what I wanted to tell Mr. Burton. I'll call his bluff. Just let him try to kill me. If he can do it, everything I've got goes to any charity you want to name. But it won't. I'm simply calling his bluff and doing something for poor old Sam. And I warn you, I'll spread it over every newspaper in England if it's the last thing I ever do in my life."

Lawrence Chase took two steps forward.

"Mina," he muttered, "be careful what you're saying. I tell you, be careful!"

"Oh, rubbish."

"I tell you, you don't know what you're saying."

"And neither do you, sir, I'm afraid," said Masters over his shoulder. "Ladies and gentlemen!" He cleared his throat and brought his fist down on the telephone table. *"If you please! Steady, now. This is a lot of hysterics; now isn't it?"*

In some fashion he managed a smile.

"Just so! And that's better, isn't it? Now Mrs. Constable," he went on in soothing tones, "why don't you just come over here and sit down nice and comfortable, eh? And we'll talk this whole thing out. Miss Keen is out there getting you some dinner"—he nodded towards the closed doors to the dining-room, from behind which they could hear the homely rattle of crockery—"and while she's getting it suppose we sit down and be sensible?"

"If you like," agreed Mina cheerfully. "I only say what I say. You can't keep me away from that telephone forever, you know."

Masters managed the parody of a wink.

"And I'll tell you another thing," he confided. "If you're worrying about this Mr. Pennick: don't. You don't need to tell everybody he's a fake. We know it."

Mina whirled round.

"Do you really mean that?"

"Lord love you, what do you think coppers are for?" asked Masters. "We know it right enough. In fact, we've just been proving it."

Outside, in the sanded path beyond the open window, there was the stir of a footstep.

Sanders—who was nearest the window—heard it but did not look round. He heard it within a layer of his consciousness, only to be remembered afterwards. For he was too intent on the faces in the bright, ornate room, where the polished oak floor made their own footfalls drown out noises beyond the light.

"It's gone bust, Mrs. Constable," the chief inspector assured her. "I'd offer you a little discount on miracles right now. Because why? Because we've just learned, from things Mr. Chase told us allied to what Miss Keen has told us, that on at least a couple of occasions our friend Mr. Ruddy Pennik was pretending to read minds when he was only passing on information received."

"I beg your pardon," interrupted Chase with hot dignity. "I'm not going to have my words twisted. *I* didn't say that. *You* chose to say it."

"Choose your own terms, sir. I don't mind."

"If I could believe that," cried Mina. "You mean that even his thought-reading was a fake?"

"It was, Mrs. Constable," agreed Masters comfortably. He glanced across at H.M., who throughout all this had said not a word. "You should have been here, sir. Lummy, it was a treat!" Then Master's face darkened. "He gave me a real turn today, and I'm not denying it. Talking about my kid! Urr! I'll give him what I think about my kid, and her that's got to have an operation tomorrow! I'd still like to know where he got that little bit. But if you're worrying about publicity, I'll give 'em a press-bulletin that'll make a proper fool of that gentleman. As for your challenges"—he gave her an odd, dry look whose meaning was not quite clear— "make 'em or not, but it's waste effort. He won't kill anybody with his ruddy Teleforce, that gentleman won't. He couldn't kill an ant with a fly-swatter. And I'll hand in my resignation tomorrow if he can."

"Listen!" said Chase abruptly.

The sharp bark of the word made them all fall silent, so that even the emphatic jingle of keys in a pocket, or Masters's still more emphatic snort, died thinly away. This time they all heard the faint rustle in the sanded path outside.

Chase hurried to the window. Sanders, who was nearest it, stared out. Stars had come out in a clear, luminous night; a night when the trees were windless and the air had a clear visibility unrelated to light. Though the path outside was empty, someone was moving away from them: moving slowly in and out under the shadows of the trees.

"That was Pennik," said Chase, clearly and thinly. "What do you suppose he's thinking about now?"

XI

YOUR BREAKFAST-THINGS, said Hilary, pulling on one glove, "are out in a line in the pantry. You can't miss them. The new bread is in the bin on the *right;* not the left: that's stale. Now are you sure you can manage? And take care of Mina too?"

"Believe it or not," Sanders told her, "I have sometimes in the past had occasion to get my own breakfast. Lord alive, woman! It is not a soul-scarifying experience, which must be approached after a night of meditation and prayer. You just shove a couple of eggs and some rashers into a greased frying-pan; and, by the time you have burned your second lot of toast, it's done. As for Mina, she is sound asleep with a quarter-grain of morphia inside her, and won't stir until nine o'clock tomorrow morning. What ails you?"

Something was wrong. And he was speaking in this fashion because he believed he felt the same influence. They waited in the dining-room, under huge dropsical pictures which (if the dark coating could have been cleared off them) might have been pictures of Gargantuan hams and vegetables. Sanders' watch said that it was twenty minutes past nine.

Hilary smoothed out the glove. Her bag was packed and waiting. Through open doors to the front of the house they could hear, faintly, a police-car throbbing in the drive.

She pulled on the second glove.

"We're all deserting you," she went on. "Like rats. Like rats off a ship. First the lovely Pennik stays out on the tiles and refuses to come into dinner. Then Larry Chase suddenly decides he has an urgent appointment and must dash back to London—"

"He has a conference with a solicitor. He told us that yesterday."

"On Sunday night? At this time? I wanted him to help wash the dishes. He said he never could stand washing dishes. If you ask me, our Larry is shy of things very different from washing dishes. But I'm not one to talk. I'm deserting you too, aren't I?" Her jerk at the glove was vicious. "The thing is, where on earth is Pennik? Why didn't he come in? Do you realize you'll be left in the house with only Pennik and Mina, of all people?"

"Never mind that. I can handle Pennik."

(He wondered if he could.)

Yet at the same time he did not want her to go. Her

color was up, and her blue eyes glittered with nervousness or excitement. She was wearing light gray, a contrast with the color of the face and eyes; with very little make-up, and a kind of freshness about her like the glow of her skin. He always remembered her like that, under a mosaic dome of lights by the dining-room table.

She picked up her bag with one hand, and extended the other.

"Well, good-by. It *has* been a week-end, hasn't it?"

"It has." He took the bag out of her hand.

They were close to the door when she stopped. "And, Jack. If anything should—"

"Look here," he protested mildly. "I am not being locked into the Bastille, never again to see the light of day. I am very comfortably housed. Dr. Edge will probably drop in about ten o'clock, to see Mina. There is beer in the pantry. There is a library I have not yet had time to investigate. Off you go; and we are seeing each other for dinner on Tuesday night?"

She nodded. He went on talking easily; and it was not until they were out in the front hall that he let a hidden worry, a hidden antagonism, flash out. Chief Inspector Masters and Sir Henry Merrivale were coming down the stairs.

"Climb into the car," he told Hilary. "Masters will drop you off at the station." He waited until she had gone out. He even closed the front door so that she was certain not to hear. Then he faced the others doggedly.

"Can I ask a question without being stepped on again?"

Masters looked surprised. "A question, Doctor? Of course," he returned, with a grin of great heartiness. "What would you be wanting to know, now?"

"What are you going to do about her?"

"Her?"

"Mrs. Constable. Has it occurred to you that she may be in a good deal of danger?"

Never before had he felt so cut off from two whom he considered his friends. Communication was a snapped line, both of thought and feeling. Even H.M., whom he would have trusted to see anything, remained somber and sour-faced. Masters was bland but positive.

"Oh? Just what kind of danger were you thinking of, Doctor? Danger from whom?"

"From Pennik. I don't think you fully understand that fellow's character. Whether he kills with thought-waves or whether he doesn't, the point is that he's capable of killing. And didn't you hear Mrs. Constable's challenge?"

"Mrs. Constable's challenge," mused the chief inspector.

97

"Yes, sir, I heard it. I've also heard the story about the boy who cried 'Wolf!' Haven't you?"

"All I remember about that story," said Sanders, "is that the wolf came."

"Well we won't worry about him just yet," said the chief inspector comfortably. "And I shouldn't let it worry you either. In fact, if I were you I should just forget all about it."

There was a silence, while Sanders stared at him.

"But when Pennik comes back—"

"He's not comin' back, son," interposed H.M. somberly. "We've just been up to his room. He's done a bunk. Packed his bag and cleared out while we were havin' a bite of dinner. And he left somethin' behind on the dressin'-table. Show it to him, Masters."

From his notebook the chief inspector took a folded sheet of note-paper, which he handed across to Sanders. On it was written in ink, and in neat small handwriting:

To the police:

I regret that certain circumstances, no less than those which may arise in the future, make it both inadvisable and inconvenient for me to remain at Fourways any longer. Lest, however, I should be thought to be running from the law, I may say that I mean to put up at the Black Swan Hotel, where I met Chief Inspector Masters this morning. It is the only hostelry I know in the district, and appeared very tolerable in the brief inspection I was able to give it. I shall be available there at any time.

Yours, etc.,

Herman Pennik

The letter, he thought, contained reason both for relief and further uneasiness. He handed it back.

"But Mrs. Constable—"

"Listen, son," said H.M., in a quiet tone he very seldom used. "I'd like to be able to think different. But the fact is, d'ye see, that the heroic and grief-stricken Mrs. Constable has been tellin' us a pack of deliberate lies."

Sanders did not know why this startled him so much; or, in a sense, shocked him. He only knew that it did.

"Want to hear what they were, son?"

"Very much."

"Item," growled H.M., running his hand round inside his collar. "Cast your mind back to that little adventure, about fifteen minutes before the murder, when Sam Constable hears the lamp go smash in your room and comes peltin'

98

down to investigate. Now, two persons gave a minute description of that, didn't they? You heard it. Young Chase described it, and Mrs. Constable described it. Chase told us how Constable came rushin' out of his bedroom, in his bare feet and bedroom slippers, stumbling all over himself to get his feet properly into the slippers. We've all had that same experience. We know how it works. It's too circumstantial. It couldn't be a mistake. It's either the truth or a plain lie."

"Well?" said Sanders—and knew what was coming.

"But what's the lady say, on the other hand? She tells us that, when Constable heard the crash and ran out, she had just finished tyin' up his shoes for him. So *she* says he was wearing shoes and socks. Again it's detailed and circumstantial. It's either truth or a plain lie. And I'm afraid, son, that it's a plain lie."

"Why couldn't Chase be lying?"

H.M. ruffled his hands across his big bald head.

"Because I know liars, son," he said rather wearily. "She's not one of the best. But if you want proof further than what's maybe cloth-headed maunderin' on my part, think back! You saw the feller, didn't you? Well? Was he wearin' shoes or slippers?"

Sanders had not before considered this. He had been too intent on other things to notice discrepancies. And, though he did not want to remember it, the scene returned with too much vividness.

"Slippers," he admitted.

"Uh-huh. So she was lying—"

"Item two," continued H.M. "You heard her swear with touchin' simplicity and fervor that she knew nothing at all about the two candles that somebody had been burnin' in her husband's bedroom? Sure. *She* hadn't been walkin' about with those candles? Maybe you didn't notice her jump when I spotted 'em, though. But we won't count that. Now, on Friday night she was wearin' a big pink padded silk dressing-gown, wasn't she? Masters and I have been snoopin' round a bit, and we've had a look at that same dressing-gown. The right-hand sleeve is still all mucked up with spots of candle-grease where her hand was shaky."

(Sanders did not question that. He did not try. For insistently there returned to his mind a memory of Mina Constable crouching in the padded chair, the padded dressing-gown drawn round her and the spots of candle-grease on the sleeve.)

"Y'see, son?" inquired H.M. meekly.

Silence.

"There's also," H.M. went on, "the question of that big press-cutting scrap-book she says she burnt. She didn't, though. You can't burn one of those whackin' tough imitation-leather books without leaving *some* trace: not unless you drop it into a furnace. But there's no furnace here, not even a single wood or coal fire where it could 'a' been burned; and no trace of a burned book either. It's all lies, son. Let her sleep. If there was just some shred of proof how she did it, she might be on her way to Kingston on a charge of murder."

"Damn and blast," said Sanders.

"Sure," agreed H.M.

"But everything she said and did— After all, what difference does it make whether Constable wore slippers instead of shoes? Or whether she burned a couple of candles and said she didn't?"

H.M. was malevolent. "I wish I knew, son. Of all the rummy clues I ever heard, there's a couple of the rummiest."

"And you also maintain," persisted Sanders, "that everything about her: her crying: her faints: her lowered vitality: even that attempted challenge to the newspapers this evening, was all a part of a hoax and a flamboyant piece of acting?"

Masters chuckled benevolently.

"Well, sir, what do you think? You notice she was very easily persuaded not to issue her challenge, don't you?"

"I think you're wrong."

"Free country, Doctor. Every man to his own opinion! And now, if you don't mind," Masters bustled out with his watch, "Sir Henry and I will have to cut along. First to Grovetop, and then on to the Black Swan to see Mr. Pennik. I don't mind telling you *there's* an interview I'm looking forward to! When Sir Henry meets him—"

"That woman is still in danger."

"All right, Doctor. You guard her. Good night, good night, good night!"

He opened the door, and motioned H.M. to precede him. H.M., picking up his ancient top-hat and his equally ancient coat from the rack beside the door, lumbered forward two steps and stopped. He turned round.

He said:

"Look here, Masters. Just supposin' this young feller happens to be right?"

Masters almost howled at him. "Now what do you want to go thinking things like that for? We've been all over this, sir. We know what we think, don't we?"

"Oh, sure. Sure. We always do. Every time anybody in this world takes a toss and goes full-tilt down a butter

slide, it comes from knowin' what he thinks. Well, let's hear the mournful numbers. What do we think?"

After looking round cautiously, Masters closed the door. Then he talked at Sanders.

"That Mrs. Constable deliberately murdered her husband, by some trick we haven't dropped to yet. Ah, and I'll tell you something else. I haven't read any of the lady's books (no fear). But my wife has; all of 'em; and she told me a thing or two before I left home. In one of the books, about an Egyptian expedition, a whole string of people were supposed to die from a curse on the Pharaoh's tomb; and it turned out that they were really polished off by some ruddy clever use of carbon monoxide gas. My wife couldn't remember exactly how the thing worked, but she said it sounded all right and you could do it at home, so she wondered whether it would work in case she ever wanted to polish me off."

Sanders shrugged his shoulders.

"All right; admit that," he said. "And in *The Double Alibi* she had the victim die from a hypodermic injection of insulin. Which is a hair-raiser, because it's scientifically sound and very nearly undetectable. I remember I said something about it to her on Friday evening. But what of that? Constable didn't die from carbon monoxide or insulin. What does it prove?"

"It proves my point," declared Masters, tapping his finger into his palm, "that a trick like this, whatever in blazes it is, would be straight up her street. If she ever set out to polish somebody off, that's just exactly how she'd go about it. Something as wild as wind and yet as domestic as cheese. Something you could do in your own home with two thimbles and a tablet of soap; and no special knowledge required."

It was at this point that an extraordinary change went over H.M.'s face. It was exactly as though he were setting and puffing out his features to deliver a resounding raspberry; but it faded off into excited wonder.

"Oh, my eye," he muttered.

"Sir?"

"Never mind, son. I was cogitatin'."

Masters turned round on him with deepest and darkest suspicion.

"I tell you I was cogitatin'!" insisted H.M. "Go on. What I was thinkin' about don't affect your case. I was only thinkin' about the spots of candle-grease on the carpet, and exactly where they were. Burn me, Masters, *why* do you always think I'm tryin' to do you in the eye?"

101

"Because usually you are," said the chief inspector briefly. "Now see here, sir—"

"Go on with your case," said Sanders. "How does Pennik fit into it?"

"Isn't it clear as daylight, Doctor? Pennik knew about it, or guessed about it. He knew when she was going to do it, and why she was going to do it. So when it happened he simply used it to catch on and bolster up his ruddy hocus-pocus of murder by telepathy. Mind you, he didn't commit himself too far by saying too much before it happened. He only said it might happen. Then it did happen; and for the first time he came out boldly and swore he did it. Eh? I'm pretty sure he wasn't in cahoots with her over it.[1] He only used her. That's why she's so blinking wild and bitter against him now. That much of her carryings-on I'll admit as genuine and sincere. Here's Pennik going about saying he did it, whereas she has thumping good reason to know he didn't do it. I ask you straight: doesn't that explain all the inconsistencies we've got on our hands?"

"It does if she's loopy," said H.M.

"I don't follow that."

"Oh, Masters, my son! Wouldn't you call it just a little bit too conscientious? Does she get as mad at him as all that just because he walks in and assumes all the blame for her own crime?"

Masters brooded. "I'm not so sure, sir. Might be the best kind of bluff."

"It might be. It might fit; in which case her 'challenge' is pure bluff? Its a good case, aside from the triflin' fact that we couldn't prove it even if we knew it was true. All I know is that parts of it *are* true. They must be; and in spite of your worryin', son"—he looked malevolently at Sanders—"that woman is as safe here tonight as though we'd got her packed in cotton-wool in the middle of the Bank of England. Now we got to be off, or we'll make Joe Keen's daughter miss her train. Goo' night, son. Come on, Masters."

Dr. Sanders stood in the doorway at Fourways and watched the tail-light of the police-car vanish among the trees. It was chillier now. He looked for a moment at the clear starlight over the trees. Then he went inside, where he closed, locked, and bolted the front door. He was alone in the

[1] In looking over my notes of this case, even now I am struck with the number of suggestions that were made about various people working as somebody else's accomplice. It will perhaps allow better concentration if I state here that the murderer in this case worked entirely alone, and had no confederate who either knew the murderer's plan or rendered material assistance in any way. The reader is warned.—J. S.

house with a quiet, pleasant little woman whom two of his colleagues believed to be a murderess. This made him smile. He was also alone with what was to prove one of the worst nights of his life.

XII

HIS FIRST SENSATION, as he remembered afterwards, was one of freedom and almost of cheerfulness.

He could settle down to read, or to consider his own personal problems, in the luxuriance of being alone. Maybe he ought not to leave all these lights blazing in somebody else's house; but they suited his mood and he did not feel of an economical turn. Remarkable, though, how wiry and receptive your nerves and ears and even eyes seemed to become under the mere weight of silence. Everything looked just a little larger and sharper than life. Everything, from the fall of your shoe on unglazed tiles to the brushing of your sleeve across the leaves of a potted palm, seemed to have a clarity of sound which shook like a note in music.

He went into the drawing-room, where the polished oak floor was even more noisy. It was growing definitely cold here, so he closed the long window. As an afterthought he went back and locked it. All the windows on this floor stretched to the ground, it occurred to him: were they all locked? When you came to consider it, such houses were nothing more than a series of open arches.

Wandering into the dining-room, he considered the great dark pictures and the massive plate on the sideboard. There was a half-finished flagon of beer in the sideboard, he remembered. He brought it out, put it down on the table with what seemed a very loud bump, and went to fetch a glass from a deep china-closet which showed him, unexpectedly, his own reflection in a mirror inside. He also brought a china ashtray from the sideboard, an ashtray which rattled and clattered and perversely bumped up against something whenever you put ash in it.

The beer, warmish, frothed a good deal. With patient effort he filled the glass, lighted a cigarette, and sat down beside the big round table to consider.

It might be interesting one day to write a monograph on the medical aspects of the emotion called fear. It had been treated before, of course; but not until he sorted out facts for his little report to Masters had he realized the depths and mists in that field called nervous shock. It was a new territory, almost a new quicksand. Several persons here had suffered from it, including Hilary. And—come to think of it—he had not yet learned what Hilary saw. Taking a more concrete example, let us suppose that Sam Constable had died of nervous shock as the result of something seen or heard or prepared for that purpose.

Behind him, the swing-door to the kitchen creaked and cracked sharply.

He did not jump up, as his impulse was. He waited for the fraction of a second, and then glanced back casually over his shoulder.

He saw nothing, knowing that he should see nothing. That jump, for which he felt annoyed, had been caused by the mere sudden movement of an inanimate thing. Drafts or contraction of wood or whatever the cause, it is the small stir of the inanimate which brushes nerves the wrong way. He noticed that the kitchen was dark; also dark was the conservatory, which he could see through a closed glass door.

But it was not the best time, probably, for analyzing the nature of nerves. Better be up and doing something. Better go up and see how Mina Constable was getting on.

Extinguishing his cigarette, he finished the beer and went upstairs. When he knocked at the door of her room he received no answer, nor did he expect one; the morphia would have done its work by that time. He opened the door very softly and looked in.

Mina's bed was empty.

The bedclothes were thrown back in some disarray, showing a sort of throat of crisp white sheets which shone in the light of the bedside lamp. Pillows were punched into confusion; and a dressing-gown and slippers, which he remembered having seen when Mina went docilely to bed at nine o'clock, had now gone. Yet the bathroom was empty. And this room and her husband's were blank dark blurs where no person could care to sit or lurk for pleasure.

"Mrs. Constable!" he called.

She ought to answer that.

"Mrs. Constable!"

There is no more disturbing realization than that a person, who is confined with you within the four walls of a house, must hear you but for some reason chooses not to reply. It is too much like an unpleasant game. Yet Mina continued to hide.

He made a search of the room, half expecting to find her in the wardrobe and wondering what he should say if he did find her there. A real seizure this time? But the slippers and dressing-gown did not fit in with that. He hurried through the bathroom, barking his shins on the bronze-painted metal of the heater and tipping over a drinking-glass, which fell with a hellish ringing clatter into the wash-basin. That noise sobered him. Quietly he set about looking into every room on that floor, including his own. Then he went downstairs, to find a slight alteration in the look of the lower hall. The tall folding doors to the drawing-room, which he was certain he had left open, were now closed.

The telephone began to ring as he pulled the doors open; it almost muddled his errand, for he never realized that the things had such a tongue. It continued to ring while he looked round the room, and angered him. Better answer it. When he picked up the receiver, he found it was still warm from recent contact with a hand.

"Hello," said a persuasive voice. "Is this Grovetop three-one?"

"No. Yes," said Sanders, clearing his throat and looking at the dial. "What is it?"

"This is the *Daily Non-Stop*. May I speak to Miss Shields, please?"

"To who? Oh! Sorry: Miss Shields is indisposed and regrets that she cannot make—"

"That's quite all right, Doctor," interposed Mina's voice, speaking at his ear. Mina's face appeared at his shoulder. Mina's arm, thin and brown and rather freckled out of the loose sleeve of the dressing-gown, moved past his own; and she took the receiver. "Hello? Yes, speaking. Well, now you've rung me back, are you convinced it wasn't a hoax? . . . Yes, yes, I quite understand you have to be careful. . . . Yes, *print* it; or as much as you dare. . . . No, that's all right; but I can't talk to you any longer, really I can't; I'm not well; yes, thank you very much. Good-by, good-by, good-by."

She clattered the receiver down on its hook and stood back.

"I'm so sorry to have to deceive you," said Mina, looking up at him after a pause. "But I told them they couldn't keep me away from the telephone forever. As soon as they'd gone, I came down here. I was waiting. They'd have stopped me."

Sanders also stood back.

"That's quite all right, Mrs. Constable."

"Now you're annoyed."

(Of course I'm annoyed. Who the hell wouldn't be annoyed?)

"That's quite all right, Mrs. Constable. If I want to make
105

a fool of myself, that's my affair." He remembered himself shouting all over the house, betraying his state of mind with every word. "But will you tell me how you manage to be so spry after that dose of morphia?"

"I didn't take it," retorted Mina, with the desperate and triumphant cunning of a genuinely ill woman. He saw that hysterical cunning, and relented. "I only pretended to take it, you see. And now I've got back at Pennik; I've got back at him. They wouldn't print all I told them, because they said it was slander or libel or something; but there's enough, there's enough, there's enough. He'll look a proper fool, M. Vaudois will. Did you know? A professor aboard our ship used to call Pennik M. Vaudois; I don't know why, but it made him look like murder. And now I've done it. I'm going upstairs now and take my medicine; then I shall be all right."

"You certainly are. Off you go, now!"

"But you'll come up with me, won't you? I'm alone, and it seems worse to be alone now than it did during the day. All the rats have left the ship. Except you."

"It's all right, Mrs. Constable. Come along."

On the landing above them the great clock rang with fluid chimes, echoing, and began to strike ten. It was twenty minutes past ten before he had got her to bed again, had seen to it that this time she swallowed the tablet, had tucked the dressing-gown round her, and heard the dull mutter of exhaustion as the drug took effect. With her head under a pillow, she crumpled up and slept.

Without dreams, he hoped. He took her pulse, studied her for a time with his watch in his hand, and turned out the light. Yet this apparently sincere woman, he reflected as he went downstairs, had lied up-hill-down-dale over every place where she could possibly have lied.

One thing, however, the sharp edge of that disappearance-scare had done for him. It had cured him (or he thought it had cured him) of nervous disturbances without foundation. Once was enough. It only left him restless and strung up beyond any hope of sleep. He knew that he ought to turn in, for he had work to do tomorrow, but he also knew that it would be useless. He prowled or sat, always coming back to the dining-room. One interval he filled up by going round and locking every door or window on the ground floor, another by glancing over a rather dull collection of books in the library. Ten-thirty rang from the clock on the stairs; then a quarter to eleven, then the hour itself.

It was close to eleven-thirty when he thought he saw

Herman Pennik's face looking at him through the glass door to the conservatory.

Sanders afterwards remembered that the tumbler, from which he had been drinking the last of the beer in the flagon, slipped through his fingers and smashed in a star of brown froth on the dining-room table. He had simply looked round, and there it was.

For some time he had been conscious of a faint noise: a noise, in fact, so dim as to be rather a vibration, a pressure on the ears, than a sound. He vaguely associated it with water, and then realized that it must be the miniature fountain in the conservatory, soberly falling after Sam Constable's death as before it. Turning round in his chair to see, he looked at the glass door of the conservatory; and Pennik looked back at him.

He was across the room so quickly that he did not remember leaving his chair. For a second he thought it might have been his own reflection, in gleams of light against a door to a dark room, until he saw Pennik's nose and fingers pressed against and flattened out in grayish-white blobs on the glass. Then Pennik bolted. Sanders threw open the door, to meet a rush of hot overscented air from the plants—and silence.

He stood in the doorway. No light, no noise, no movement of any kind, until he blundered forward and set moving a jungle-brush of sound by walking into plants. He could not remember the position of the light-switch. Groping through the aisles, he knew that to search here was useless; and for another reason. One of the long stained-glass windows, which he had locked a while ago, was now open: a way of escape.

Mina Constable?

Mina Constable, upstairs and half-drugged?

He tried not to run when he went upstairs and hurried into the dark room, only to find another false alarm. She was no more dead or hurt than he was: breathing quietly and regularly in sleep. Yet this time he took no chances. He locked the door to the bathroom, saw that the windows were locked, and, when he went out into the hall again, locked the door on the outside and kept the key.

These continued false alarms were worse than a real happening. Yet he had seen Pennik; or hadn't he? Suddenly he knew that he was not sure. It had been no more than a flash across the tail of the eye, an image conjured out of his own imagination, or (he boggled at the thought) a projected image. But the open window? He might have left that open himself; now that he reflected, he was almost sure he had.

That was a little better. However, he did not go far away from Mina's bedroom; he sat down on the top step of the stairs. His breathing quieted, his thoughts revolved round the ease with which phantoms could be evoked, he lighted another cigarette and watched the smoke. The clock chimed the quarter to midnight. Feeling easy again, he wandered downstairs—

The telephone was ringing again.

Better answer it.

"Hello?" said a pleasant voice. "Grovetop three-one? This is the *Daily Trumpeter*—"

Sanders wearily started to lower the receiver. "I'm sorry," he said, "very-sorry-no-statement-to-make-this—"

"Hold on!" said the voice, with such urgency that he stopped in spite of himself. "Don't ring off, will you? I don't want any story. I want to give you one."

"What?"

"Is Miss Mina Shields all right? You know what I mean."

"No, I don't know what you mean. Of course she's all right. Why?"

"Who is this speaking, please?"

"My name is Sanders. I'm a friend of the family. Why did you ask whether she is all right?"

"*Dr.* Sanders?" asked the voice quickly. "Doctor, you ought to know this. Mr. Herman Pennik has just rung up this office."

"Yes?" said Sanders—knowing what was coming.

"He said that Miss Shields would probably die before midnight tonight. He wants us to make clear that he doesn't promise it, or say that it's certain, but he thinks he'll have succeeded in killing her by then. Naturally we don't pay much attention to his claims; but we thought we'd better give you the opportunity to contra—"

"Wait! Where was he 'phoning from, do you know?"

Slight pause. "Place called the Black Swan Hotel, about four miles away from you."

"You're sure of that?"

"Yes. I checked back."

"How long ago did he ring?"

"About ten minutes. We're considering what's best to be done about it, Doctor, and if you would care to assist us by making a state—"

"There is no truth in it. Mrs. Constable is comfortably asleep with her door locked, and nobody can get near her. She is absolutely all right. Please accept that from me."

He put down the receiver with jingling finality; he stared at the bay windows, and fingered the key in his pocket.

Was she all right?

Shatteringly, at his elbow, the telephone rang again.

"Grovetop three-one? This is the *News-Record*. Sorry to trouble you, but some remarkable claims were made to us this morning by a man named Herman Pennik. Now he has just rung up the office to say—"

"I know. He proposed to kill Mrs. Constable by what he calls Teleforce. He is very modest about it, and doesn't entirely promise he can do the trick—"

"Not exactly," said the voice. "That's what he said fifteen minutes ago. Now he says she's dead."

For a time Sanders looked at the number on the white dial before him. Without listening to what the person at the other end of the wire was saying, he replaced the phone.

He would not be gulled again. It had been all imagination that he thought he saw Herman Pennik in this house, for at that time Herman Pennik had been at the Black Swan Hotel four miles away. Everything was imagination. Yet the fact that it had been such vivid imagination, the fact that Pennik's image had been stamped on that glass as clearly as the prints of his nose and fingers, was what made Sanders's scalp stir with the remembrance of that hard sandy head as a reality.

He had seen it. By the Lord, he had.

Again the telephone clattered out.

"Grove top three-one? This is the *Daily Wireless*—"

This time Sanders put down the receiver with nicety and care. Taking the key to Mina's room out of his pocket, he crossed the room and went upstairs and it was not until he had nearly reached the top of the stairs that he began to run. He fitted the key into the lock, opened the door, and went across to the bed.

* * *

When he came out again, a few minutes later, he had only one idea. Mina was still lying in the bed, but her posture was no longer peaceful except in the thin sense that death is peaceful. Poor devil, poor woman whom he had liked so much, poor pathetic lump of clay lying with arms and legs asprawl. Yet he had only one idea: he must somehow shut off the noise of that telephone, still ringing violently and incessantly downstairs.

Part III

TERROR:

Concerning Meaningless Clues

FLASHES FROM EVERYWHERE

Daily Non-Stop

Monday, May 2, 1938

MINA SHIELDS DEFIES MYSTIC, DIES; SECOND DEATH FROM UNKNOWN FORCE.

Daily Trumpeter

TELEFORCE: NEW MENACE TO MANKIND?

Daily News-Record

STUDENT FORETELLS TO NEWS-RECORD DEATH FROM ALLEGED THOUGHT-RAYS.

What is Teleforce?

Evening Griddle

(MONDAY NIGHT FINAL)

NO SIGN OF DEATH:
Terror Stalks in Surrey As Teleforce Claims Next Victim! (Exclusive!)

... but we 'eard it. Yerce! Me and me 'usband 'eard it on the wireless. And I said to me 'usband, I said, 'Well, if yer can't trust the B.B.C., then 'oo *can* yer trust?' That's what I said, 'If yer can't trust the B.B.C., 'oo *can* yer trust?' Cor

lumme, people ain't 'arf talkin' about it. Nuffing else wher-
ever yer go. Poor Mrs. Drew, fair got the wind up she 'as;
not 'arf; 'er Bert works in a garridge in Grovetop; didn't yer
know? 'Reckon 'e ought to be 'anged,' she says, 'this Pennik
ought.' 'Let 'im kill old 'Itler,' I says; 'let 'im kill old 'Itler,
and then we shall see.' I said to me 'usband; knows all about
it; ow, yerce, reads all the science bits in the papers; I said,
'But wot is this Teleforce?' 'E says, 'Ow, it's big, it is.
Like wireless, only bigger.' But I said, 'What'll they do to
this Pennik, that's what I wanter know? Will they 'ang 'im?
What'll they *do* to 'im?'

Another pint, please, miss.

Ta.

Now, old man, I'm sorry to say this, but I'm afraid you're
a reactionary. Yes, old man, I'm afraid that's just what you
are: a reactionary. No offense, I hope, but you'd be the first
to admit yourself you're a bit of a reactionary.

Believe it, old man? Why not? That's science for you. I
mean, look at how the times are moving. I mean, thirty or
forty years ago you'd have said wireless was impossible. Now
wouldn't you, old man? I mean, if you'd been alive then?
And yet there it is right bang in your own house, and all
you've got to do is twiddle a little knob and there you are.
See what I mean, old man?

Gummy! In thirty or forty years you'll be able to turn
on this Teleforce and kill your boss or Hitler or anybody you
damn well please. Gummy! Wouldn't *I* show 'em a thing or
two, if I knew how to work it! Pop pop pop pop pop. Like
a machine-gun. All the same, old man, I mean to say.
This Pennik. He can't do that. I mean, people like Einstein
and H. G. Wells are all very well but thanks old man I don't
mind if I do.

Another of the same, please, miss.

Ta.

Evening Griddle? New York calling. Go ahe-ea-d.

Hello? *Evening Griddle?* Let me talk to Ray Dodsworth,
will you?

Yeah, that's right: Dodsworth.

Hello? Ray? This is Louie Westerham of the *Floodlight.*
Howzit, Ray? Look: for crissake what's all this about a
Czecho-Slovakian scientist getting ready to knock off Hitler
with a death-ray?

What?

So it's all a lot of hooey?

What do you mean, it's a better story than that?

What?

Look, Ray, can I depend on that?

Story! Holy jumping—why, it's the biggest thing that—

111

wait a minute, wait a minute; let's see how it looks in a head. T-E-L-E—holy jumping—

What?

What do you mean, 'go easy'?

Oh, for crissake, Ray, why bother about that? It's new, ain't it? It's big, ain't it? Suppose nobody does know what it is; that won't keep 'em from talking, will it? We'll sell Tele-force to the American people, that's what we'll do. We'll make every man, woman, and child in this country Teleforce-conscious. Now wait, Ray; don't go 'way; I want you to talk to—

Allo! Allo!

Ne coupez pas, mademoiselle, ne coupez pas. Quelqu'un sur la ligne. Rétirez-vous, imbécile!

Is it again the British Ministry for War?

Bon!

Ah, my friend, it is still you?

I spoke, my friend, to offer you my sincerest congratula-tions. Of a truth it is magnificent. It will be of an inestima-ble service to the Entente Cordiale, will it not?

Ha ha.

We know of what I speak, do we not? Boum! The machine which your engineers have constructed?

No, no, I say no more. I do not press you. It is necessary to be discreet. I only offer congratulations.

Your tone is admirable. I too suspect that the wire is tapped.

But our engineers may call on you, perhaps?

I cannot understand you. The wire makes sputtering sounds; it is tapped. Yes, it is beautiful weather here in Paris. The tulips are out in the gardens of the Tuileries.

A'voir, my friend.

XIII

ON TUESDAY IT RAINED. It was raining in a solid sheet when Dr. Sanders got out of the Underground at Trafalgar Square and hurried across to the restaurant at the top of Whitehall where he was to meet Masters and H.M. for a conference over lunch.

He was relieved to be back in town again, in the steamy bustle where fantasies could be forgotten. But something fol-lowed and caught up with him; with the difference that whereas in the country it had been only a whisper, here it was several million voices. From the table behind the big plate-glass window giving on the street, where Masters rose to meet him, he could see newspaper bills. And they were enough.

H.M. was only a few minutes late. They saw him get out of his car and waddle in through the rain, in a large transparent oilskin with a hood, which swathed him entirely (including his hat) and made him resemble a particularly malevolent ghost in a cloud of ectoplasm.

He disentangled himself from this, tossed it to a waiter, and sniffed the steam of good cooking. Masters rose at him.

"You promised, sir—"

H.M. howled back.

"It's no good goin' for me, Masters," he said. "I couldn't go down to Fourways yesterday. I couldn't. There's blue blazes to pay here; and unless I can get myself out of this I'm headed for the House of Lords as straight as an onion to Covent Garden."

"Trouble?"

"Trouble?" said H.M., sticking the end of his napkin under his collar and looking up over the menu. "Oh, no. We nearly had an international situation on our hands, that's all. It's better now. Or at least I hope it is. I'd like to know what fathead started that report about us havin' a death-ray that would knock any bomber out of the sky if it wasn't more'n half a mile up. We're supposed to be crafty. Crafty. Oh, my eye. You know, Masters, it seems like every time a mess starts in this world it's our fellers who have to go out and smooth it over; and all we get for our pains is a kick in the pants for not bein' more active."

Masters pointed to a newspaper bill in the rain.

"But how long is this nonsense going on, sir?"

"I dunno. I'm hopin' for a short row and a merry one."

"But Pennik can't do that!" Masters pointed out.

"Without doubt, my old one. Only he's doin' it."

"It's this campaign in the newspapers. I never saw anything like it in all my born days. Trams, tubes, buses; nothing but Teleforce, Teleforce, Teleforce, and what do we propose to do about it? Very nastily said, too. It's a disgrace, they say. One gentleman buttonholed me in the train this morning and quite seriously suggested sticking Pennik away in a zinc-lined box like a tube of radium. It's the newspapers; and I wish I knew who was encouraging them."

H.M. tapped his chest with the menu.

"I'm encouragin' 'em," he said.

"What?"

"Sure. Note, son, that there ain't a soul in Fleet Street who claims Pennik is a true prophet. There's a very strong tinge

113

of The Bird hoverin' round every line that's written. And if I can manage—"

"But people are believing it!"

"Oh, yes. Pennik's mustard. Wait till you hear him on the wireless tomorrow night."

"Goddelmighty," said Masters. "You don't mean they're going to let him broadcast over the B.B.C?"

"No. But they are in France. He goes on over Radio Brittany at 7.15; commercial program; sponsored by Creemona Cheese Biscuits. Y' know, Masters"—H.M. ruffled his hands across his big bald head—"there are features of our modern life that puzzle me. They do honestly. How that's supposed to be a great recommendation for a product beats me. 'Here we are, ladies and gentlemen. Listen to Herman Pennik, who knocks 'em off without even the aid of Creemona Cheese Biscuits.' "

"And I suppose you encouraged that too, sir?"

"Uh. Well. I didn't altogether discourage it."

Masters did not say anything. He studied H.M. as though he could think of a place of incarceration for him much more suitable than the House of Lords.

And H.M. was not joking. He drew himself up.

"I'm the old man, son," he said with great dignity. "You trust me and everything will be all right. I've got my reasons. Only—"

"Only?"

"Well, if the thing won't work and I take a toss over this, I hate to think what's goin' to happen. I'll be packing my bag and departin' for Siberia with such promptness as to baffle the eyesight."

"You will that," said the chief inspector grimly; and Sanders knew that H.M. was really worried.

"Which is why," he returned, "we got to get down to business and do it straightaway. I want every fact I can lay my hands on. I want every dagger in the arsenal, because Pennik's got a few himself. I've been reading your report." He looked at Sanders. "And yours, son. You did the postmortem on Mrs. Constable yesterday?"

"Yes," said Sanders.

"And still no sign of what caused death?"

"No. Except that she was so chronically run down in every organ, so burnt out except for actual physical strength, that she was the easiest possible victim—"

"For whatever it was?"

"Yes."

"Uh-huh. Finally, I want your whole story. I want to hear everything that happened to you on Sunday night, after we

114

left you to your fate. And Mrs. Constable to hers, God help us. Now tell me: slow, steady, and careful."

Sanders told him. It lasted through the soup-course and halfway through the beef; it was the dozenth time he had told it, but he omitted nothing. H.M., his napkin stuck firmly into his collar, listened while he ate; occasionally he would stop and peer over a loaded fork. What parts of the story struck him as significant Sanders could not tell, though at times his eye was curious.

At the end of it H.M. put down his knife and fork.

"So," he muttered, folding his arms. "So!"

"It'd seem, sir," interposed Masters, *"it'd seem* we may have made a bit of a mistake about Mrs. Constable."

"Oh? And that makes you still more dubious, hey? If I'm so cocky about thinkin' I'm on the right track in this business, I got to explain how that mistake came to be made, haven't I? I wonder if you can guess."

"I don't want to guess; I want to know. That's to say, if you know."

H.M. reflected.

"We'll round this up. Tell me, Masters: is it absolutely certain that Pennik's alibi for Sunday night is air-tight?"

Masters nodded firmly.

"Not a doubt of it. He put up at the Black Swan, as he said he was going to. You remember that you and I went over there and tried to see him; but he got on his high and mighty horse and refused to see us."

"Well?"

"Well, he arrived at the Black Swan at about nine o'clock. From that time on, until he went to bed at well past twelve, he was never out of the sight of at least two witnesses. Oh, ah! Did it deliberately, of course. He kept a group of them up on a little drinking party after the bar closed. They thought he was a bit touched in the head, and you can't blame 'em. Frothing at the mouth, and so on—"

"Did he do that?"

"He did. They even kept him in sight when he was making his telephone calls, though there was a lot of noise and he spoke low and they didn't hear what he was saying. However, from nine o'clock to well past twelve he's definitely got an alibi that can't be shaken."

Masters paused. He drew a deep breath. Then his blood-pressure went up like a thermometer.

"I know it can't be shaken," he insisted. "The only trouble is that Dr. Sanders here swears he saw Pennik prowling through Fourways at half-past eleven."

There was a silence. H.M. looked round at Sanders.

115

"You're sure of that, son?"

Sanders nodded. On that rainy afternoon, even in the crowded and noisy restaurant, the atmosphere of the twilight house was back again. He too well remembered the nose and five fingers pressed against that glass door to the conservatory, and Pennik's face behind.

"Yes. It was either Pennik or his ghost or his twin brother."

"His ghost, maybe," commented H.M. without inflection or surprise. "Sort of astral projection. I told you he was mustard."

"Astral projection be blowed," said Masters, going more red. "Only—lummy! Are you telling me, sir, that he not only can polish people off without a mark left on their bodies, but he can send his ghost to do it for him? Are you telling me that?"

"Well, how do you explain it?"

"I don't," said the chief inspector. "Not yet. All I know is I'm going mad. I'm slowly going stark, staring, raving—"

"Now, now!" urged H.M., giving a deprecating look round over his spectacles, and turning back to Masters with a soothing air. "Just keep your shirt on, and stop poundin' on that table. Be dignified. Like me. Ho ho!" A ghoulish grin went over his face. "I'm as dignified as even Squiffy could want. Eat your cheese and think of Marcus Aurelius. How's everything at home? How's the kid?"

Masters's face lit up.

"Survived the operation beautifully. Everything's fine, I'm glad to say. Mrs. M.'s with her now. I've been running about a good bit—"

"Sure. So your brain won't work."

"Much obliged, sir."

"That's all right. Looky here. I'm trying to extract from you your meed of information. The last time I saw you, you had only one object. The last time I saw you, you were goin' bald-headed to find something out about Pennik. Have you found out anything about him?"

Masters was himself again.

"Ah! I have, just a bit. Not much, but I'm grateful for anything."

"Well?"

"Part of it I got from Mr. Chase, and part of it by a piece of luck from the proprietor of the Black Swan Hotel." Masters frowned. "As you say, the trouble so far has been to find out something about Mr. Ruddy Pennik, who he is or what he does or where he comes from. I saw Mr. Chase

116

yesterday. He seems to be the only person now remaining alive who knows anything at all about Pennik."

H.M. opened his eyes.

"Very cheerin' thought, that is. I hope it comforts him."

"As a matter of fact, sir, I—hurrum!—I asked Mr. Chase whether he could manage to drop in here and see us today. I thought you might like to talk to him. But that's by the way. I thought of getting a line on Pennik through his universities. Which were Oxford and Heidelberg, according to Mr. Chase. But Oxford doesn't know anything about him. And neither does Heidelberg, except that he took a degree there about fifteen years ago, with all kinds of honors for (stop a bit) metaphysics. He spelled his first name with two 'n's' then."

"Did he, now?"

"The only other bit comes from the Black Swan. Now everybody, when they first meet Pennik, gets an idea that he's some sort of foreigner; but they can't think why. I did myself, and hanged if *I* know why. The proprietor of the Black Swan thought so too. He wanted Pennik to sign the foreign-visitors register. Pennik got annoyed, and said no, and pulled out a passport on the Union of South Africa. The proprietor was convinced, but he wasn't certain, so he jotted down the number of the passport on the q.t. Still, I thought it was worth while cabling to get a report, if possible, on the holder of that passport? Eh?"

H.M. grunted. "Any reply?"

"No, I'm sorry to say."

"And he scrapes through there too," growled H.M. "Burn me, they won't leave any indications or hentracks, will they? Or—will they? Take Mrs. Constable's murder, for instance. Even you will admit it was a murder now. We've just heard the story of the funny business from Sanders. I take it you've been all over the ground? Looked for the fingerprints and the stray cuff-links and whatnot?"

"Lord knows I have!"

"Yes. Find anything?"

"No, sir, we did not find anything. We combed every inch of the room where that lady died, and every other inch of the place as well, and we got absolutely nothing. Fingerprints? Oh, ah! A whole crop of 'em. But then everybody had been through that place at one time or another."

He bent forward earnestly, tapping the table with a knife.

"There was the poor lady lying in bed, in a nightgown and that pink dressing-gown, and the bedclothes kicked back. She'd undoubtedly put up a struggle, a real struggle, as the doctor will tell you—"

117

H.M. looked up.

"Hold on! A physical struggle?"

The chief inspector hesitated, and looked at Sanders.

"I shouldn't have said so," the latter replied, with a vivid vision of the bed and its occupant. "There were no marks or bruises on her, in any case. I should have said a struggle in the sense of a hard seizure like the one she described her husband having out in the hall before he died."

There was a slight shiver in the overheated room.

"Yes; but," argued H.M., "keeping this to the physical plane, could anybody have got at her for a physical struggle?"

Sanders considered.

"The chief inspector and I have been arguing that. It's remotely possible; but I doubt it. I last saw her alive at half-past eleven. I then locked up the room, locking the door to the bathroom and the door to the hall as I went out. After that I sat on the stairs for fifteen minutes. At a quarter to twelve I went downstairs—just as the telephone rang. I spoke to the newspapers and hurried back upstairs again within (I am sure) two or three minutes at the most.

"Now, this isn't a 'hermetically sealed room.' The locks on those doors are very old-fashioned and could have been housed in half a dozen ways. For instance, somebody could have gone in through the bathroom door while I was sitting on the stairs outside the other door. Afterwards there are several ways by which the murderer could have gone out again by the bathroom door and turned the key from outside, leaving it locked again. Granted. But if she had been murdered by a physical attack at any time while I was sitting at the top of the stairs just outside the hall door, I'm damned certain I should have heard it."

"H'mf. You weren't very far away from the door, son?"

"No. Only about eight feet. And, as Masters says, she struggled violently before she died on that bed. I'm certain I couldn't have helped hearing it."

"Fair enough. Shut up, Masters! And there wasn't a sound?"

"No. Nothing at all. Which means that the attack must have taken place during the two or three minutes while I was downstairs at the telephone. All right; I admit it did. In that case the murderer would have had to get through a locked door, kill Mrs. Constable after a struggle by a means that left no trace, and get out again. The murderer could have done that, yes. He could have left the doors locked behind him, as I said a minute ago. But it seems a remarkably short space of time for it to happen in, that's all."

H. M. spoke slowly.

"So she died alone," he said. "Like her husband in the hall."

Into Masters's face had come a quiet affability, such a blandness that H.M. regarded him with suspicion.

"Just a moment, sir," he interposed. "Just a moment, *if* you please. Now, you say that there was nobody in that house on Sunday night except Dr. Sanders and Mrs. Constable. You say there was no third person?"

"I dunno. We're still debatin' whether Pennik's astral projection was there."

Masters's epithet turned Pennik's astral projection into something much shorter and less dignified.

"—because, sir, I'm in a position to prove—*to prove*— that there was a third person there."

"Well?"

"You remember those two green candles on the chest-of-drawers in Mr. Constable's room?"

"I do," said H.M.; and his eyes narrowed.

"Just before you and I left Fourways on Sunday night, we had a look into Pennik's room and found him gone. Just so! We also had a look into Mr. Constable's room. Just so! You pointed out those two green candles to me, and showed how both of em' were burned down about half an inch?"

"Get on with it, son! Well?"

Masters sat back.

"After Mrs. Constable's death," he said, "the same two candles were both burned down another half-inch."

XIV

I DON'T SEE WHAT it's got to do with us," pursued Masters. "Or with the death of either Mr. or Mrs. Constable. It's not what you'd call a clue." He chuckled a little. "Oh, I've had my ideas, I'm bound to admit. What I thought of first off was a poisoned candle. I've read a story (in fact, I've read two stories) in which a bloke was polished off with a poisoned candle. But the doctor here swears blue that neither of the victims died from poison, solid, liquid, or gaseous. And that's good enough for me."

He raised one finger impressively.

"It proves blinking little about the murders. But it does more or less prove there was a third person at Fourways on Sunday night. You and I, Sir Henry, were the last to leave; and the candles hadn't been burned their extra half inch them.... daresay, Doctor, *you* didn't burn 'em?"

"No. I certainly didn't."

"Just so." Here the chief inspector hesitated. "And no reason, is there, why the dead lady should have burned 'em herself? Stop: I know what you'll say. She might have. Admitted. But why should she? Does it seem likely? No. Unless it was suicide. But then the candles weren't poisoned, so they couldn't have killed anybody. Oh, lummy, lead me to a lunatic asylum."

At last H.M. spoke.

"That tears it," he said.

"What tears it?"

"The candles. I'm pretty sure I'm on the right track now. I say, Masters. Any fingerprints on 'em?"

"No."

"Any more spots of candle-grease? You know, like the spots on the carpet in Constable's room, whose position I kept pointin' out to you?"

"Nary a spot."

H.M. grunted. "No. I didn't think there would be. This time the murderer was more careful."

"Was he, now?" muttered the chief inspector, eying H.M. with a strained and corked expression. "So the murderer *was* in the house on Sunday night, eh? I'm going to talk to you straight, Sir Henry. If you've got any notion how this was done, or how Mr. Ruddy Pennik managed to be in two places at once, or what those even ruddier candles mean, tell me flat out and don't talk flummery. I'm not in the mood for it."

H.M. grunted again. "I'm not either, if it comes to that. Burn me, Masters, didn't you ever feel you were just on the edge of something, not quite seein' it, not quite, but *almost* getting the—" He slid his fists along the table-cloth. "Almost? That's all. It's like trackin' back something you've just dreamed. It's a spiritual experience you'd best avoid. Tell me one more thing, and I'll exchange information for information. That big presscutting scrap-book of Mrs. Constable's: have you found it yet?"

"No."

"Did you look for it?"

"Ho! Did we look for it?" said Masters, with a certain sarcasm. "Between me and the superintendent and his men we've been over every inch of that house. And I mean every inch. It's not in the house. But does that surprise me? Not so you'd notice it. At the end of the week-end, all the guests walked away from that house carrying bags. It went away

120

in one of those bags, that's all; somebody pinched it."

"It's a possibility. Sure. The only objection to it from my point of view is that I don't believe it. I said this before, and in spite of all the burstin' dams I'll say it again. Mina Constable hid that book before she was murdered. If I ever saw a thing in a human face, I saw that in hers; and I'll bet you my hat to a tanner it's still in the house."

The chief inspector mustered all his force of reasonableness; you could see him doing it.

"Dr. Sanders!" he said. "You're the only one who's seen this scrap-book. About how big was it?"

Sanders considered.

"About eighteen inches high, an inch or so thick, and ten or twelve inches broad, I should say."

"Eighteen inches high," continued Masters, holding his hand at that height from the floor, "and ten or twelve inches broad. What you'd call a stunner of a big book. Outstanding. And bound in heavy, stiff, imitation leather. She couldn't have burnt it, as you said yourself; she couldn't have destroyed it. She didn't leave the house at any time. Would you like to tell me *where* in the house she could have hidden a big book like that so that we didn't find it?"

"I dunno, son. I'm bein' stubborn."

"You are. You mean you think it contains the secret of how all this hocus-pocus was worked?"

"Somethin' like that. Maybe."

"If it does," said Masters with restraint, "by George! it ought to be bought for the nation and put in the British Museum. In the first place it's invisible. In the second place it contains the secret of why two green candles are burned every time a person dies. In the third place it shows how Pennik can be in the barparlor of a country hotel and at the same time in the conservatory of a house four miles away—"

"Uh-huh. I admit that. Pennik's the problem; and yet, d'ye know, it may not be so difficult after all. From what I've seen of Pennik—"

Masters stopped him. Masters said:

"From what you've seen of Pennik? But you haven't seen him yet! He wouldn't meet us at the Black Swan on Sunday night. You haven't seen him at all."

"Oh, yes, I have," said H.M. He removed his glasses, which gave his eyes a different, rather caved-in expression of bleariness; it suddenly turned him into a stranger. After looking at the glasses through the light, he replaced them. But for a moment he had really looked like the old man.

"Oh, yes, I have," he repeated. "Like young Chase on a

121

certain interestin' occasion, I didn't meet him and I didn't talk to him; but I saw him."

"When? Where?"

"Last night, in the Gold Grill-Room of the Corinthian Hotel. I'm well treated, I am. I've got two daughters whose greatest pleasure in life is to make me lose sleep. For every extra hour of sleep they can make me lose, it's one up to them. So I got dragged off for an aftertheater supper. And there was Pennik in the Gold Grill-Room of the Corinthian, blossomin' out in all his grandeur. Havin' supper with him was Hilary Keen."

The chief inspector whistled.

Sanders, on the other hand, wondered whether he could ever leave off doubting anything or anyone in this world. He could not decipher the expression on H.M.'s face.

"Well, what of it?" he demanded; and yet jealousy struck as sharp and quick as a dart in a board. "Why shouldn't she? Though I'm having dinner with her tonight myself, and I hadn't heard anything about it. But I can't afford places like the Corinthian."

"If I thought," muttered the chief inspector, "that that young lady was in cahoots with Pennik—"

H.M.'s weary gesture cut short his excitement.

"Oh, Masters, my son. No! Pennik's not in cahoots with anybody; Pennik's the lone wolf. But don't you see the real point I'm drivin' at? There she was, all colored up and halfway out of a gown like my two gals. And yet she was scared, Masters; blind scared and watchin' Pennik out of the corner of her eye even when he only lifted his hand to call a waiter."

He paused.

"As for Pennik, Pennik wasn't too happy about one thing. That grill-room's got lots of glare and glitter and red plush, but it's a tiny little place. When it's overcrowded, the effect on the nerves of anybody who can't stand being shut in—like Pennik—must be pretty raw. All that kept him going was to look at her. Y'see, he's fallen for her in a way I don't like one little bit. And that brings us to the point."

He peered round at Sanders.

"I haven't said much about your affairs, son. What you're beginning to feel for Joe Keen's daughter may be only action-on-the-rebound or it may be the real thing. That's not important at the moment. What's important is this: at the rate things are goin' now, as sure as God made little apples, you and Pennik are due to collide with a smash. Had you thought about that?"

"No."

"Then think about it, son," said H.M. somberly. "Because once before, Masters tells me—hullo!"

He broke off, drawing his eyebrows together. Hilary Keen in the flesh, followed by Lawrence Chase, had just come through the revolving door of the restaurant, stamping and shaking rain from their waterproofs. Lowering her umbrella, Hilary glanced out rather apprehensively at the street. The storm, which seemed to have been dying down, had swung back again. A glint of lightning looked pale over the solidness of Whitehall; and, with a shake in that curtain, a faint crackle of thunder exploded along the sky and joined the rain.

Chase ducked his head in such a way as to tilt the water from the brim of his bowler hat. He looked up under it.

"Good afternoon, good afternoon," he said. "Anybody who says 'speak of the devil' will hereby and on the instant receive today's cliché cup. At the same time, I've got a distinct feeling you were just discussing either Hilary or myself. Am I correct?—as Pennik would say?"

Hilary tried to keep up the same light atmosphere. She and Sanders looked at each other, and both looked away again.

"You're quite right," agreed H.M., beckoning to a waiter. "Sit down, both of you. Have a coffee with us. And a cigar."

"I don't want a cigar, really," said Hilary, taking off her hat and shaking back her rich brown hair. Sanders set out a chair for her. "And I can only stop a moment. I don't get two and a half hours for lunch like some people. But I was on my way back to Richmond Terrace, and I met this tempter, and—I was curious."

Chase tossed his cigarette-case on the table.

"As a matter of fact," he admitted, "so was I. And still am."

"Oh, ah?" asked Masters affably. "About what, sir?"

"If I knew that," said Chase, "I wouldn't be curious. About why you wanted to see me, among other things. Is anything else up? Anything besides what we know, that is? My God, poor old Mina!"

The edges of his eyelids were pinkish. He hitched his chair closer to the table.

"I wouldn't have believed it. It's the worst mess ever devised by man, beast, or what's-its-name. Look round you. Look out there—newspaper-bills. Look in here—newspapers. That table, and that table, and that table." He glanced back quickly. "Er—I say, you don't think anybody knows *we're* connected with it, do you?"

"Well, sir, they won't if you keep your voice down."

123

Chase seemed to dwindle.

"Sorry," he whispered. "But I warned Mina, and she wouldn't listen. It's not that I think this fellow has any supernatural power; it's only that these things keep on happening. Now I've got to straighten things out. You probably know that Sam was a distant relative of mine."

"Is that so, now?" inquired Masters, with interest.

"Yes; didn't you see it in the obituary notice? His father's name was Lawrence Chase Constable. I'm a second-cousin." Chase looked glum. "Not that I inherit any of his money, worse luck."

"No?"

"No. Well, except for a hundred pounds, which hardly counts. The trouble is, who does inherit it? Am I speaking in confidence?"

"Entirely, sir. Entirely!"

"Sam's will," Chase explained, opening his cigarette-case, "left everything entirely and unconditionally to Mina. But Mina, who never thought of such things, died without leaving a will. And Mina has no kin whatever, not a surviving relative in the world. Which means that legally Mina's estate, and Sam's very large estate on top of that, must revert to the Crown.

"Now that will cause a dust-up for fair, because the whole thing will certainly be contested by Sam's relatives. Not by me, though! In the first place, I'm appointed joint executor and trustee of Sam's estate with an old moss-back named Rich, Sir John Rich. In the second place, Sam's other surviving relatives are a sister and two first-cousins. If they win their claim, the sister will grab the lot; or what she doesn't grab will be taken by the first-cousins; and I should be nowhere even if I tried. That's the position, quite frankly. All I get is the dirty work of administering the estate and a kick in the backside whatever happens. Ah, well. The thrice-damned Pennik—"

He straightened the shoulders of his very elegant coat, he lighted a cigarette with concentration, and evidently decided to say no more.

"Bad luck, sir," condoled Masters.

"Ah, well. It's all in the game. What really matters is that poor old Sam and Mina are both dead."

"Yes, sir. But—"

"But what?"

The now-too-affable chief inspector produced a metaphorical hand-grenade, examined it, pulled out the pin, and dropped it among them. You could almost see him searching for an excuse to drop it.

124

Masters frowned.

"Nothing, sir. Only best not to speak too harshly of Mr. Pennik in present company. Eh?"

"Present company?"

"I mean in front of Miss Keen."

"Look here, what's Hilary got to do with all this?"

Masters assumed a heavy air of surprise. "Well, that's to say: Miss Keen is a great friend of Mr. Pennik. Aren't you, miss? After all, going out to a slap-up supper with him on the night after Mrs. Constable died—"

Hilary had not spoken.

Her chair was cramped in close to Sanders's, but she did not turn her head. He could see only the smooth line of her hair, cut rather long and curling in below the ears, and the smooth line of her neck above the plain dark-blue dress. But he felt her breathe.

The uncomfortable pause was only prolonged by the waiter bringing coffee-cups and rattling them.

Then Hilary raised her head. She spoke to H.M.

"Why do you dislike me so much, Sir Henry?" she asked.

"*Me?* Dislike you?"

"Yes. You do, don't you? Is it because you're a friend of Sir Dennis Blystone? Is it?"

"My dear girl, I don't know what you're talkin' about. What's Denny Blystone got to do with this?"

"Never mind," said Hilary, picking up a match-box and playing with it. "I saw you at the Corinthian last night. Looking and looking and looking and looking. You pretended not to see us, but you even stumbled past our table so that you could get a good look. I suppose it was you who told the chief inspector about it?"

For a moment H.M. did not reply. He seemed oddly fussed. Making a careful selection of a cigar from a tray of boxes the waiter handed round, he growled and glowered.

"Well, y' know—you were there, weren't you?"

"Yes. Oh, God, yes. I was there."

"Of your own free will?"

"Of my own free will."

"And it's a mighty public place, the Corinthian is. At any minute I expected a squad of reporters to come chasin' in and set off a lot of flash-bulbs—"

"As a matter of fact, they did. When we were leaving."

"And did you like that?"

"No. I hated it," said Hilary. She put down the match-box. "You have a lot of power." she went on quietly. "I mean the power to make other people think and feel as you

125

think and feel. Please don't judge too soon. Please don't jump to conclusions before you know why certain things are done."

"I'm not," said H.M. with equal quietness. "Honest, I wish you'd sort of accept the fact that my gapin' and starin' wasn't at you. And I blundered past your table to get a good look at Pinnik's hands."

She frowned. "His hands?"

"His hands," agreed H.M. "At a pinch, y'know, I might even accept the possibility that you mean better than you seem to mean."

Hilary sat back, releasing her breath. Sanders laughed to get rid of a certain tension.

"Will somebody tell me what this is all about?" he asked. "We're not here to talk about social evenings, are we? Why shouldn't she go out to supper with whoever she pleases?"

"Of course. Why not?" said Hilary coldly. "It was only that the chief inspector brought it up."

"Now, miss!—"

"And after all," pursued Sanders, "she's going out to dinner with *me* tonight, if it comes to that. Aren't you?"

"Yes, of course, Jack. Only—"

"Well, aren't you?"

"Yes, yes, of course. Besides, this isn't the place to talk about that. I've got to get back to the office. Please excuse me." Finishing her coffee she got up and pulled the waterproof round her shoulders. For the first time she faced him. Her manner was one of quiet efficiency: a reserve, a poise which was not shaken.

"Right, then," said Sanders cheerfully. "I'll call for you at seven-thirty sharp. Don't be late."

"Jack—"

"Here, you've got to have a taxi. You can't walk to Richmond Terrace in all this."

"Jack, may I speak to you a moment? The rest of you will excuse us, won't you?"

"Miss," said Chief Inspector Masters, with a curious look at her, "all this may be no business of ours. On the other hand (excuse me) it may be. I'd just like to bet you, now, that I know what you're going to tell him. And anything about Mr. Ruddy Pennik, anything at all about him or the people he's with, for whatever reason, interests me. *Why* can't you go out to dinner with anybody else tonight?"

He got to his feet.

Outside the great dingy oblong of the plate-glass window, a figure moved along in the rain; it turned in at the restaurant, navigated the revolving door, and came in. Herman

Pennik, removing his sodden hat and coat, beckoned imperiously to a waiter even as he turned to smile at them.

XV

THE MANGO-TREE WAS GROWING.

That was how Sanders saw Pennik's character. New tentacles were stirring out from under the cloth, and coming to blossom.

The worst of it was that they all had to pretend this was only an ordinary lunch, such as a few other people were eating in the now nearly empty restaurant. The steamy air, which had set a film over mirrors and decorations alike, was now subsiding. Over empty tables waiters slapped with their cloths at ancient crumbs. In the midst of this somnolence the party could not raise their voices, could not sit in any but stiff and constrained attitudes, whatever might be going to happen.

Pennik spoke first. It was an optical illusion that his face or the least detail of his appearance had changed: it had not. Yet there was a new set about him, a new cause for satisfaction, which Sanders did not yet understand.

"Sir Henry Merrivale?" inquired Pennik, with his light eyes fixed.

"That's right. Join us?"

"Thank you."

He handed his coat and hat to the waiter; and it was in the waiter's face, not in that of any of the others, that you saw reflected the emotional state round that table. In the waiter's face you saw sudden recognition. Taking Pennik's things, he turned round and walked rapidly away.

"I must be going," said Hilary. "I really must. Jack, if I could have a word with you?"

"Please sit down, Miss Keen," Pennik requested. His tone was formal, but inside him Sanders felt he was holding his thick ribs with amusement. That was it: he somehow conveyed the impression of being thicker, not only of body and face but perhaps even of mind. "No, no, you must not go. If you are late at the office, all that can be arranged."

"I only wish it could."

"Do you? If everything else were as easy!" said Pennik. " 'And you should have the sun and moon to wear, If I were king.' "

"That would be very nice," said Hilary.

She sat down.

"How do you do, Mr. Masters?" pursued Pennik, to a chief inspector who was watching him as warily as you might watch a cat at which it may soon be necessary to throw a bottle. "And you, Mr. Chase?"

"Sorry. Got to go. You'll excuse me," said Chase.

He got up stiffly and walked out of the restaurant, whirling his waterproof behind him wthout even bothering to put it on. They saw him standing just outside, bare-headed and semi-bald in the rain, peering up and down to decide in which direction his appointment lay. He collided with a little group of loungers who had huddled under the shelter of the overhang at the door, and were looking steadily into the restaurant.

Indubitably, something was going to happen.

"I regret," Pennik continued, again fixing his attention on H.M., "I genuinely regret having had to turn you away from the Black Swan the other night. For I have looked forward to a meeting. Under the circumstances, however, I felt that to see you would be a disturbing influence. Can you understand that?"

H.M. had got his cigar lighted.

"No apology necessary, son. But what are you doin' here now?"

"To tell you the truth, I was following Miss Keen."

"Then it was you—" Hilary began.

"Following you in the taxi? Yes, my poppet, I am afraid it was. I like looking at you. Yes, I honestly do like looking at you, if you follow my meaning. You stimulate me. Under your inspiration I feel that even a modest fellow like myself might do great things." Hiliary's face flamed, but she did not dare comment. Pennik was opening and shutting his hands. "When I saw all of our—er—protagonists seated round the council board here, I could not resist joining in. For one thing, I wanted to see Chief Inspector Masters."

Masters stiffened.

"I wanted to ask him a question," explained Pennik.

"If there are any questions being asked hereabouts," Masters said, "I'll ask 'em, if you please. And I've got a question or two for you, Mr. Pennik. What are you doing in London? What's your permanent address, in case we want to get hold of you? You were last at the Black Swan Hotel. Well?"

Pennik smiled.

"Well, I don't live there, you know. I have a flat in Bloomsbury; a modest flat, as suits my tastes. I will write you the address. Er—what I really wanted to know, Mr. Masters, was this. Would there be any objection to my leaving the country?"

A blow in the solar-plexus could not have been worse.

"Leaving the country?" breathed Masters. "Yes, sir, there smacking well would be an objection to your leaving the country. If you think you can start all this rumpus and then walk out, you'll soon find out you can't."

Again Pennik smiled. Though his little, light, flickering eyes were on Hilary, he gave the question his attention.

"Be comforted, Mr. Masters. I have no intention of deserting you. I meant for a few hours only, on a visit to France. I have received a signal honor in being asked to make a radio broadcast—"

"Oh, ah, yes," said Masters maliciously. "I remember. For the cheese company, wasn't it?"

Pennik laughed outright. It gave him an odd look, as though his face were unused to laughter and these new sensations produced queer wrinkles when he did laugh. He seemed genuinely to like the chief inspector; in fact, he bore malice towards nobody.

"No. Hadn't you heard? All that is changed. I have been officially invited to speak over the French government radio station tomorrow night. I shall speak first in French and then in English. Nine-forty-five to ten-fifteen is the time, in case you are interested." His forehead was ruffled with an annoyance not unmixed with amusement. "You know, my good friend, I am afraid the French have rather misunderstood the nature of my claims. All these nonsensical rumors of death-machines and such claptrap—"

He shook his head.

"They will mislead themselves, gentlemen. They will persist in attributing to me powers I don't have and never claimed to have. Heaven knows my thesis is modest enough. It is only surprising because, in its present scientific application, it is new." Here Pennik hesitated a little; Sanders wondered why. "I do not want them, therefore, to be misled by such tales and be disappointed. At the same time, when they hear what I have to say I don't think they will be disappointed. By God, gentlemen, the million people who hear me shall not be disappointed."

They all looked at him.

"Just a minute, son," said H.M. He put down his cigar on the edge of his plate. "Do you mean you're proposin' to kill somebody else?"

"Yes," said Pennik.

Again it was perhaps a full minute before anybody spoke. Then, anticipating any objection, Pennik explained himself with painstaking lucidity.

"You hardly need to point out to me gentlemen, that so

129

far I have put myself consistently in the wrong. I admit that. I am no master of strategy. I am a hunam being, and liable to act in a fit of impulse. I killed Mr. Constable deliberately, in the firm and solemn conviction that I was doing good by it. But Mrs. Constable's death—well, why not? Why not? If I acted in anger, why not?"

Masters's tone was flat.

"So you did that," he said, "because I said you couldn't kill an ant with a fly-swatter."

"I accepted her challenge. Now she is dead. But hear me a little further!" He tapped his blunt forefinger on the table. "I am not going to abuse a force which seems so simple to me and so mysterious to you. I said it must be used for good; and I meant just that. But I will not fail to use an opportunity like the present one. Think of what it means. To me has been given an opportunity such as has been granted to few men in the history of the world. I am explaining to children something they do not understand. I must prove it to them by nursery instances. Very well. When I speak to them tomorrow night, they will not be satisfied with talk. I will take a human life like a globe of glass in my hands, and smash it down on the floor before them: then they can see for themselves. I will tell them who is going to die, and where, and how. When they have seen the bone crack and the heart stop, they may possibly understand that I mean what I say."

He drew in his breath. His excitement simmered down, and now he became cheerful with a restrained and ghoulish cheerfulness.

"Too much talk, too much talk," he added, rubbing his hands together briskly. "As Antony said to Cleopatra (eh, Miss Keen?) I am not here to talk. But there is something about your expression, Mr. Masters, if you will excuse me for saying so, which always impels me to get above myself. Anyhow, that is what I propose to do. And I really do not see how you are going to stop me."

"Steady, Masters!" said H.M. sharply. "Sit down."

"But—"

"I said sit down, son."

The chair creaked. All this time H.M. had continued to smoke with unhurried placidness; but he trimmed the ash off his cigar after almost every puff. Dr. Sanders, however, was watching Pennik. And as Pennik leaned across the table towards Hilary during the first part of what was just said, he had never before noticed that Pennik had such a blubber-like mouth.

"If this gentleman," began the chief inspector, "thinks he

can go over to France and show off, *and* if he thinks I can't top him, then, by George!—"

"Are you goin' to be quiet?" interrupted H.M. He turned back to Pennik. "Well—now. If you want to go and make his splash, it's your business. I don't see you'll be needed for anything tomorrow. There's the inquest tomorrow afternoon, of course, but your testimony won't be needed for that."

Pennik showed quick interest.

"The inquest? What inquest?"

"On Sam Constable, the first victim."

"I don't think I understand you, sir. There was an inquest on Mr. Constable. And it was adjourned."

"That's right, son. But since by law it's got to be held sooner or later, they're goin' to hold it tomorrow and get it over with."

Pennik sat up straight.

"I still don't think I understand."

"Looky here," said H.M., rubbing his hands rather desperately over his forehead. "A man dies, d'ye see? The police think there may have been dirty work." (Here Pennik smiled.) "So they get the inquest adjourned so's they can work on it. But if there's not enough evidence of any kind against anybody then as a matter o' law the coroner has got to hold an inquest. They do that so that they can officially record the cause of death. A coroner's inquest is an inquiry into what caused death."

"But they will not be able to tell what caused his death, will they?"

"No, they won't."

"Then why hold the inquest?"

With a powerful effort H.M. kept his temper.

"I dunno," he said. "It's only the law. Lord love a duck, I didn't make it. Don't blame me. You got to have pity on our blindness; you got to remember that it's not every day a coroner has to hold an inquest on the victim of a telepathic conk over the onion. But, before the red specks start dancin' in front of my eyes, try to accept it. It's a matter of form: they'll return an open verdict sayin' they don't know how he died, that's all. So if you want to go to Paris or Timbuctoo, go ahead. You're not a witness."

"I am aware," said Pennik, enjoying himself, "that I am not a witness. But I am the murderer, and therefore I feel some slight interest in the proceedings. When is this inquest to be held?"

"Three o'clock tomorrow afternoon."

"Where?"

131

"At Grovetop. Look here, you're not thinking of goin'?"
Pennik opened his eyes.

"Sir," he replied, "you must excuse my morbid interest
in these public spectacles; but if you think I shall remain
away from it you do not know your man. I may be only the
murderer, but I am curious to hear what they say about
me." He looked thoughtful. "Three o'clock: yes, that can
be managed. An Air France plane is at my disposal, you
may be glad to hear. I can attend the inquest and still be
in plenty of time for Paris that night. I will even make a
statement, if you like. It may assist the coroner in his unfortunate dilemma."

Chief Inspector Masters looked at him.

"You're not (hurrum!) you're not by any chance afraid
of being lynched, are you sir?"

Pennik laughed.

"No. You don't know your own countrymen, my friend.
They may talk a great deal in private; but the quality
which comes from an ingrained horror of making a scene will
keep them quiet in public. If I am presented to one of them
the worst he will do is cut me dead; and I must contrive to
put up with that."

"So you mean to go down there in all your glory, do
you?"

"Yes."

"And you seriously intend to go to Paris and—and—"

"Kill someone else? Yes, I do. With the best of motives
I do. Tell me: do you think I am a fraud now?"

Masters gripped the edge of the table.

"Why don't you tell me, Mr. Pennik? You're the thought-
reading bloke. Or pretend to be. Why don't you tell me?"

"With pleasure. You are thinking that I really did commit these murders; but that I did it in some commonplace
physical way you have not as yet fathomed. Is that correct?
Ah, I see by your face it is. Well, since the 'commonplace
physical way' must be much more curious than any modest
claim I make, I have no objection."

"You haven't given any thought to the choice of the
next victim, have you?"

"It will not be you, Chief Inspector. At heart you are not
a bad fellow, and in your own way you are useful. No; in—

Hilary spoke in a small, quiet voice.

"I am sorry; I simply can't stay any longer. I must get
back to the office, and that's all there is to it."

Pennik was deprecating but firm. "My dear, your lightest
whim shall be indulged. But that is not a whim; it is depres-

132

sing nonsense. Didn't you hear what I said? All that can be adjusted."

"Oh, what's the good of talking like that? I don't want anything adjusted. I only want to get out of here. Pull your chair—"

"I am sorry," said Pennik his face clouding, "that I was rather abrupt about revealing my plans. But I could not resist the expressive faces of these gentlemen, and so I was a little premature. Listen in pity while I explain what I mean. I don't want you to go back to the office. In fact, I had rather hoped to persuade you to come with me to Paris."

For the first time since Pennik's arrival, Dr. Sanders spoke.

"Take your hand off her arm," he said.

It was as though everything in the restaurant had come to a standstill. And this was true in a literal sense as well. Though he was not aware of it, Sanders was the first to raise his voice above the studied muttering of the group by the window. He did not speak very loudly even then; but it was like a stone flung through the window. And in the background, the movement of waiters ceased.

"I beg your pardon?"

"I said, take your hand off her arm," Sanders repeated.

Their voices were clearly audible now. Pennik hitched his chair round.

"Ah, my friend the doctor," he said with an air of enlightenment. "I had not noticed you. How do you do, sir? You sat there so quietly, doubtless thinking long, long thoughts, that I have been ill-mannered enough to overlook your presence."

"I wonder if you can guess what the thoughts were."

Pennik made a weary gesture.

"Sir, we have had all this out before. Several times I feared I should have difficulties with you; once, at the Black Swan Hotel on Sunday morning, I was almost certain of it. But let me play the peacemaker. Please do not trouble me with parlor-games now. That business is of no consequence. It was an *hors d'œuvre,* deliberately designed to catch the attention—"

"Oh."

"And may I ask why you say that?"

"Because that's what I thought it was," said Sanders.

Beside them, the big plate-glass window went white with lightning, picking out every detail down to the turn of a lip or the design on a spoon. But Pennik had his back to it, so that Sanders could not see his face. He wished he could see it, for he had a feeling that the momentary change in

133

the aspect of the window was no greater than the momentary change in Pennik's features. Thunder exploded after it, spreading out and losing itself in the curtain of the rain.

Pennik spoke quietly.

"I still don't understand."

"Well, this thought-reading. Masters got it out of Larry Chase on Sunday night that you'd been fishing for information about everybody. With this 'reading-the-subconscious-mind' business you had us both coming and going. If we had something deeply worrying us, and you said, 'This is what is in your subconscious mind,' we couldn't very well deny it, could we? But all you needed was information. For the rest, intelligent deductive work combined with what in a book I went after the other night, is called Muscle-reading—"

Hilary Keen, moving behind Pennik's back, was making frantic signals to him. But Sanders paid no attention.

"So if you really killed those two people—"

"*If* I killed them?" repeated Pennik. "You said the same thing once before, if I remember correctly. And I must beg leave to give you the same answer and the same warning, which you were prudent enough not to disregard. Are you challenging me, sir?"

Sanders pushed his coffee-cup to one side.

"Yes," he said.

XVI

THAT IT WOULD ever stop raining seemed open to doubt. When the 5.20 train pulled out of Charing Cross, immersed in steam like a kettle, little could be seen from the windows. But the train was almost empty, so that they had a first-class compartment to themselves, and two of them were walking up and down within its confines.

It was barely five minutes later when H.M. spoke.

He said:

"For the love of Esau, can't this caterpillar go any faster?"

"Perhaps I'd better go up and speak to the engine-driver," suggested Masters, not without sarcasm. "Give him half a crown, or something. Why the rush, sir? Fourways waited for you yesterday, when you promised to come down and didn't. Why can't it wait now?"

H.M. did not answer this. He sighted over his spectacles,

put his fists on his hips, and glared at Dr. John Sanders who was sitting down.

"You young ass!" he said.

But Masters was pleased. "How do you feel, Doctor?" he asked jocularly. "No sudden palpitations of the heart coming on? No cold sweats or whatnot? Lummy, it did my heart good, and that's a fact! I mean to say, giving it to him bang in the snoot when he was so sure you wouldn't."

"You think this is funny?" inquired H.M. "Shut up, Masters! Now listen to me, son. Why did you do it?"

Sanders rose to this.

"Well, who does Pennik think he is, anyway? A sort of god who can walk about telling people when they'll die and who they'll go to dinner with? His Teleforce is rubbish and you know it as well as I do. All right: let him go ahead and press the switch. We'll see what happens."

"H'm," grunted H.M., scratching the side of his jaw. "Got the wind up, have you?"

Sanders was honest.

"Yes, in a way I have. A little."

"Then why did you do it?"

(Why not admit it? Why not acknowledge that Hilary's blue eyes, Hilary's laugh, Hilary as she appeared to him in imagination now, had brought this about inevitably? Where Hilary was concerned, he and Pennik were like two dogs round a bitch. The simile was not a pretty or pleasant one; and he disliked himself even for thinking of it in connection with Hilary; but, if you faced it, it amounted to that. Nor was there anything of the *preux chevalier* about Pennik. Pennik would kill him if he could, and that was that too. He remembered Pennik calling for his hat and coat, bowing, and walking quietly out of the restaurant into the rain: in itself, when you remembered Pennik's past behavior, the most dangerous sign of all.)

Sanders looked up. "Haven't you got any idea why I did it?"

"Me?" said H.M. "Oh, sure. It's not insight I lack, if that needs any; it's the ability to prevent people doin' fatheaded things after I've expressly warned 'em not to. Pennik was waitin' for you. I hope you noticed that? But oh, no. Down went the gage of battle on the floor, and I hope you're feelin' proud of yourself. In spite of all the signs and warnings for five days—"

"But—"

"—you still couldn't take a hint. Why do you think that gal, Joe Keen's daughter, has been going about with Pennik and pampering his vanity so religiously? It's to prevent

135

just exactly what happened this afternoon. It's to prevent Pennik from roundin' on you."

The wheels of the train rattled and clacked under them.

"Do you mean that?" Sanders asked quickly.

"Oh, son, do I mean it! Sure I mean it. I know it. Don't you realize Pennik wants you out of the way? Don't you know he's been waitin' for a legitimate excuse to show his claws? That's the trouble. Pennik, within his limits, is a perfectly honest man."

Chief Inspector Masters made a noise.

H.M. looked at him.

"He is, though, Masters. You give me just one more raspberry, and I'll chuck this case straight back at you."

"Now, now, Sir Henry! All I meant——"

"Pennik's got a conscience. I admit he can be pretty unpleasant at times. I've also got a suspicion he's going off his onion; and, unless somebody can right him, he'll go completely off it. But he honestly has got a conscience that bothers him about Sanders. Little devil says yes. Conscience says no. Little devil says, 'Go on; soak him.' Conscience says, 'No; if you did that it would be out of pure jealousy of anybody who comes near her, and would show you were no superman.' Little devil says, 'It'd be in the interests of science.' Conscience says, 'Science my foot.' But now you've given him an excuse; and conscience goes overboard. He'll make you the next victim, if he can."

Masters looked even more worried.

"Hold on, sir! Does that mean you think he *will* do it?"

"If he can," repeated H.M. stubbornly. "No, I don't go that far. I'll give you consolation. In point o' fact, I think Sanders is pretty safe——"

"Yes, sir, that may be all very well," the chief inspector objected. "But that's what you said about Mrs. Constable too; and she's as dead as King Tut now."

"You're a fine pair of Job's comforters, aren't you?" interposed Sanders, not without reason. "A couple of damned old ghouls, if you will excuse the plain speaking. Would you like to order my shroud now, or can it wait until we get back to town?"

H.M. was soothing.

"Now, son, you're all right. You'll be quite all right if you——"

"I know. If I just trust the old man. Very well; consider the trust applied."

He brooded.

"All the same, up to now I always believed I lived in an ordered, ordinary world where nothing much ever hap-

136

pened. I rather envied Mar—that is, I envied people who could travel on voyages to Japan. In actual fact, nothing much has changed. I still eat and sleep as usual. All the wall-paper looks the same, and I don't get any more money. But I feel I've stepped over into a new kind of world where anything can happen."

"That's what we shall all be feeling," the chief inspector decided gloomily, "if all this flummery about Teleforce is allowed to go on. Teleforce! Did you hear 'em back at the railway station? And that woman sticking her head out of the train window? And at the book-stall? I wish we'd had time to get an evening paper, though. We might see if we can get one when the train stops next."

Obediently the train did stop, with a sudden flight and an equally sudden pull-up like a ballet dancer. Masters disappeared into the streaming dimness and returned with an armful of newspapers.

"H'm," said H.M.

There was a brief, rustling pause after the train had pulled out again.

"This," said H.M., "is pilin' Babel on top of Pisa. The scientific swells have now weighed into the controversy. 'Professor Huxdane, interviewed, consented to say one word: "Balderdash." ' (That'll make Pennik foam.) Professor Trippletts, on the other hand, while admittin' the theoretical possibility of such a weapon, says that the idea is not new. (That'll make him foam still more.) Yes, good enough." H.M. glowered at Sanders. "If only you hadn't butted in! If only you had kept quiet in front of Pennik!"

Dr. Sanders sat back.

"One question," he said. "Will you tell me why *I* am the villain of the piece? Why pitch into me? I've offered to call Pennik's bluff for you in the only possible way. Instead of giving me at least a word of thanks, you're going on as though I had spoiled some scheme of yours."

"You have, son."

"How?"

"That's the blinkin' awful cussedness of it," said H.M. wearily. "I was being crafty; I had everything all planned out. I was goin' to snaffle Pennik just like that." He snapped his fingers. "At least, I had a forty-sixty chance to do it, which is the most you can hope for in this world. Now you've reduced it to ten-ninety. Oh, my eye. That's why we're goin' down to Fourways in such a rush. I've got two more chances—"

"To get Pennik?" demanded Masters.

"That's right."

"To get him when?"

"Tomorrow, if we're lucky."

Masters eyed him. "Well, you'd better not be too long about it, sir. Mind, I don't for a minute believe a word of all this rubbish. All the same, what if Pennik decides to polish off the doctor here before then?"

"No," said H.M., shaking his head quite seriously. "There's twenty-four hours' grace there. Pennik won't move until he makes his speech at Paris tomorrow night—"

"Ha ha ha," said Sanders.

"Be quiet, will you?" ordered H.M. with austerity. "You're not in this. And, as I was sayin', Masters, until he gets ready to bust his bombshell on the floor then. We're all right for the moment."

"I hope you know what you're doing, sir. But I tell you straight, I'm beginning to think you're clean daft. You don't mean you're going to *let* him make that speech? You can't mean that. I can think of half a dozen ways to stop him; easy ways; eh?"

"Tut, tut. Why stop him?"

Masters grew very quiet.

"Then there's another thing," the chief inspector went on, his eye and brow darkening with suspicion. He held up a newspaper. "Have you seen this? The *Evening Planet?*"

H.M. said, rather guiltily, that he hadn't. He asked what was in it.

"I'll tell you what's in it," replied Masters. "There are two pictures of me in it. 'Chief Inspector Masters as Himself.' Then, 'Chief Inspector Masters Disguised as a East End Tough.' The picture of me as myself looks about fifty times tougher than the one of me disguised as an East End tough. But never mind that. I've been (as you would say) sitting and thinking, and blowed if I can remember than one person who had a copy of that picture of me disguised. Did *you* give it to this paper?"

"Now, now."

"Did you?"

"Just keep your shirt on, Masters."

"I'll try to. I've had a bit of an idea, too, that it was you who wrote that full-column letter in the *Daily Wireless*. Now I don't say you're daft as a March hare, sir; I don't *say* it. But when they stick you in the House of Lords I only hope I'm in the gallery to see, that's all. And what are we doing now, going down to Surrey? What do you expect to find there?"

H.M. was stubborn.

"For one thing," he insisted, "I got to find that press-cutting scrap-book of Mrs. Constable's."

"Oh, ah? That? In spite of all I tell you, you still think it's in the house?"

"Yes."

"And where do you think of looking for it?"

"That's just it. I dunno."

Masters gave him up. The blurred windows of the compartment whitened with lightning, and thunder descended like falling masonry to mingle with the rattle and click of the wheels. None of them spoke until the train drew in at Camberdene, where Superintendent Belcher, in response to Master's telegram, was waiting for them with a car.

And none of them, perhaps liked driving through the open country in a thunderstorm. Fourways looked as black as the rain when they drew up before it, and the grounds had turned to a swamp. It was more than ever a gutted house, a hollow house, a dead house. Superintendent Belcher had a key to the front door; inside, the rain on the roof sounded like a heavy hammering.

"Now that we're here—?" suggested Masters, when they had turned on a blaze of lights.

H.M. peered round the front hall.

"Don't hurry me. Lemme think. Ah, I got it! When you looked for that scrap-book, what about the conservatory? Did you give the conservatory a good going over?"

"You can bet we did. If you're thinking the book may have been hidden under one of the plants, that's out too. We didn't uproot 'em all, naturally; but the soil in those boxes and pots was so dry that we'd have noticed any disturbance."

"All the same, let's have a ·look."

Drawing-room, dining-room, conservatory. All as Sanders remembered them on the night Mina Constable died. On the dining-room table, under the glowing mosaic dome, the fragments of broken glass still lay in a sticky dried puddle where Sanders had dropped the tumbler when he thought he saw Pennik looking at him.

They re-created the past like a scent or a sound.

Pennik couldn't do anything. Pennik was a burst bogy. Pennik had been told off to his face. All the same—

H.M. had opened the glass door to the conservatory, and was bending close to blink at it.

"If you're looking for fingerprints," observed Masters with a sour grin, "you can save your eyesight for brick walls. There aren't any. Yes, I know the doctor said Pennik shoved his nose and his fingers against that glass; we didn't

139

neglect that. But either they were wiped off afterwards, or else they never were there."

Sanders refused to be drawn.

"So now I'm accused of seeing things?"

"Don't forget the astral projection," growled H.M., wagging the door back and forth. "I say, son. Did you see anything of Pennik except his hand and face?"

"Not clearly, no."

"Did you hear him when he ran away?"

"No, I can't say I did. But I'll swear he was there; there was no jiggery-pokery about that."

Pennik couldn't do anything. Yet his image, huge and ugly and dead-looking, seemed to gather and spread through Fourways.

It was Masters who pushed past H.M. and found the switch in the conservatory. The clusters of luminous fruit bloomed again under corners of the glass roof; and the din of rain beating on that glass dome was so deafening that they had to raise their voices in order to make each other hear. But it was a relief not to see Pennik sitting in a wicker chair among the semi-tropical plants. H.M. wandered to the dry fountain in the middle of the maze.

"Hoy!" he bellowed.

"What?"

"A very important question, son. When you saw Pennik through that door on Sunday night, and ran out here was this little fountain working?"

"No."

"You're sure of that, now?" insisted H.M., poking out one finger.

"I'd swear to it. I remember how dead quiet the place was. What's more, I remember passing the fountain. But why?"

"Only," said H.M. mildy, "this. If that's so, it's one of the most important pieces of evidence in the case."

Masters was at his side in a hurry. "Steady a bit! An important piece of evidence? You think that's important with regard to whether Pennik was or wasn't here? Or has anything to do with explaining his being here? But what about the fountain? it's an ordinary Gamage garden fountain; pumps up the same couple of gallons of water and uses 'em over and over again. I had a look at it, because I was thinking of buying one once myself."

"Whether you were thinkin' of buyin' one or not, Masters, it's still important. And I don't care how it works. That's not the point. Now let's see." He sniffed round the over-gilded, over-decorated lounge. "Any more doors here? Ah!

140

One. Goes to the kitchen, does it? I thought so. But there don't appear to be any back stairs. Make note of that: no back stairs."

H.M. was peering into the kitchen. Again Masters followed him.

"But—"

"On the other hand," persisted H.M., muttering rapidly to himself and making fussed gestures to keep Masters away, "our late friend Sam Constable's bedroom is directly over the dining-room back there. I seem to remember Mrs. Constable tellin' me that. Yes. Also, I seem to remember seeing a balcony outside one of his bedroom windows, with stone stairs leadin' down to the ground. (If you don't get away, Masters, I'll murder you.) So you could go from the dining-room to that bedroom upstairs without being seen; and come down again too. If we—"

"God!" said the chief inspector involuntarily.

It was not the glare of lightning through the glass roof which made them all jump, though it turned the whole conservatory to a blaze of deathly daylight and put the same pallor on their faces. It was, instead, the enormous crash of thunder which began in a long splitting noise as though the glass roof were crumpling, and then exploded close over their heads to the end of the peal. The dome vibrated to it; one of the small panes in the roof did, in fact, fall and smash on the tiles; and the rain poured through. But all sights or sounds were entangled with each other and happened at once. They saw each other's faces in such pallor because, in the instant of the lightning-flash, every light in the house went out.

"That's torn it," said H.M.'s voice out of the dark.

Superintendent Belcher's voice spoke cheerfully. "It's all right. I've got an electric lantern here. What was it, do you think? Wires down outside, or a fuse blown?"

Masters was not so easy. The shock of that assault still made the room tremble, and the darkness was dense. He spoke loudly above the rain.

"Wires down outside, I should think. They've got so many extra fittings that they're on distributing fuses, one to two or three rooms; and you wouldn't blow out the whole lot at one go unless—"

"Fuse-box," said H.M. suddenly.

"What's that, sir?"

"I said fuse-box. Masters, when you went over this house so thoroughly, did you look inside the fuse-box?"

"No; why should I? I'll swear it wasn't touched before or after Mrs. Constable's death—"

141

"I wasn't thinkin' about it in connection with anybody's death. I was thinking about it," answered H.M.'s voice in the dark, "as the one perfect hiding-place for a flat book eighteen inches high by ten inches broad."

After a pause he added:

"Where is the box?"

"As a matter of fact, it's at the back of the cupboard in Mrs. Constable's bedroom," said Masters. "And we're going up there now."

The beam of the superintendent's lantern went ahead of them. In the forlorn bedroom upstairs, and in the side of the room farthest from the bed, was a large wardrobe cupboard with folding doors. Just above the shelf inside was the black-painted iron cover of the box, held upright by two light screws: a large box, some two feet high by a foot and a half broad. Standing on a chair, Masters carefully undid the screws. As the cover fell, a tall thin book in colors of black and gilt flopped out into his face, and dropped with a thud into the cover again.

"So that's it," snarled Masters.

"That's it, son. Serene and untouched where Mina Constable shoved it away as long ago as the night her husband died. Also, the perfect hidin'-place. You look at a fuse-box; and it never enters your head that there could be anything inside it except fuses; it's all too snug and close. But the cover don't fit in close against the contents: it can't. And if you want a place to hide your money where no burglar will look for it, take a tip from Mina Constable. It was one of her more ingenious ideas."

Masters jumped down from the chair.

"Ingenious ideas, eh?" he said, and shook the book in the air. "Just so. Got the bounder, anyway!" He shook it more savagely. "You think this is what we want?"

"Yes. Maybe. If it contains what I hope it does—Masters, we've got Pennik. Put it down on the table and let's have a dekko at it."

The light was held for them. While the rain splashed the windows, Masters put *New Ways of Committing Murder* on the dressing-table, and the others bent over his shoulder when he opened the book.

It was a grisly exhibit, in its way. It contained, neatly pasted in, a long series of press-cuttings all dealing with violent death in one form or another. They seemed to have been collected over a period of seven or eight years. Some were so old as to have had the paper turn dingy; others were frayed or ragged as though they had lain long in a drawer before their owner decided to make the collection;

142

still others looked fresh. Though in a few cases the date and the name of the paper had been written above the article, as a rule they bore a question-mark or were left blank. Some were from popular magazines; one or two from a medical journal. Not even any chronology in dates had been kept; 1937 came before 1935, and 1932 turned up between both. Over everything you could see the clever, untidy mind of Mina Constable.

H.M. had already uttered a groan. But he uttered a deeper one when they found, on the last page but one, an oblong piece of the page—article, name of paper, and date, if any —jaggedly cut out with a pair of scissors.

"She was takin' no chances," said H.M. "And she could burn that much of it, anyway. Masters, we're licked."

"Did you hope for as much as that from the book?"

"I don't mean it does us down entirely. Humph, maybe not. But I sort of had a feeling that I could prove I was right to myself, and prove it to other people too. If there'd been one little thing in this book, just one little thing—"

He tapped it with his finger. Afterwards he blundered across in the dark and sat down in a big chair. Faint lightning showed against the streaming windows behind him.

Masters shook his head.

"Afraid it's not much good, sir. If we had any ghost of a line to work on at all, I could have put the organization to work and it's ten to one we'd have run down the press-cutting you want. But there's not a ruddy thing to go by! We don't know what paper it might have been in: not even the country, because there are American and French here too. We don't know the day or the month or even the year. We don't even know what kind of an article we're looking for. If"—the chief inspector's voice yelped out with exasperation —"if you could just give me some idea what line you're working on, and what it is you want to prove?"

H.M. put his head in his hands. Dimly they could see that he was ruffling the two tufts of hair at either side of his temples.

"Uh-huh. Sure. I know all the difficulties. Mina Shields didn't have a secretary. She didn't even subscribe to a press-cutting bureau: I took mighty good care to look into that. As to what I want to prove, I can tell you short and sweet."

"Well?"

"I want to prove that a person may be dead, and yet at the same time be alive."

There was nobody in that room who liked the surroundings any better for this remark. Nor was the situation improved by H.M.'s ghostly chuckle.

"Ho ho. So you're convinced I'm off my onion at last, are you? Ruin of noble intellect. No, my lad. I mean exactly what I say. You're also overlookin' the motive in this case.[1] You wouldn't believe me when I told you there was such a thing as a Judas Window; but I showed you one, didn't I?"

"Maybe you did and maybe you didn't. But you're blooming well not going to show me a living corpse, and neither is anybody else. Not while I keep my own sanity you won't. I'm fed up, Sir Henry, and that's a fact. I thought you'd gone the limit before, but this beats anything I ever heard of. You can take your astral projections and your green candles and your Gamage fountains and your living corpses, and you can—"

"Oho? Scared, are you?"

"May I ask, Sir Henry, who you're calling scared?"

"You, Masters. You've really got the wind up at last. You're beginning to be scared of this house and everything in it. Now aren't you?"

"No, sir, I am not. I deny—"

"Look at you jump, then, over a little bit of thunder! Ain't you ashamed of yourself: honestly, now?"

"Steady on!" advised Dr. Sanders, in genuine concern. "You'll have him chewing the carpet in a minute."

"Listen to me," said H.M. suddenly, in such a sharp, quiet voice that they all fell silent. Sanders almost imagined that he could see a wicked eye gleam from the chair. "Ah, that's better. Now then: do you want to catch the murderer?"

"Of course I want to catch the murderer."

"Right! Then if you won't listen to scientific facts, I'll give you somethin' more practical to chew on than the carpet. Listen to our line of attack. Our attack begins tomorrow. It may take a lot of moves and a long time, but we got a chance and that's all I want. We start at the inquest. Now Pennik thinks he's goin' to make an unholy spectacle of himself at that inquest. He's not; or at least we make him think he's not. We've got to get permission for this, but I think I can wangle it. We issue a statement that—"

---

[1] A very just remark, I can see now. The motive for murder, though fully indicated in the text, is not obvious on the surface; and it involves, indeed, a legal point. Anyone interested in solving the problem may be advised to look carefully below the surface. The reader is warned.—J.S.

Part IV

MORNING:

Concerning the End of It

PRESS

Daily Non-Stop

Wednesday, May 4, 1938

(banner headline)

PENNIK BARRED FROM INQUEST
ON ALLEGED VICTIM:
TRIES TELEFORCE TONIGHT

Daily Trumpeter

CONSTABLE INQUEST
'NOT OPEN TO PUBLIC':
Government Muddle.
TELEFORCE—PARIS TONIGHT.

News-Record

PENNIK PROMISES NEW VICTIM;
ANSWERS CHALLENGE TONIGHT.
But Self-Styled Killer Cannot
Attend Inquest on his Victim.

Daily Wireless

SIR HENRY MERRIVALE:
Exclusive Interview.

145

TELEFORCE,   TELEFORCE,   TELEFORCE,   TELEFORCE,

9.45.   9.45.   9.45.   9.45.

... yet smile as we may over certain statements which have been forced upon our attention, the thoughtful man cannot but view with concern a more serious consideration which has today arisen: a threat to those individual liberties which we justly hold so dear. An inquest held behind locked doors, an inquest to which the general public are denied entrance, is a bold step for which some explanation is surely due. The Government have acted wisely and well; now let them inquire into the identity of, and deal suitably with, the author of this remarkable measure, the responsibility for which cannot rest entirely upon the shoulders of Mr. Freedyce the coroner.

Goin' out to see what 'appens, Mrs. Topham?
Cor lumme, not 'arf!

XVII

THE TOWN HALL at Grovetop, where the inquest was held, was a more pretentious example of Victorian stone scrollwork than the town seemed to deserve. But there was nothing pretentious about the part of it where the inquest took place. This was a long, low, semi-underground room, through whose barred windows you could see the legs of passers-by on the green outside. It smelt like a schoolroom. It was dark and nearly always chilly, despite the dingy asbestos-covered furnace-pipes across the ceiling; and echoes went up from the stone floor.

A white-shaded lamp hung down over the coroner's table, with the witness-chair beside it. A sort of dais held the jury, who breathed hard. The rest of that dim room was taken up with rows of naked chairs; for only a few people sat in the front row. But if business here seemed cold and formal, it was counteracted by the jovial roar of sound outside. You could see many legs (and faces) beyond the windows.

"I will have silence in this court," said the coroner, flinging his notes all over the table. "This is really intolerable. Sergeant!"

"Yes, sir?"

"Be good enough to close that window. We cannot even hear what the witness is saying."

"Very good, sir."

"I cannot endure this. What are all those people doing there? Why don't you disperse them?"

146

"Well, sir, it's a pretty big crowd. They're piled up twenty deep from Cross's end of the High Street to the main road. I never saw such a jam hereabouts since they brought down a zep on Heidegger's farm during the war."

"Sergeant, I am not concerned if the entire population of London has chosen to honor us. I have my instructions and I mean to abide by them. Go and send them away. Is the arm of the law entirely powerless?—Good God, what is that?"

"It sounds like an accordion, sir."

"Does it, indeed?"

"Yes, sir. Joe Crowley playing *John Peel*. He—"

"I do not care if it is Rachmaninoff playing his *Prelude*. He cannot play it outside my court. Will you go and send them away?"

"Very good, sir."

"Yes. Now. Gentlemen of this jury. I am very sorry, gentlemen, to have both you and myself subjected to this annoyance. If you can shut your ears against it, let us proceed with the examination of the last witness. Dr. Sanders."

Sanders, in the witness-chair, looked round. He was thinking that he had never seen a drearier-looking place than this long schoolroom. Out of the gloom the wooden faces of H.M., of Masters, of Superintendent Belcher, of Dr. Edge, of Lawrence Chase, who had formally identified the body. All of them were very quiet.

But it seemed to him that the jury were bursting.

"Now, Doctor! You have given us a very clear and concise statement as to your examination of the deceased, both immediately after death and at the postmortem. You would say that your examination was exhaustive?"

"I should."

"I take it, then, that you agree with the opinion already given to us by Dr. Edge?"

"I do."

"*Now, then! Move along there! Mo-ove along!*"

"*Ere! 'Oo yer shovin?*"

"*Mo-ove along, now! Mo-ove along!*"

"*Yah! Think yer almighty big in that 'elmet, don'tcher? Boo! Sssss! Boo!*"

"*All together, boys:*

"*D'ye ken Bobbie Peel with his helmet so gay,*
D'ye ken Bobbie Peel at the break of day—"

"Will someone be good enough to close that other window? Thank you, Inspector. I would rather stifle than go

147

deaf. A strong line, I am afraid, must be taken. Now, Dr
Sanders."

Sanders gave mechanical replies. His head ached dull
from sitting up all night over books, and the noise outside
did not soothe it. Nagging at the back of his mind was always the realization that Hilary had not gone out with him
last night after all, so the first round went to Pennik.

"You further tell us, Doctor, that no organ necessary to
life was in any way injured?"

"That is correct."

"And that, though there are causes by which this condition could have been produced, it is impossible to tell
which one of those causes (if any) was responsible for
Mr. Constable's death?"

"Yes."

(Damn Pennik and everything connected with him. I
could not have slept last night if I had tried. This mere
business of suggestion is enough to make the nerves crawl.
You imagine things. It's past three o'clock now. The sun
will go down presently. Pennik tries out his game on me
between nine-forty-five and ten-fifteen tonight. Seven hours
to go.)

"Tell me, Doctor. The deceased did not die instantly?"

"No. quickly, but not instantly. Within two minutes, at
any rate."

"Should you say that he died in pain?"

"In a great deal of pain, yes."

(Rather humiliating, though, to go round to Hilary's tiny
bed-sitting-room flat in Westminster; to reserve a table for
them at the Corinthian Grill-Room; and then to find she
had gone out already with Pennik, leaving regrets with a
charwoman. There was that note, though. 'Please trust me;
that's all; I'm working with your H.M. now, and he's got a
plan.' But what plan?)

"*May* I have your attention, Doctor?"

"I beg your pardon."

(But what plan? What was behind H.M.'s wooden look?)

"Let us clear up one thing now, Doctor. You place no belief, then, in any suggestion of a supernatural or even super-
normal cause of death?"

"No belief whatever."

"Would you go so far as to say that such a suggestion was
nonsense?"

"I should."

"In conclusion: we may sum up your opinion by saying
that it is impossible for you or I or anyone else to deter-
mine the cause of death?"

148

"Yes."

"Thank you, Doctor; that will be all."

One of the jurymen, a red-headed wiry man in a tall collar, who had been fidgeting even more than the others, managed to clear his throat.

"Hold on!" he said. "Excuse me, Mr. Coroner, but are we allowed to ask a question?"

"Yes, certainly. Please ask the witness any question you think may be relevant."

The red-headed man sat forward with his hands on his knees.

"Wot about Teleforce?" he demanded.

A stir went through the jury, who came forward as though they had been pulled to a similar position. The foreman, a stout man who owned the most flourishing public-house in Grovetop, looked annoyed, as though he had not been quick enough off the mark to put the question himself. But he repeated the question.

"I have never heard of it," Sanders said curtly.

"Don't you read the newspapers sir?"

"I mean that I have never heard of it scientifically. If you ask me my opinion of it, I can only join Professor Hux-lane in calling it balderdash."

"But—"

"Gentlemen," interrupted the coroner coldly, "I am sorry to curtail your natural and commendable wish to weigh matters thoroughly; but I must ask you to confine your questions to points which are relevant to this inquiry. You have heard the medical evidence. Your decision must be based on that and that alone. I do not merely request you to do this, gentlemen; I am afraid I must *instruct* you to do it."

Once their spell of silence had been broken, most of the jury were shivering with such repressed eagerness that several of them spoke at once.

"But that's not right," somebody threw at the coroner.

"Sir, are you presuming to question my conduct of this inquiry?"

"Doctors," said an obscure, furred voice of contempt. "Doctors! You take my wife. When she died, the doctor said—"

"I have said, gentlemen, that I mean to have silence; and have silence I will. Is that quite clear?"

"Good Lord, there he is!"

"Who?"

"I say, Sally, quick! Here, I'll hold you up. Getting out of that car."

"Waow!"

149

"Blimey, it is too. I seen 'is pitcher. Oi, old cock: wot about killin' my missus?"

"And now, gentlemen, I am afraid I must ask you to direct your attention towards me rather than looking up towards those windows. What lies outside these walls does not, I need scarcely point out, concern us. Thank you, Dr. Sanders: the jury have no further questions. They are satisfied."

"Murderer, that's what he is!"

"Ssss! Boo! Ssss! Boo!"

"Here, I say! Fair play. Give the man a chance. What's he done?"

"What's he done? He's Nazi, didn't you know that?"

"What are they saying? What is it?"

"Nazi. Great friend of Hitler."

"Ah. True as gospel. Heard it at the pub last night. Big fat gentleman from London; bald-headed; got a title; said—"

"—that evidence, and only evidence, gentlemen of this jury, must concern us. Dr. Sanders being the last witness we are to hear, it now devolves upon me to give you a brief summary of the facts to the end of assisting you in forming your verdict. And I fear, gentlemen, that there is only one verdict you can give me. However, let me put the considerations to you in—"

Sanders tiptoed past the few others in the court, still sitting motionless as dummies in the chairs of the front row. He cast a brief glance at H.M., whose eyes were closed, his arms folded, and his corporation rising and falling gently as though in sleep. Masters, on the alert, never looked away from the coroner. But Dr. Sanders's nerves crawled and at the moment he wanted to smoke more than anything else in the world.

Pushing open the creaky door, he edged out into an underground passage which was equipped with a small window and a rubbish-bin; and he met Herman Pennik coming down the stairs.

The westering sun was full on Pennik's face through the window, so that for a few seconds Sanders was in shadow. He surprised on Pennik's face a dream; and it was a dream of pure power. Sun touched the thick eye-lids and seemed to make the eyes bulge. He was dressed for traveling; nea cap and coat, and he carried a suitcase. Yet he hesitated a little when he saw the little underground room, for he did no seem to like little underground rooms. But he had not ye reached the bottom step when a policeman stepped in from of him.

"Yes, sir? And what would you be wanting?"

"I have a fancy, my friend, to attend the Constable inquest."

"Are you a witness?"

"No."

"Press and public not allowed. Up you go, now."

"I have a fancy to make a statement. I am told that anyone who so chooses has a legal right to attend an inquest and give testimony."

"Not to this one they haven't. Not by my orders."

"But you don't understand. I am Herman Pennik. I am the fairly well-known person who killed—"

"In that case," said the constable imperturbably, "go up to the charge-room and give yourself up. I don't care who you killed; you've got no business here."

"Are you trying," began Pennik, "to—"

For an instant it was touch and go. He had lifted his thick hand, and he was going to slash it across the constable's face as casually and contemptuously as he might have struck a cobweb out of the way.

But he lowered his hand.

The constable looked at him curiously.

"I don't know what you meant to do, my bucko," he said, "but you go trying any games like that and you'll see trouble."

The door to the inquest-room creaked again. H.M., his fists on his hips, pushed through.

"That's all right, son," he told the constable. "Let him come down. The coroner's just about finished in there. And I want to see him."

Pennik descended the steps. Setting down his suitcase on the floor, he removed his gloves and put them into the pocket of his tan topcoat. He ignored Sanders altogether.

"Ah, so the inquest is over?" he asked. "I am sorry. I was so unfortunate as to be held up. I go from here to Croydon airport, to save time, which is the reason for the bag and—"

"You're sartorial magnificence itself, son," said H.M., eying him. "I was just wonderin' if you'd turn up."

"Yes. Now we must try to penetrate *your* mental defenses, Sir Henry," Pennik spoke with the air of a sympathetic dentist, "and see what is going on. I confess the decision of the Home Office to hold this inquest in private intrigued me. Particularly, I was curious as to why your friends the newspapers were excluded. I did not see a reporter anywhere. I also wondered whether the whole affair might not be a bait, a challenge, a dare to me."

H.M. shook his head.

"No, son. I didn't want you to come. I didn't for a fact.

151

But, now that you're here, I think you might as well com
in and hear the verdict."

"Ah, the effort is to frighten me?" said Pennik, an
laughed in his face. "Now that is unworthy of you, if I ma
say so." In moving closer to H.M., he nearly brushed San
ders's elbow, but remained coolly and contemptuously uncon
scious of him. "I have taken legal counsel. I know quite wel
I have established, that I cannot be convicted of any crim
whatever."

"Yes, that's right. You can't be convicted of any crim
whatever. But just come in and hear the verdict. That's i
I say, Masters'—he spoke over his shoulder as the chief in
spector emerged—"just take his other arm, will you? We'r
goin' in to hear the verdict."

"May I ask what you're doing?"

"We're goin' in to hear the verdict. Phew, you use scen
don't you? Or is it hair-oil?"

"Would you mind taking your hand off my arm?"

"That's right, this way. We'll sit down at the back of th
room, where they won't see us."

The mutter of noise outside, which had dwindled in th
passage, now struck out at them from the inquest-room. Aft
ernoon shadows were gathering in that already dark room
where legs and faces still shifted beyond the windows.

"Well, gentlemen of the jury, have you reached a verdict?

It was remarkable how the jury seemed to come togethe
like a Rugby scrum, and then fold apart again to present
united front. It was at this minute that somebody stuck
flash-bulb and camera against one of the windows; the ligl
glared out into the room, showing Pennik between his tw
escorts. The foreman, already red in the face, was on hi
feet. He held a piece of paper, which he contemplated wit
a scowling brow.

"Mr. Coroner."

"Yes, yes? One moment!"

This time, outside the windows, there was a genuine polic
charge. The legs scattered. As though his wits scattered to
the foreman looked up over his shoulder. Then he settle
himself again, grimly.

"Mr. Coroner," he said, "before we give you our verdic
can I ask a question?"

"Yes, yes, of course, if you really think it is necessary
What did you wish to know?"

"Mr. Coroner, are you bound to accept whatever verdi
we give you, now?"

"Of course."

"Well, some of us weren't properly sure," persisted th

foreman. "Laws being what they are, with the brewers and all. Is there a kind of judge, or court of appeal, or something like that, that can take back our verdict and say it's n.b.g.?"

"No, certainly not. And I see no reason for such terms or such language, Mr. Foreman. This is not a court of law. It is an inquiry, and I must act as you direct. But surely—"

The foreman drew a deep breath, holding up a huge hand to forestall further comment.

"Ah, that's what I wanted to know." He glanced at the paper in his other hand. "We, the jury," he roared from the depths of his throat, "find that the deceased who came to its death was deliberately murdered by Pennik, using a thing called Teleforce—"

The coroner was on his feet. Sanders never forgot the effect of it. In his evident legal agitation the coroner had forgotten the hanging lamp over the table. His forehead struck the edge of the thin white glass shade, which gave out a ringing note like a bell. He reached up to steady the wildly swinging cord of the lamp as he spoke.

"Gentlemen, please, one moment!"

"Told you 'e wouldn't like it, Ted," said a voice.

"I cannot interfere with your verdict, of course. I have no wish to do so. You are the judges of the facts, not I. But before your verdict is recorded let me beg of you to stop and consider. —You are asking me to commit Mr. Pennik for trial on a charge of murder?"

"Yes, Mr. Coroner, we are."

"But do you realize that such a trial would be a farce? Do you realize that they could not possibly convict him?"

The little red-headed juror stuck out his neck.

"Then they ought to be ashamed of themselves," he said. "If a murderer is going to be allowed to run around loose, what's to become of any of us? We don't care what the doctors say. It's in all the papers, *all* of 'em; and if it's in all the papers it's not politics: it's true. It was even in the *Daily Wireless;* that ought to be conservative enough for you; interview with a big pot named Sir Henry Somebody. If they can't convict him that's their business, and more shame to em; but at least we've done our bit."

"'At's telling him. Charley," said the approving voice.

"But, gentlemen, for the last time let me implore you to stop and consider! Have you considered, for one thing, how much a trial for murder costs the taxpayers?"

"'Ow much?" asked the approving voice, with quick interest.

153

"Well, that is hardly germane to our inquiry—"

"Ah, but you said it was," the approving voice pointed out.

"If you press me, I believe it costs about five thousand pounds."

"Five thousand pounds?"

"Yes, gentlemen, about that. Now, come! Does not that consideration weigh with you in the least?"

The foreman's brow darkened.

"Yes, it thundering well does," he said. "If they can throw money down the drain like they do *on* the things they do, why, I say, they can thundering well spend a little bit of it on upholding the laws of this country. There was a gentleman in my bar-parlor last night; stout gentleman; very pleasant-spoken; said exactly that. If they can throw—"

The coroner bowed his head.

"We need not carry the discussion any further, gentlemen. I am ready to hear your verdict."

He listened gravely while it was read again.

Sanders was watching his face. Sanders did not dare look at either H.M., or at Masters, or at Pennik sitting between them. The coroner's pale, dry face was very close to the white lamp; and on it Sanders could have sworn he saw, very briefly, the faint turn of a smile.

"Thank you, Mr. Foreman. —Is the police-officer in charge of this case in court?"

At the back of the long, dim room, Masters got to his feet.

"Ah, Chief Inspector? By virtue of the authority invested in me, I must instruct you to apprehend—"

"He's here, sir," replied Masters, putting his hand on Pennik's shoulder. "Get up, Mr. Pennik. Walk forward and see the coroner."

The jury were on their feet. Sanders did not see Pennik's face and he did not want to see it. He remembered as a grotesque touch that Masters, with one hand on Pennik's arm, was carrying in his other hand Pennik's new and shining suitcase. The windows were now entirely darkened by police legs.

"Mr. Herman Pennik?" asked the coroner.

Pennik merely bowed.

"I am afraid, Mr. Pennik, that I must commit you for trial. Chief Inspector Masters will tell you that you need no say anything at this time, but that, if you do, it will be taken down in writing and may be used as evidence. I further—"

Pennik spoke very clearly, "Mr. Coroner, I am not certain whether to be amused or annoyed. This situation is fantastic

154

You have said yourself that the trial will be a farce."

"I quite agree. If you have, contrary to my instructions, been present at this inquest," the coroner told him in a curious tone, "you will be aware that I could not have given your case fairer treatment had I been briefed in your defense. But I have no alternative."

"It is unreasonable; it is not justice. Still, if you insist, I must give in with as good a grace as I may. I am willing to stand my trial whenever you think it is necessary. You know where to find me. In the meantime, however, I have a very important mission to undertake: a visit to Paris. I will, of course, give bond for my reappearance. But if you will excuse me now—"

Two police constables moved out and stood in front of the door.

The coroner shook his head.

"I fear, Mr. Pennik," he said grimly, "that it is not quite so simple as all that. You will not go to Paris or anywhere else. You will be committed to jail pending your trial; and that will be the limit of your activities for the present."

It was perhaps three seconds before Pennik spoke. Sanders saw his shoulders seem to broaden under the festive topcoat.

"You do not mean—you cannot mean I shall be under restraint? Locked up? Not in a cell?"

"Naturally. That is the customary proceeding. You cannot expect to be treated any better or any worse than others who are committed to trial for murder."

"But I cannot be convicted," said Pennik, with a desperate reasonableness. "I am quite safe. You tell me that in so many words. It is raving lunacy to lock up a man who cannot be convicted. Because a parcel of thick-witted yokels choose to make a decision at variance with all law or sense—"

"What's that you're giving us?" demanded the foreman of the jury, jumping down from the dais.

The coroner turned swiftly.

"Gentlemen of the jury, before you leave for your homes would you be good enough to file into that room (there) by that door? I should like to say a few words to you before you disperse. Please do not argue the matter, but oblige me by going at once. I shall not detain you long— Mr. Pennik, I cannot argue the matter with you any further. Chief Inspector, I leave the prisoner in your charge."

Pennik's voice rose.

"But when is this trial? How long am I to be kept under restraint?"

"I cannot tell you that exactly. This is the beginning of May. You will probably come up for trial at the Kingston Assizes some time late in July. I obviously cannot give you any information more exact than that."

"*Three months?*"

"Roughly, yes."

Despite Pennik's heavy chest and shoulders, Sanders still would not have believed there was so much power in them. Pennik moved with such blinding swiftness that Masters's finger-nails scratched vainly across the cloth of the topcoat, and missed their grip. It was a heavy table, an oak table; but Pennik had it into the air with one enormous heave, his hands on either side, and he would have brought it down on the coroner's face and head like the crash of a slab of stone if his ankle had not twisted under him. The table wavered, a weight in the sky; Masters had him round the waist and shoulders half a second later; the table wavered still more, and thudded to the floor as two more men fastened on Pennik.

The coroner, though he was white to the lips, merely touched his spectacles as though to make sure they were still on his nose.

"That will do, I think. You have him, Chief Inspector?"

"Got him fast, sir."

"I think it would be as well not to risk anything. After an outburst of that kind, you may use your own discretion as to the sort of cell to which Mr. Pennik is confined. Mr Pennik, you have asked for the exact letter of the law; and that is what you are receiving. I notice that you appear to retch violently at a taste of your own medicine. Now, gentlemen of the jury, if you will kindly follow me?"

With a heavy shuffling of feet, the jury filed out, and the coroner shepherded them. Pennik was left alone with his other captors in the dark and darkening room. Sanders still could not see his face, but the gaiety of his tan topcoat and traveling-cap were eloquent.

Then Pennik spoke again.

"God in heaven," he said, suddenly putting his knuckle at the corners of his eyes without turning round, "you can't do this. It is monstrous, It is brutal. It is pure torture. Three months in a cell; three months locked up; three months to go mad in. I can't stand it. I demand the law."

H.M. spoke very quietly. He had lumbered up with surprisingly little noise, and he was standing at the other side of Pennik. He took a chair from the front row and set it out.

"Sit down, son," he said.

XVIII

POLICE-CONSTABLE LEONARD RIDDLE, of C Division, had a beat along which, it is true, little in the way of violence or crime ever happened. And P.C. Riddle was content to have it so.

He liked his beat not only for the mingled life and quiet of it, but for the pleasurable feeling it gave him of having some acquaintance with the nobs, of being behind the scenes, of, unobtrusively, helping tend the lares and penates of an admirable house. His beat skirted Park Lane, took him along Mount Street to Berkeley Square, down round the curve of Curzon Street, and back to Park Lane again. Odd how much information you picked up about people, even when they never noticed you. You could tell how things were going; who went where; what the domestic troubles were; all of a good many who were aware of you only as something to say good-night to.

P. C. Riddle had his favorite people, as he had his favored parts of the beat. Few of them he knew as names, though many chauffeurs were his friends. But many were ticketed in his mind as numbers, with some corresponding description, as a cloakroom attendant will ticket hordes by a catchphrase and return the right hat without any slip of paper to identify it. Sometimes he felt fatherly and a trifle godlike. When someone in private life told him he was a student of human nature, he was pleased.

This term had even, in fact, been applied by one of his numbers. There was a night when number eleven D'Orsay Street (junior, not the old man) was coming home from a cocktail-party at three o'clock in the morning; and number eleven D'Orsay Street had draped himself over a pillar-box and insisted on talking first about astronomy and then about the perfidious nature of woman. Having just been given the raspberry by his fiancée, number eleven was in a philosophic mood. In the course of his remarks he had called P.C. Riddle a student of human nature: just as we all, when whiffled, like to think that the person we are talking to is as profound as we are. But he had always liked number eleven afterwards; it was one more reason why D'Orsay Street, a little cul-de-sac off Mount Street, was of interest to him.

And it was the cause of a new, unpleasant interest now. Riddle knew a few names there. Number nine, for example,

157

was a fine Regency mansion now turned into flats with incredibly steep rents. Mr. and Mrs. Constable had occupied the flat on the first floor. In common with most of London, Riddle knew all about the Constable family; but he had known a little about them before the crimes whose echoes had stirred even into Mayfair.

Mrs. Constable, for instance. She had several times tried to ask him questions about the police, poor lady. Once she had come bouncing down the steps into the street, bobbing along beside him, holding her hat while she tried to keep pace with him—and if there is anything your constable dislikes, it is having someone walk along the beat with him —while she poured out queries.

For several nights P.C. Riddle had been thinking about her. It is too much to say that he was haunted; he was not haunted by anything. But in the midst of the uproar, while Teleforce shouted from the newspaper bills and animated the street-corners, he always walked slowly when he passed number nine D'Orsay Street. And he thought.

He was not concerned with the investigation of crime. In fact, when once they raided a number off Curzon Street and found a gambling house, he was startled; well as he knew the neighborhood, he had no idea of this until he got his instructions; and he felt annoyed with the gambling house for not knowing about it. But, again in common with most of London, he found himself groping for explanations. He didn't like to think about it; he didn't like to think about anything that disturbed him. He could not help himself.

On that gusty Wednesday night—following the inquest on the body of Mr. Constable in the afternoon—his eye had been caught by a newspaper bill in Park Lane. He had not seen an evening paper; he had not had time. In a hazy way he had hoped that they would do something to this here Pennik. But the bill stared out at him in red letters.

PENNIK IN PARIS

Anger stirred in P.C. Riddle's soul, stirred and spread like glue out of a bottle. So they'd let him go. So he'd be at it again. And this time Lord only knew how far the monkey would go. During near-war-cries Riddle had had much the same feeling: that you couldn't trust the world at all: that in the course of only a few days you were suddenly bang against the unbelievable, with everything turning upside down.

At the mouth of Mount Street he slowed down his tread.

He was half tempted to do something he had never done in his life. For he had a pal who had got on: who was, in fact, a sergeant in the fingerprint department of the division. Riddle was half tempted to ring up Billy Wynne (he could use the 'phone at number four, the chemist's) and tell him a theory which had remained stubbornly in his head for days. Of course, Billy wasn't one of the high muck-a-mucks. But he was C.I.D. anyway, and would know who to go to. Riddle himself knew none of the high muck-a-mucks. He did happen to know one of the Yard chief inspectors, Masters, by sight; only a couple of years ago there had been a row in Lancaster Mews, near here, when the Ten Teacups case blew up. Also, there was the old gentleman named Merrivale. But, on the whole, better speak to Billy Wynne and let him do it.

Ring up Billy?

No; better not. Only get a ticking-off it if he did, and serve him right.

P.C. Riddle resumed his steady tread along a dim and apparently deserted street. There was a high, clear moon, and a warmish gusty wind which chased a discarded newspaper across the pavement ahead of him.

Steady growl of traffic from beyond; steady watchtick; everything steady. It was twenty minutes to ten. Pennik in Paris, Pennik in Paris, Pennik in Paris. Here: wasn't Pennik due to speak over Paris P.T.T. at a quarter to ten? The fruiterer at four-b Russell Lane, the little alley only a step away, had a wireless; and it would be easy to drop in for a few minutes' listening. But better not. He had to meet his sergeant at ten; this round had to be spaced as steady as a clock.

P.C. Riddle, crushing down temptation again, kept to his regular tread and turned into the little cul-de-sac called D'Orsay Street.

Here, halfway into it, he stopped.

There was an unusual noise.

Riddle knew the proper noises of his streets as a man knows street-noises from a familiar room. Anything out of line registered in his mind seconds before he began to think about it. This was not a loud noise, but he tracked it along carefully to where the super-swank number nine thrust its heavy masonry at the moon.

Beside number nine, whose first-floor flat had been occupied by Mr. and Mrs. Constable, was a tall narrow gate with fancy iron grilling. Behind number nine, Riddle knew, was a deep garden enclosed by high walls; and this gate opened on a little passage leading back to the garden. The gate was now open. It clicked and rattled very slightly in the gusts of wind. Even from a distance, if you kept a sharp eye out, you could see it move. In four years of patrolling this district, Riddle had never known it to be open before.

Mr. and Mrs. Constable were dead, so they couldn't have opened the gate. The tenant of the ground-floor flat, to Riddle's certain knowledge, was away from home. About the tenant of the top floor, he wasn't sure; that one had been at least until recently in the south of France, and might or might not have returned. But when the the top-floor tenant was at home there were always lights and sometimes sounds of revelry. Not a light showed anywhere at number nine; and the gate continued to creak.

Riddle pushed it open, and walked back to the garden.

The garden was mostly grass and trees. A thin, clear moon shone down into it, throwing the back of the house into shadow. Riddle could make out that the back of the house was a literal whited sepulcher of whitewash, dingy and peeling; that each floor had a long iron balcony stretching across it, with an ornamental iron handrail and separate sets of stairs leading down, so that each tenant had access to the garden.

Keeping into shadow by the house, Riddle peered out into this garden.

He saw Pennik there.

There could be no mistaking that face turned up to the moonlight, the face that had turned and stared through the newspapers in every possible combination of face and profile. A chestnut tree, new and rich with foliage, threw a dense shadow on the edge of the grass; but Pennik—his eyes on the house—moved out from under it.

He was hatless, and his face (perhaps from a trick of the moonlight) looked bloated like a drowned man's. Riddle saw him slide his hand into his pocket and draw something out. Despite the vast whisper of wind in foliage, all sounds were whittled down to such a fine point that Riddle distinctly heard the click, and saw moonlight run along the blade, as Pennik pressed the button of the clasp-knife.

Then Pennik, slipping the open knife into his pocket, moved out softly towards the house.

P.C. Riddle moved with him—sideways in shadow as Pennik moved forward. When Pennik put his foot on the first step of the iron stairway, Riddle was close enough to breathe on him. He almost put his hand on Pennik's as the latter took hold of the hand-rail. But Riddle did not do that; he waited until Pennik was a half a dozen steps up, and followed.

That grotesque, monkey-like climb in the dark was done in silence. Pennik did not look round. Or at least Riddle hoped it was done in silence. If he had any thoughts at all, it was a confused shouting to himself that he had been right after all. He ought to have rung up Bill Wynne. Might have done himself a bit of good.

Never mind. Leonard Riddle had his own satisfaction. He could tell 'em a thing or two, if he wanted to. So again Pennik was in two places at once, was he? No, he wasn't. Len Riddle could tell 'em why he wasn't. In London they might know a lot about detective work, but they didn't know anything about poachers—

The iron stairway creaked faintly. Pennik ahead was almost up to the first floor; Riddle could see the windows against the dingy whitewash. Then Pennik stopped, and Riddle also stopped so abruptly that he almost made the whole stairway shake. There was another man on the balcony just over their heads.

Riddle could not make out the face of the other man, who was of medium size and wore a soft hat and had his hand on the rail of the balcony. Riddle had a feeling that he was young; he also had a feeling that Pennik, as Pennik's head appeared like a jack-in-the-box over the edge of the balcony, gave the other man a shock he refused to acknowledge. The two faced each other, and seemed to brace themselves.

In barely a whisper, so that it was difficult to distinguish the words, Pennik spoke.

"Good evening, Dr. Sanders," he said.

(Sanders? Sanders? Wasn't that name familiar?)

The young man moved out and stood squarely at the top of the stairs. He also spoke in a whisper.

"What are you doing here?"

"I have come to settle matters, Dr. Sanders," said Pennik.

In the distance, muffled by the night mutter, the bell of St. Ald's Church struck the quarter-hour to ten. Pennik, throwing back his head and lifting his wrist, strained his eyes to peer at his wrist-watch in the dark. What he saw seemed to give him great satisfaction.

"Quite correct," he whispered. "And what are *you* doing here, Doctor?"

"I wish I knew," said the other man, taking a hard grip on the rail of the balcony. "I wish to God I knew. I wish they'd tell me."

"I can tell you," Pennik answered, and made a bound for the top step.

This was where P.C. Riddle acted. He was not dramatic about it; it was not in his nature to be dramatic. He merely

161

took the remaining steps at a couple of long, efficient strides, and tapped Pennik smartly on the shoulder from behind. At the same time he unhooked the bull's eye lantern from his belt, switched it on, and turned the beam into Pennik's face as the latter swung round.

"Now, then," said P.C. Riddle. "What's all this?"

The question was rhetorical. What answer he expected he did not know himself. But the last thing he expected was the expression of the face turned round towards him in the beam of his lantern. So stealthy had been Pennik's movements that the result was startling and almost shocking. Pennik's face looked queer and bloated because the man had been crying: crying like a child; crying until his eyelids were puffy and the whites of the eyes showed streaked with pink. He put up a hand to shield those eyes from the light. The corners of his mouth turned down—and he whimpered.

There was a stir of footsteps on the iron plates of the balcony. They were cautious steps, but plain as a noise of rats. The beam of an electric torch appeared and fastened on Riddle.

"What in hell's name are you doing?" muttered a voice, and it seemed impossible to get so much concentrated savagery of exasperation in words spoken under the breath. "Put out that light!"

Both lights vanished after Riddle had turned his upwards. But what he saw so startled him that he risked one more gleam again afterwards to make sure. The speaker had been Chief Inspector Masters, who pulled his bowler hat down on his head and brushed the light away as though he were brushing something off his face. Beside him stood the old gentleman Riddle remembered from the Lancaster Mews row. Then, on the breezy balcony of a lightless house, P.C. Riddle tried to gather together his wits.

"What is it?" muttered Masters. "What do you want?"

"Gate open, sir—" replied Riddle automatically. Then the more important matter wormed uppermost. "I've got Pennik," he added, and fastened his free hand on Pennik's collar.

"Yes, yes, that's all right. Hop it now, d'ye hear. Hop it! No, stand by; we may need you."

"Sir, this Pennik. He's not in Paris. I know how he did it. The same as the poachers did in Lancashire. My Dad——"

"Let him go! What do you think you're doing?"

"Begging your pardon, sir: I was going to get in touch with Billy Wynne, but I'd like you to listen to me. They were twin brothers, the finest poaching team that ever deviled the magistrates. Tom and Harry Godden; one of them

162

would clean up Sir Mark Wilman's park under the keeper's nose, but he'd have an alibi because the other would be at the pub with a dozen witnesses to prove——"

"Are you off your chump?"

"There's two of Pennik," persisted Riddle, tightening his grip. "I thought it was so before, sir; and I know it now."

"Steady, son," interposed a heavy voice. Riddle heard Sir Henry Merrivale breathe in the gloom. "Keep your shirt on, Masters. Y'know, in a way he's quite right."

"Thank you, sir. My Dad——"

"Now, now! But let him go, son; take your hand off him. He hasn't done anything."

"But these murders, sir——"

"He hasn't done any murders, son."

Riddle's hand fell, the more so as this time there was no mistaking the look about Chief Inspector Masters in the gloom. It was the young man called Sanders who spoke. He spoke quietly and reasonably; yet Riddle had a feeling that he meant to be answered, and Riddle would have been impelled to answer him if he could.

Sanders said: "Look here, sir, this has got to be a showdown. The time for hocus-pocus is past. You tell me what I'm to do; and I do it. You tell me how deeply I'm involved, and what to be careful of, and how I must help you; but it's only fair to give me a shot at what's going on."

"Uh-huh. Well? What is it?"

"Do you say now that Pennik didn't do the murders?"

"He didn't do anything," returned the heavy voice, dully and rather wearily. "He didn't do any murders; he don't even know a thing about any murders. He's absolutely innocent o' crime or complicity in crime of any kind at all."

Below them on the tall balcony, wind frothed in the leaves of the garden.

"There," pursued the heavy, eerie voice. "There you are. That's the hobgoblin that's been frettin' you, and frettin' the world, for nearly a week. But come along with me. 'll show you a real hobgoblin, if you like."

He moved along towards the iron stairway towards the balcony of the floor above. For all his breadth and lumbering movement he made little noise. Sanders followed him.

"But this is the Constables' flat! This one. Here, on this floor. This is where they lived. Why are we going upstairs?"

That whole unnatural colloquy, taking place in explosive whispers, was beginning to wear on the nerves of everyone present. The steep stairway creaked. H.M. went ahead, and the others followed. Up at the top floor there was a gleam of moonlight through iron ribs and slats. Almost at the top

163

of the stairs. H.M. hesitated and turned round. The moonlight shone on his spectacles, and on the nap of the ancient top-hat that was pushed to the back of his head. His thick arms were outstretched as though to bar the top of the stairs. Just as he turned round, they all heard, thinly but shrilly ringing, the front doorbell of the top-floor flat.

"I expect that's the real murderer ringin' at the bell now," muttered H.M. "Listen to me. We're going' to look in through some windows that have been left open for us. If anybody speaks while we're up on this balcony, I'll murder him. I just want to tell you that up here is the flat of the person toward whom the whole scheme of the dirty work has been directed almost from the beginning; and that person is supposed to die tonight. Come on."

His coat disappeared. Above them there was no hood to the balcony. Moonlight silvered the tiles of the roof, and the long windows that stretched to the floor. These windows opened out like doors; two of them stood several inches open now. Inside were heavy pink draperies probably half an inch thick; and these also had been left partly open. There was a slight mist of unreality about the scene, since, in addition to the padded draperies, curtains of very fine-spun gold mesh had been drawn across the windows. No breath of air stirred them. As though through a film of gauze, the watchers looked into the dimly lighted box beyond.

It was a woman's bedroom or boudoir after the French fashion of the middle eighteenth century. The wall-panels were of silk, alternating in mirrors with gilt medallion heads. The bed at their left, a sort of indoor tent, was draped and billowing from a gilded circle of wood in the ceiling; and from this ceiling the chandelier hung in weight of crystal. But there were no lights except two electric wall-candles burning. Someone whom they could not see, presumably the owner of the flat, sat in a high wing chair with its back to the windows.

They had already heard the murderer ringing at the doorbell. A voice from the wing chair called back a request to come in. There was a noise of footsteps coming through other rooms in the flat.

Dr. Sanders, who felt his heart bump as though with physical fall, was gripped by H.M. and thrust towards the gap in two of the curtains. Directly across from him there was a door. That door opened, and the visitor came in.

It was P.C. Riddle who disobeyed H.M.'s orders.

He spoke in a hacking, shattering whisper almost against Sanders's ear.

"But I know who that is, sir," he seemed half to shout

"I've often seen her here at her stepmother's flat. That's Miss Hilary Keen."

THE MIST OF UNREALITY about that scene behind the gold gauze, the two electric candles throwing their light dimly on silk wall-panels, the hush given to footsteps and even voices by very thick carpeting, all these things kept the brains of the watchers dulled like an opiate.

In the midst of this finery, Hilary looked deprecating and rather apologetic.

True enough, there was a somewhat breathless air about her, and a faint color in her cheeks; but this might have come from walking too fast up the stairs. For she carried under one arm a sizeable squarish parcel wrapped in brown paper. She wore a tailored suit of dark green tweed, and a soft hat which shaded her eyes. Despite her deprecating air, her smile was the straightforward smile that all the watchers had seen.

A crow of pleasure or welcome issued from the chair where her hostess, and stepmother, was sitting.

"Hilary, my dear! How *nice* of you to come!"

And her hostess bounced up.

By moving his head sideways, Sanders could now see Mrs. Joseph Keen reflected in one of the long mirrors across the room. She was a small, plumpish, extremely good-looking blonde, with long ringlets which fell past her shoulders, large lips, and narrow twinkling eyes. She could not have been much older than Hilary herself; and beside Hilary she looked tiny. She was wearing a heavy lace negligee which went with her air of silk sleekness. Running to Hilary, she kissed her smackingly on both cheeks.

"How are you, Cynthia dear?" said Hilary, allowing herself to be kissed.

"I knew you would come," said Cynthia triumphantly. "I promised there shouldn't be anybody else here, and there isn't! Hilary, you wretch. I've been running after you for days and days and days—"

"But you only got back from the Riviera on Sunday," protested Hilary. She paused, and added in a curious voice: "How was the Riviera?"

"Heavenly! Absolutely heavenly!"

"I imagine it was."

"Oh, it was. I met the nicest—but never mind that. You

165

know what I want to hear. All about P-e-n-n-i-k. Hilary, you've become positively famous; all these terrible things in the papers; I can't think what's come over us. And you there in the middle of it all, all the thrilling things and everything. And that's not all. Pennik. They say he'd do anything for you; they say he adores you; positively dotes on you."

"I suppose he does, rather."

"Stella Erskine saw you both at Borononi's last night. Stella said she saw him lean over and kiss your hand in public. Well, I mean! Aren't you thrilled? *I* should be. Like being taken out by Hitler or Mussolini; only more so, if you know what I mean. Hilary, people positively run after me when they know I'm related to you. But you will tell me first, won't you? You will tell me all about it?"

"You shall hear all about it, Cynthia dear. I promise you that."

Cynthia wriggled with pleasure.

"That's my Hilary. Now come over here and sit down, do. I can't wait to hear about it. Is he nice? Has he—you know what I mean, dear? Yet, I mean? They say it's a real *grande passion,* like those French kings who tear about in the stories, and whoop it up so." Her forehead clouded, though not seriously. She half laughed. "Stella says I'd better be careful. She says she heard that Pennik said I wasn't fit to live, because I took your father's money from you or something like that. How absurd. Isn't it, dear? But don't stand there like that, please. Take off your things. And what on earth is that you've got under your arm?"

"A little present for you."

Cynthia's eyes opened, and she flushed with pleasure.

"For me? Oh, Hilary, how *nice* of you. And that reminds me. I brought you something from the Riviera too; it isn't much, but it was the best watch they had in the shop, and it's got diamond movements or something, whatever that means. There now, I've gone and told you what it was, but never mind. What's in yours? What is it? Let me open it."

"You'll know in just a minute, Cynthia dear," said Hillary.

Eluding the other's hands, she put down the parcel on the ledge of the white marble mantelpiece. Smiling, she took off her hat and shook back her rich brown hair.

"Hilary! Is anything wrong? You're trembling!"

"Nothing at all, Cynthia dear. May I use your bathroom for a moment?"

"Of course," said Cynthia, smiling at her rather archly Though Hilary kept her own mechanical smile in the dimness of the room, she gave her companion back a long, curious look; and Sanders's heart turned cold inside him. Then,

166

picking up her handbag with a swift movement, Hilary strode with the same swift movements across to the bathroom. She went in and closed the door.

Sanders could hear somebody's watch ticking. He did not think; he did not dare think. Once he had taken a step forward as though to interrupt, but H.M.'s hand fell with a crushing grip on his shoulder.

Cynthia Keen hummed a little to herself; looked at herself in a mirror with her head on one side; turned round slowly, examining herself; laughed a little with excitement; lighted a cigarette from a box on a little table beside the wing chair; and put the cigarette out again immediately. She was evidently so avid to hear the details that she could not stand still. Then the bathroom door opened; and the atmosphere of that over-decorated room changed as palpably as though a cold current of air had been turned into it.

Yet it would be difficult to say just how or why the atmosphere had changed. The dim electric candles were burning near Hilary's face, one on either side of the bathroom door just above her. They threw slanting shadows. They showed that Hilary's color was perhaps a little higher, and that she was breathing perhaps a little faster; nothing more. She kept her pleasant, poised, rather heavy look. Keeping both hands behind her, she used one of them to push the door shut.

Hilary took a step forward.

Cynthia half laughed.

"Darling, what on earth is the matter? I never saw such an absolute *juggins!* Is anything wrong?"

Hilary took another step forward, her hands still behind her back.

"Hilary!"

"No, really," said Hilary, breaking the tension by speaking in her quiet, pleasant voice. "There's nothing wrong with me, Cynthia dear. Only—"

She had nearly reached the chair. By this time, even outside the window they could smell faintly the new odor in that overheated room: the odor of chloroform. Cynthia must have smelled it too, or must have caught another sort of atmosphere which surrounded Hilary; for she turned in such a way that her face was repeated in several mirrors, and all the faces were white. Nor did Hilary raise her voice in speaking: it was only the contrast between the quiet tones and the meaning of what she said.

"Only I'm going to kill you as I killed Mina Constable," said Hilary—and flung herself on the other woman.

She spoke almost too soon.

Sanders could have told her that to administer chloroform to a fighting patient is not so easy as the layman supposes. The face-cloth, which she had saturated with it, almost slipped out of her hand; and Cynthia Keen was on the edge of being able to scream, for they saw her teeth before her head was buried in the crook of Hilary's arm. Both were carried over out of sight into the deep chair. Only the flapping, panting noises beat against the back of the chair and shook it partly round. It was a full minute before Cynthia's legs, the feet in white satin mules, ceased to kick and presently fell.

Hilary got up and backed away.

She was bent forward almost double, so that the sides of her hair had fallen over her face, and she was breathing hard. Her blue eyes were blank, yet at the same time intensely watchful; they roamed into corners, they were poised as though every nerve were listening, they probed even the silence.

Then she examined herself. One of her stockings had laddered. She automatically put her finger to her lips, moistened it, and ran it along the edge of the stocking before she straightened up. Slowing down her panting breaths, pushing back her hair she went to look at her now-pale face in the mirror over the mantelpiece. Yet she never left off that strung-up watchfulness, turning round and round as she moved, round and round, as though wondering if something would surprise her in a corner. The silence held too heavy; there was not even a clock.

As though remembering, she ran and turned the key in the lock of the door. Then, hastily, she broke the string of the brown paper parcel on the mantelpiece. It seemed to contain a large box of stiff cardboard, which in turn contained several articles. First she took out several lengths of very heavy but soft-looking black plaited cord, evidently the cord of a dressing-gown cut into pieces. Next she took a pair of rubber gloves, and rolled them expertly on her hands.

Half carrying, half dragging the unconscious woman, her face suddenly showing red and ugly with a grimace over Cynthia's lace-covered shoulder, Hilary supported her to the bed. She rolled her on to the bed, into the darkness under that muffling fall of brocaded canopy-curtains.

For the first time Hilary spoke aloud.

"I shall have to undress you, Cynthia dear," she said. "People have to be undressed before they can die in the way the other two died. After you're undressed, we will just tie you up with these, which are soft and won't leave bruises on you. Then"—she raced back to the mantelpiece, returning with a handkerchief and several strips of sticking-plaster—"we'll put this in your mouth, and fasten it with the plaster to finish the gag. I want *you* to be fully awake when you die."

Hilary sprang up and round again, her eyes searching.

The fine lightness and grace of her movements, like that of a dancer, was in contrast to the expression of her eyes. Those eyes moved towards the windows, hesitated, and moved back. On the bed the other woman uttered a faint moan.

"Yes, you will be coming round in a moment," said Hilary quickly. "That must be seen to."

Two minutes later she pulled up the bed coverlet over the stirring and muttering woman, who now could not move her arms or legs.

"Cynthia. Can you hear me?

"If I dared. I wonder if I dare take that gag out. If I dared.

"Cynthia!"

Inside the canopy showed only a blob of darkness, which Hilary's arm shook. Then Hilary herself seemed to wake up. Across the room there was a fat, squat-legged cabinet of gilt and lacquer-work, its front painted with a pastoral scene of Watteau shepherds and shepherdesses. It held, ingeniously concealed, a radio. Hilary clicked the switch, but no answering light showed against the glass inside. She hurriedly examined the base-plug, which was connected; again she clicked the dead switch back and forth.

"Cynthia, why won't this radio work?"

There was no reply.

Hilary went over to the bed and spoke in a tone of quiet reasonableness. "You see, I have got to hear Pennik speaking, poor lamb. He is going to announce your death, and I want to know when to kill you. Teleforce isn't much good unless I give it a little help unknown to him. As the dear chief inspector once truly said, Pennik couldn't kill an ant with a fly-swatter—though he quite sincerely thinks he can; and it's gone to his head."

She bent closer.

"You would be surprised at the trouble I had persuading him to kill you. He was *so* set on making an example of Jack Sanders instead; and how he ranted and swaggered and threw his weight about! I had it all nicely arranged, too, before Dr. Sanders butted in and challenged him. Then I had to go to work all over again. But I managed to persuade him (if you know what I mean, Cynthia? And of course you do) to choose you instead. He keeps telling me that he would give me the sun and moon to wear, if he were

169

king; so he could hardly fail to agree to a modest little request like killing you."

Hilary laughed a little. Her enormous vitality, her warm and living aliveness of personality, flooded up into it. But that mood changed very quickly. Her feet planted wide apart, her hands on her hips, she again bent forward like a mother over a cradle.

"So you wanted to hear all about it, Cynthia? You wanted to hear all about Pennik, and what he does, and who he is? You shall hear it: I promised you. To put it vulgarly, you thought I had picked a nice soft spot for myself, didn't you? You shall hear how soft it is. Do you know who Pennik is? Do you know what he is?"

She reached into the darkness of the bed. There was a tearing sound; she plucked away several strips of sticking-plaster, and extricated the handkerchief from Cynthia Keen's mouth. She threw the handkerchief on the floor.

"Do you, Cynthia?"

The whimper from the bed was still unintelligible.

"He is an East African mulatto," said Hilary. "His father was a white hunter of good family, or so he says. His mother was a Matabele savage. His grandfather was a Bantu fetish-man, or witch-doctor; and he was brought up in a Matabele hut until he was eight years old."

Outside the window, several persons looked at each other.

As an arrow strikes dead to the center of the target, as by the sound of the bat the cleanness of the hit can be told, so the essential *rightness* of those words came back. They stirred dozens of memories. They made dozens of pictures. They created an image of Pennik, fitting together all the contradictions at once.

"You've seen him in public," said Hilary. "Look at his mouth, and his nose, and his jaw. Look at the shape of his head and body. Above everything look at the little blue half-moons at the base of his finger-nails. You can't be mistaken, even when you see how he acts. He keeps a dreadful restraint on himself. He doesn't even drink. And yet he's a misfit. In his soul he's three-quarters cultured gentleman and one part superstitious savage; but watch, over and over and over again, the tail wagging the dog. That's the nice soft spot I've picked for myself, Cynthia darling: the black boy."

Hilary was never still. She moved away from the bed. Now her cheeks were more deeply flushed; and she shivered. Back and forth she went, with little short steps.

"Anyway, he was and is very intelligent. You can't deny that. They saw that when he was a boy; and an English

170

priest and a German doctor took over his education. They took him away from the fetish-man, and sold the fetish-man's ivory so that he wasn't swindled, and got enough money to keep the boy-wonder for life. But I wish the fetish-man grandfather hadn't got into his skin so much. He did; and I have to stand it—for a little while, at least. The fetish-man taught him too much. I wish he hadn't seen the fetish-man mumbling spells in a hut, and striking down somebody a hundred miles away. He believes in it. He saw it work. All the rest of his life he's been trying to explain it scientifically. He's been at the science of the mind, the science of the mind, the science of the mind; thinking there was a great power somewhere; thinking he could put a scientific net round it, and define its terms and mark it out and use it. He's got a power. I don't deny it, in its way. But it's not that.

"And then something snaps in his head sometimes, and he reverts to type. I don't mind that in the least, because it's given little Hilary what she wants; or it will, when I've watched you die. He reverted to type last Friday night, at the Constables', when we couldn't keep the conversation off a certain subject.

"You must hear about that. We were sitting in the conservatory, Sam Constable and Mina Constable and Dr. Sanders and Larry Chase and myself, and not understanding what was under the surface. I wish *I* had understood it then. But I didn't. Nobody did. That smoothed-faced gentleman, perfect gentleman, Samuel Hobart Constable, had already been baiting Pennik until he couldn't stand much more of it. Then dear Dr. Sanders set the real ball rolling by saying, 'We will pass over the question of whether you could kill a man by thinking about him, like a Bantu witch-doctor.'

"Pennik himself had already made a slip by using a 'savage' as an illustration in an argument, and correcting himself quickly. But after that we couldn't keep off the subject. Chef's caps came into the talk; and Mr. Constable said, with that oh-so-nice-sneer of his, that Pennik would look well in a chef's cap. Mina Constable asked whether Dumas didn't once cook a dinner for the gourmets of France; and Dumas, as you probably don't know, was an octoroon. Samuel Hobart finished it by saying, 'If I can dress for dinner among a lot of damned niggers, I can dress for dinner in my own house.' And the light went out in my little mulatto's brain. He said Samuel Hobart would die.

"And he would have died, if a Bantu spell could have killed him. That's what Pennik put on him over the salad-bowl. That's what scared that woman-servant and her son
171

so much that they ran away from the house. That's why Pennik gets to a state of frothing at the mouth. That's why he came to me first, and attempted that highly inartistic seduction before dinner—really, Cynthia dear, I hope most of your own clients are better—and told me he would kill Samuel Hobart as a sacrifice to me, and said he would strew rubies at my feet; and in short, my dear, for the moment at least, he really did frighten little Hilary out of her wits. I was terribly impressed. For Samuel Hobart did die, just as Pennik said he would. But the amusing part of the whole thing is that Pennik had nothing to do with it. The little Matabele boy is quite harmless, if you know how to manage him. All the same, he was a nice cover for me when I killed Mina Constable. I killed Mina so that she shouldn't blab the real truth about Sam's death, and then I could go on and do the real work—that is, attending to you—still under cover of Pennik's mysterious powers. Pennik's mysterious rubbish.

"I know exactly what I'm doing, angel. I know that I'm in for some awkward suspicions and some awkward questions. But I'm used to that. I rather like dealing with men in that way. The point is that, no matter how much they suspect or think they suspect, they'll never be able to prove anything. Even if they do burst Pennik's bubble they'll still suspect him, and I shall be sitting most dainty and pretty (as usual) because I've got a really noble alibi for the death of Samuel Hobart Constable."

Whereupon Hilary Keen made the mistake she could perhaps not help making. She lost her head. Her face was pink. She had started talking, and she could not stop.

"I'm tired of playing things safe and sound, when people like you can get all they want just for the whistling. I made up my mind I was going to see you in your grave just as soon as I heard the real truth about how Samuel Hobart Constable died.

"I didn't kill him, Cynthia—did I tell you that? No, no. Up to the day after he died my thoughts were as innocent and pure as they ever have been. Otherwise I shouldn't have been so free about admitting to Dr. Sanders that I wanted to see you dead. I heard the truth about Samuel Hobart's death because for two nights afterwards I slept in the same room with Mina; and Mina, as everybody knows, talks in her sleep. First I fitted together one bit of it; and then I fitted together another bit of it; and then I saw how I could use Pennik to cover me like a sheet in getting at you.

"In law, you could say that Samuel Hobart's death was an accident. It was in mechanics; but it wasn't really an

172

accident. Pennik was responsible for it. If Pennik hadn't said what he did, and done what he did, and prophesied death at Fourways before eight o'clock, Samuel Hobart would be alive and strutting at this time. It was bound to happen. If I had only listened to that conversation beforehand, I could have seen it coming at us like an express-train. People all acted according to their natures, each as he had to; and Samuel Hobart's fat little carcass got the benefit of it. *I* got the benefit of the rest of it. Now you'll see how he died, because you're going to die like that too."

Sanders knew the expression on Hilary's face—he had seen it under the mosaic dome in the dining-room, her color up and her eyes glittering, when she took leave of him a few hours before the death of Mina Constable.

She crossed over to the mantelpiece, and put her hand into the cardboard box.

"If the radio won't work," she said practically, "it won't work. And that's that. I've got oceans of time anyway, before the announcement. I want you to pay close attention, Cynthia. It's the loveliest little way of killing people I've heard of. And needs no knowledge, or heaven knows *I* couldn't have managed it. Chief Inspector Masters said another thing that was as true as gospel. I sneaked up to listen to what they were saying at the door, before they put me on the train I didn't take; and he said, 'Something as wild as wind and yet as domestic as cheese. Something you could do in your own house with two thimbles and a tablet of soap.' And that was quite right. Soap! Soap! That reminds me. You'll have to wait a minute!"

She flew into the bathroom, and a moment later two taps were turned on with a roaring rush of water.

"I don't have to be careful about the noise here," she explained, reappearing in the door, "the way I had to be careful at Fourways when I got rid of Mina. Poor old thick-witted nice Dr. Sanders heard the water running out; but *he* thought it was the fountain in the conservatory. He even saw me then. But I'd borrowed one of Pennik's masks. His fetish-man's masks. Have you ever seen them? No, of course you haven't. I gave Dr. Sanders quite a scare.

"I rather failed with that boy, Cynthia. I nagged and nagged at him to make violent love to me; I even sat down with him in the dark so he'd do it. But he wouldn't. He's still violently in love with some silly wench like you, on a cruise now; he thinks she's been deceiving him, as she probably has; but he simply can't get over it and the rebound wasn't enough. I nearly managed it, though. He said I was

173

like 'the heroine of a thriller'; and I thought that was much the best way to play my part. Don't you think so?

"It was rather a good bit of business, because he's awfully easy to lie to and I knew if he caught me at Fourways on Sunday night I could make him swear to protect me. He could be lots of help. He has been. But I had rather to snub and slight poor Larry Chase, after giving Larry some encouragement to take me there.

"Do you know, Cynthia, I'm beginning positively to like you. You don't know the relief it is not to be Miss-Dignified-on - your - Poise - Little - Dog - Dingo - Fetch - and - Carry - for - Everybody, just for a little while anyway. I think I got all my best tricks and ideas from you. I've studied you ever since you married my father. Only, worst luck, the at least tolerable number of men who fall for me never seem to have any money. You always were lucky like that... *Naughty!* No you don't!"

The woman on the bed, thrashing under the coverlet, screamed. Hilary was at her side, quiet and poised and cool again.

"Like Pennik, I'm talking too much," said Hilary coldly and easily. "Don't shout like that again. Do you know, I had thought of putting lighted matches to your feet before I did what I'm going to do. I don't suppose they would bother about a little burn or two like that afterwards, and it would so please me. Anyhow, get ready; I've got to carry you now."

Cynthia Keen's voice, coughing but unexpectedly clear, spoke out.

"No, you don't," she said.

"Why don't I, my dear?"

"Because of all those people out on the balcony," said Cynthia. "I've got some modesty left, in spite of what you say. I've got most of these damned knots loose, and I can reach this negligee now; but I think they might have told me what you were going to do."

"All right, boys," said H.M. in an ordinary tone.

He threw the window wide open, pushed draperies and curtains to one side, and stepped into the room.

XX

YES," SAID H.M., holding up a tall glass to the light and stirring the sugar in it, "I'll tell you all about it, son. Masters and I couldn't tell you before, because we were afraid you

174

would blow the gaff to the gal, even if you didn't mean to. But you deserve to know. It's a very simple story, son."

"Including," asked Dr. Sanders, "the method of murder that's 'something you could do at home with two thimbles and a tablet of soap'?"

H.M. nodded. And Chief Inspector Masters grinned.

They were sitting, towards dawn on that same morning, in H.M.'s office up all the flights of stairs at the back of Whitehall. For some hours the telephone had been ringing, and H.M. had been giving the same gleeful instructions over and over again. The same broad desk, the same flexible-necked lamp, the same iron safe that contained bottles and glasses: these were familiar as well.

"H'mf," said H.M., sniffing, sipping the tall glass, and blowing down the stem of a black pipe in rapid and successive movements. "It requires very little sittin' and thinkin' once you've got the central fact. Which is this: That a man may be dead, and yet at the same time alive; and that there's only one medical or physiological cause which can put him in a state like that. Masters here carried on something awful when I first said it, but it's sober fact."

He reflected.

"The best way of approach is by simply *tellin'* you the story just as it happened, from the start of the whole mess last Friday night. Hilary Keen—well," he peered over his spectacles, "we won't talk too much about her; but she said a true thing. She said it was practically inevitable, because all the people there acted accordin' to their characters. And they did.

"Now I want you to imagine you're back at Fourways, beside the fountain in that conservatory, at round about seven-thirty on Friday night. A clean sheet is before you; the dead are alive; and the whole thing is about to happen all over again. Pennik has just exploded a mine by announcin' that Sam Constable will probably die before eight o'clock.

"But what did Pennik actually say? Did he say (at that time) that *he* would do the killing? Not a bit of it! Did anybody understand him to mean that he would do the killing? No! You'd been playin' at mind-reading. So Hilary Keen immediately asked, 'Do you mean that it's in someone's mind to kill Mr. Constable within a very short time?' And Pennik, smilin' affirmatively, answers, 'Perhaps.'

"Now each of you took that proposition, and interpreted it each accordin' to his own nature. None of you thought of Pennik as the possible murderer: in fact, it startled the daylights out of you when later Pennik coolly announced what he had really meant. What you all thought he meant was

175

that somebody else in that house had conceived a plan to kill Constable; and that Pennik had read the guilty thought. Is that a fair statement, son?"

Sanders nodded.

"It is," he admitted, and thought again of the over-heated conservatory.

"Well, and what was the effect of it on your two hosts? What was the effect on Sam and Mina Constable? Just reflect on that. Constable, as pure a hypochondriac as I ever heard of, first thought of a seizure and then instantly thought of murder before murder had even been suggested. Back he came to the same old idea that he'd been talkin' about for so long: that his youngish, attractive wife might murder him. It was three-fourths a joke, of course. He didn't really and seriously believe she ever would. But he was the sort who likes to try out that kind of thing on a wife, three-fourths as a joke but one-fourth as a warning not to try any games. Everything he said was sprinkled and peppered with references to that. He even indicated how she might kill him. 'Mina will be the death of me yet, dropping things.' And more directly, 'Will she kill me and make it look like an accident, like that case in the papers?' Hah! That was a side-thrust they both understood, because the case was in Mina's scrap-book.

"So—while he looked accusingly at her—what do you imagine his wife was thinkin'? She'd heard this before. She was an imaginative woman, ill and unstrung from the backwash of malaria, jumping at every shadow. She really did worship that old blister. So it was, 'Poor old Sam thinks I might kill him, and of course I never would; but suppose I *should*, without meaning to?' At that time she believed in Pennik with fervency. And up sprang this prophecy, which she could only take as applyin' to her. The hobgoblin was: 'If I should kill him, they would hang me.' It was a pretty bad thought.

"And Pennik?

"Pennik was responsible for it all.

"It's Pennik's case. He's the god from the machine. His personality was a whole heap more powerful than you thought. He took a group of ordinary, bickerin' human people; and before he got through with you he had each of you thinking exactly the thoughts you shouldn't. He had *you*, young feller, thinking you didn't actually care a rap for Marcia Blystone. He had Hilary Keen pondering very unpleasant thoughts about her stepmother. He had Sam Constable half afraid his wife would kill him, and Mina Constable terrorized for fear she might. The emotional pressure was stoked up too high. Somethin' was bound to blow up. And it did.

"At seven-thirty the Constables retire to their rooms to dress. That woman, with her shaky hands and her frightened imagination, has got to draw Samuel's bath and put the studs in his shirt. He's already hinted, downstairs, how she might kill him even while dressin' him. Suppose she did? Suppose she had a subconscious (cor, how fond and afraid of that word we all are!) a subconscious wish to kill him? That's the worst thought of all.

"Now, did Samuel immediately step in and get his bath as soon as they went to their room? Later she said he did; she said he'd finished his bath, and was dressed to such an extent that she was tyin' up his shoes, just before he hopped down to investigate the smashing of the lamp in the other room at a quarter to eight. But she was lyin', as we proved. At a quarter to eight he was wearin' a dressing-gown and slippers, and nothing else. That was because he hadn't yet had his bath. He'd spent so much time jawin' away to her—and making her more nervous—that he was only just ready to step into the tub when the lamp-smash happened. He went to see what it was; he returned; and he got into the tub between a quarter to eight and eight o'clock.

"Ah, now we're sort of approaching!

"Samuel was always complainin' of the cold. He couldn't get the house warm enough. In fact, the last thing he groused about to high heaven, before your party broke up at seven-thirty, was the coldness of the house. Well, what's he done to take care of this mania of his in a room where people really *do* feel the cold: I mean the bathroom?"

H.M. looked malevolently at Sanders.

"You, son. On a couple of later occasions you saw in the bathroom a portable electric heater. A two-bar, or two-unit, heater. In fact, on one occasion you fell bang over the thing, didn't you? Yet it's very rummy—I repeat: very rummy—that, though you saw a heater there on Saturday and Sunday, you didn't see one there on Friday night when you looked into the bathroom only a little while after Sam Constable's death."

It was true.

Sanders had in his mind only too clear a picture of that damp-smelling bathroom, when he had gone into it to search in the medicine-cabinet for an opiate to administer to Mina Constable. He had noted every object in the bathroom on Friday night; and there had been no heater there. But later it obtruded itself on the notice: a bronze-painted affair over which both he and Mina had at different times stumbled.

"And," he said suddenly, "the bathroom still smelt damp—"

"Sure," growled H.M. "Because Samuel Hobart didn't ge[t] his bath until it was past quarter to eight. Burn me, I ca[n] see him and I can hear him!

"He climbed in. He squawked to high heaven about draft[s] and the cold. There was his wife flutterin' around him as h[e] made his valet flutter. And he was king and emperor. An[d] automatically and without thinkin', just as he'd done [a] thousand times to his valet, he bawled to her to put th[e] portable heater closer to the bath. And the subconsciou[s] fear or wish got hold of her, just as she was afraid it would[.] And she automatically picked it up in those hands of her[s] that can't hold a glass. And all of a sudden, as she lifte[d] it, they both thought of the same thing. She slipped; and th[e] electric heater dropped into the bath.

"That's all, gents.

"Certain death, that's all."

H.M. drew a deep breath.

"Y'see, son, here in town the London County Counci[l] have quite rightly got almost morbid rules about electric fit[-] tings in bathrooms. They won't even allow an electric light[-] switch inside the door. But to pick up a two-bar heater an[d] move it about near bath-water is just plain suicidal lunacy[.]

"If it falls into the water, the thing short-circuits with [a] bang. The full weight of the house current goes through th[e] best conductor of electricity known—water—and though th[e] body of a victim sittin' in it up to his shoulders. It won['t] leave a mark or burn on the body, because the area's to[o] distributed. It won't leave any sign at all, except dilate[d] eye-pupils. There were two cases of it recently, at Bristo[l] and poor old Mina Constable knew it only too well, becaus[e] she had the press-cutting in her scrap-book. And the voltag[e] don't matter; 210 kills.

"She was the death of him, dropping things. And the ver[y] thing she was most awful cussed scared of was the thin[g] that really happened.

"Well, what next? She stood there in the dark, with [a] wet-splashed bathroom and a dead husband. *(No, don't inter[-] rupt me!)* She had to find out if it was so. The lights ha[d] been put out when the fuse blew. But, as we found ou[t] Fourways is on a system of what they call distributing fuse[s:] two or three rooms to each fuse. The only lights that ha[d] gone out in the house were the lights in her room in th[e] bathroom, and in Samuel Hobart's room.

"There were a couple of candles standing on a chest-of[-] drawers in her husband's bedroom. She ran in, lit the candle[s] and brought 'em tearin' back to the bathroom to see wha[t] was what. But, in addition to droppin' wax on her sleeve[,]

178

she also dropped two blobs of grease on the carpet. One was by the leg of the bed, and the other was by the door of the bathroom. Remember, son? We were talkin' to her on Sunday afternoon, and she was standing in the doorway of the bathroom? I told you to look at the wax-stains, one by the bed and one beside where she was standin'? Uh-huh. We gave her a bad time then, and I'm sorry as blazes; but that's how it happened.

"Well, her husband was dead.

"And they'd hang her now.

"You know what that woman's character was. She saw in her mind, in blazin' colors on vellum, the judge and the scaffold and herself on it. Pennik's hocus-pocus got hold of her imagination and swept it away. Nobody would believe it was an accident now. Samuel Hobart had practically said in front of witnesses that she'd kill him: 'and make it look like an accident, like that case in the papers.' She's even thought of it herself as a method of murder for a book; she *was* guilty. Oh, my eye.

"Standin' there in that bathroom with the candle held up, you know what she thought about. Little devil whistles to her and says, 'Couldn't you pretend you didn't do it?' She says, 'No, no, I loved him and I won't.' 'But you didn't mean to do it.' 'Never mind that.' 'You could,' little devil says, 'if you could get him out of that bath and not let on the bath had anything to do with it.'

"It's simple enough. She was no-end fond of him; but she couldn't stand the thought of bein' arrested and hanged. She never thought faster or in more of a fever. Mina Shields, professionally, worked it out in two minutes. She once wrote a detective story (here, I say! Didn't young Chase comment on this?) where the murderer killed his victim in one place and then moved the body somewhere else and pretended the victim died there."

Sanders nodded gloomily.

"Yes," he agreed. "Chase did comment on it. It was my introduction to Mina Constable: he said he refused to believe it could be done."

"I see. Ideas bein' in the air, hey? Well, her mind worked exactly along the same lines again. Move the body.

"It was easy enough to put the lights on again, unknown to anybody else. The fuse-box was in the cupboard in her bedroom. She shoved in a spare fuse, and put the candles back on the chest-of-drawers in the other room. The next part was pretty horrible for her, because she had to dress him. Gents, I saw her on Sunday—and I tell you that only the thought of the hangman kept her goin'. Keep in mind

179

her later actions and you'll understand. It was easy enough to move him; he wasn't a heavyweight and you noticed her strong wrists. I've seen little women handle dead-drunk men and undress 'em and put 'em to bed without trouble. What she did was the reverse. She had a good ten minutes to work in. The clothes were laid out, and the studs and links were in the shirt.

"What she thought would be the worst part was gettin' him out in the hall. She pulled him out there and propped him over that hand-rail, as though he'd fallen across it. The hand-rail held up his body with the weight supported on each side.

"But it wasn't the worst part of it.

"Not by a jugful!

"Gents," said H.M., with a long, reflective, evil look at his two companions, "next came those screams. Everybody who heard 'em was just about paralyzed. I've heard they hardly sounded human. She stood in the door of her room and went on screamin' as though she'd gone mad; and she very nearly had. She wasn't acting. Oh, no. After super-human labor to avoid the hangman, she'd got a dead lump of clay out and poised over the rail. And, just as she was lookin' back at him before she closed the door, *she saw him move.*

"Just note very carefully, young feller, that no independent witness ever saw Sam Constable actually standin' on his feet. You didn't; and you were out in that hall almost as soon as the woman started to scream. There was no sign of the 'dancing and staggering' she invented to protect herself. You saw him saggin' across the rail, just as she had left him with one of his hands on the newel-post. But you did see him move.

"You saw his body twitch; and one of his hands go up in a little jerk—so—and the fingers start to twitch. He was inert across that rail, yet he managed to move his back and hand. The symptoms are pretty characteristic, hey? Yes."

He turned to Masters. "The doc'll tell you, son, that there's only one form of death in which a man can be officially pronounced dead, and have his heart stop; and you can show signs of life minutes afterwards. That's death from electric shock."[1]

"It was known to happen in the old days of official execution by electricity in America, before they knew quite as much as they know now. When a feller gets only one shock

[1]*See Taylor's Principles and Practices of Medical Jurisprudence* electricity, Vol. I, pp. 560-573.

nd that an accidental one in his own home, you can often
et signs of life by givin' him artificial respiration. Mind
ow, Masters: I said *signs* of life. No artificial respiration
ver invented can keep that heart beatin' for long. The vic-
m's a goner if his heart's stopped to begin with. But you
ay get the same signs as Sanders here saw Constable make.
nd why? Because, all unknown to herself, Mina Constable
ad just been givin' him a very violent kind of artificial
spiration by dressing him.

"At the end of that feverish work, when she pressed him
orward on the hand-rail, she'd flogged just a flicker of life
to him. A stir; a groan; not much more. But, by the blinkin'
wful cussedness of things, Sanders here felt that flicker of
fe go out—and naturally thought it was the real time of
eath.

"Lord, who can blame him? Who'd suspect revival from
lectric shock in the case of a man who, by all the evidence
nd testimony, merely falls down and dies in his own hall?
t was a kind of second death. It threw everything wrong re-
ardin' the time and place and manner of death. It made us
ok straight in the wrong direction. I don't trust this young
ller as a detective, but I do trust him as a doctor; and
ere's nobody alive who could have seen what had happened.
t was cussedness and it was a part of the same inevitability.
inally, it nearly finished Mrs. Constable."

"Thank you," said Sanders.

He was remembering Mina in her bedroom just after that
eath. Her stark bewilderment, and her rapid-beating pulse
f physical exertion. Her words, 'But he's not *really* dead!
e's not. I saw—' could be completed in a different way
ow. 'You would know. You're a doctor. You would know,
ouldn't you?"

Yes, he could trace every turn of her feelings, the self-
ontempt she showed and the hesitation she had on the
erge of blurting out everything then and there.

"And you'll also," pursued H.M. dryly, "trace without much
ifficulty the state of her feelings when, coolly and calmly,
ennik announces to everybody that *he* killed Samuel Ho-
art by Teleforce. It'll give you just a faint glimmerin' sus-
icion why she suddenly rounded on Pennik and screamed
at he was a fraud and a crook. Here he was, gently
ayin' he'd eliminated a useless member of society, and
uildin' up a great reputation on it: while she had only dead
lay that she couldn't even nurse. The trouble was, she
ouldn't speak. She wanted him shown up more than any-
ing in the world. She was so anxious to challenge his

181

Teleforce that we couldn't do anything with her. But sh
couldn't speak.

"And there we'll leave Mrs. Constable. She wasn't a mu
derer. She was a decent woman tryin' to save her own ski
After the accident she'd hidden the wet, blown-out electr
heater in the wardrobe; and the next day she exchang
it for a good one among the hundred heaters in that hous
She hid the scrap-book after she saw Sanders lookin' at
after the time Sanders *didn't* see any heater in the bat
room. She passes on. And we consider the not-too-appetizi
figure of the murderer—the real murderer—the only murder
in this case.

"I mean Hilary Keen, whose stepmother had only a lif
interest in Joe Keen's fortune, which would have reverted
Hilary at her death."

Chief Inspector Masters grunted, looking up from his not
book. Behind the broad desk, whose goose-neck lamp w
pushed nearly flat down to its surface, H.M. leaned back
his swivel-chair. He shaded his eyes and spectacles with on
hand. The corners of his mouth were turned down; and h
still drew noisily at the empty pipe. But Sanders had
feeling that a small, sharp eye was being turned towar
him from under the shadow of that hand.

H.M. spoke.

"No," he said, "I didn't like her. And she was clev
enough to see it. I knew her father. And she's bad stoc
son; though I couldn't very well have told you, or you
have jumped down my throat for persecutin' a poor chiva
rous gal. You didn't fall for her, though she tried h
damnedest to make you do it, because you could 'a' been us
ful. I'm a bit glad you didn't fall for her, too, since it's duca
to an old shoe that she's goin' to hang."

(That was the first word that really hurt.)

"No need to jump, son. It's not pleasant, but then neith
was she. If I were you I'd put this down to experience, ar
not say much about it to Marcia Blystone when she ge
home in June. You heard Joe Keen's daughter talkin' wh
she was off-guard, so I don't need to say much more abo
her character: strong practical intelligence plus arrested em
tional development. She was on to things fast enough. He
was Herman Pennik ridin' high and wide, utterly convince
he'd killed Sam Constable; utterly convinced he wielded
power so strong that it scared even Pennik. That was Pe
nik's state of mind. She saw how he could be used."

H.M.'s face resumed its malevolent scowl.

"Ah! But now lemme tell you about *my* side of it. Yo
two dragged me into this case on Sunday afternoon. I g

own there for a peaceful afternoon, worried as blazes, with
the House of Lords gibberin' at me from every bench;
nd what do I find? I find a ruddy loonybin. All you can do
gabble about people killing other people by thought-
waves. Mrs. Constable begs me, on bended knees and with
ars in her eyes, to unmask Pennik—and at the same time
he tells me a pack of lies.

"Well, what did I think? What would anybody think? I
greed with Masters that, if there had been any murderin'
one, Mrs. Constable had done it herself. I said she was in
o danger; I said she was as safe as though she was packed
cotton wool in the middle of the Bank of England; and
still maintain I had a right to say it.

"But Pennik worried me. And if Mrs. Constable had killed
er husband, I couldn't think for the life of me how she
ad done it. All I knew was that that bathroom was mixed
p in it somehow. All trails led to the bathroom. The candle-
rease spots led there. Mrs. Constable had lied about the
me her husband took his bath. Sanders had given a careful
escription of the bathroom just after Constable's death, and
aid there was no electric heater in it: but I could see for
yself on Sunday afternoon a biggish bronze-painted heater
ere large as life, and it didn't seem reasonable that a
an who felt the cold like that would have failed to keep a
eater in the one room where he was most likely to need it.

"I was awful dense, Masters. But then I was worried;
nd I had to get over that hurdle of a doctor swearin'
onstable had died in the hall. It wasn't until late Sunday
ight, when I was back at home sittin' and thinkin', that
occurred to me somebody needed to burn candles in
at bathroom because the ordinary lights were blown out;
nd the ordinary lights were blown out because somebody
ad dropped a missing electric fire into the bath. It'd ex-
lain the revived corpse. It was the only thing that'd explain
e dilated eye-pupils.

"That looked as though Pennik must be in cahoots with
Irs. Constable: Pennik to star-gaze with Teleforce, Mrs.
onstable for the real work. I went to sleep happily dreamin'
f what I'd do to 'em—and woke up to find Mrs. Constable
lished off, and Pennik *again* with an alibi.

"Then I got mad.

"The Teleforce issue was raisin' blue blazes. I was so
ed up with business that I didn't get a full report on Mrs.
onstable's death until Tuesday at lunch. Then I heard
hat both of you had to say. That tore it. I knew I was
ght because (a) the candles had been burnin' again, and
b) Sanders, sitting in the dining-room almost directly under

that bathroom upstairs, had noticed a vibrating, continue[d]
sound of running water which didn't come from the founta[in]
in the conservatory."

There was a silence. Sanders nodded glumly.

"I see. It was the water running into the bathtub."

"No, son."

"What do you mean, no?"

"It was the water running *out* of the tub," answere[d]
H.M. "Y'see, it's easy to fill a bath practically in silence,
the murderer wanted to do. Just fill it slowly. It isn't like
that through those thick walls you would have heard t[he]
bath bein' filled. But what can't be stopped, what does pr[o]
duce that vibratin' noise you heard, is the water goin' wi[th]
an unchecked rush down the drainpipe when it's emptie[d].
And that's why you heard it at all. The water was goi[n']
down; down in a pipe past the dining-room, to drain awa[y].
And so you heard it. And so it seemed pretty plain th[at]
Hilary Keen was the murderer."

Chief Inspector Masters sat up. "Hold on, sir! I do[n't]
follow that."

"No?" said H.M. "Look at the other evidence. What d[o]
Sanders tell us about Sunday night at Fourways? He ga[ve]
Mrs. Constable her morphia tablet, tucked her into be[d]
and came downstairs from her room at about twenty minut[es]
past ten. At shortly before half-past eleven he heard th[e]
sound of runnin' water, and he looked round, and he sa[w]
Pennik's 'astral projection' (ho!) looking at him from t[he]
conservatory. He searched the conservatory—without res[ult]
—and then tore upstairs to make sure Mrs. Constable w[as]
all right. She was apparently right as rain, sleepin' pea[ce]
fully.

"But in that case when did she die? For fifteen minut[es]
after that, Sanders sat down on the steps not eight fe[et]
away from the door in a dead quiet house. If you['re]
goin' to tell me that durin' those fifteen minutes the m[ur]
derer went through all the motions: draggin' an only ha[lf]
drugged woman, who'd be certain to wake up partial[ly]
splashin' her into the bath: droppin' the heater, which mak[es]
a very loud flash and crackle: dressin' her, draggin' h[er]
back, puttin' her to bed again with all the trimmings:
you're goin' to tell me all that happened then, and a m[an]
eight feet away from the door didn't hear a single solita[ry]
sound—Masters, I'll just make an impolite noise like th[at].
Likewise if you tell me it all happened durin' the tw[o]
minutes Sanders was downstairs answering the phone. N[o].
Allied with the fact that water was running out of the ba[th]
tub shortly before eleven-thirty, it means only one thing.

184

"Mina Constable was dead before eleven-thirty. But Sanders found a livin', breathin' woman tucked into that bed at eleven-thirty. It's true, as he told us, that he didn't turn on the light when he went in. It's true he left Mina Constable with her head buried under a pillow. It's true he left her wearin' a heavy padded dressing-gown too big for her. But that living woman in the dark couldn't have been Mina Constable. And if it wasn't Mina Constable, just focus your wits for half a second and ask yourself who it must have been."

It was the creepiest part of the business Sanders remembered. He and Masters looked at each other, and H.M. nodded.

"Sure, son. Joe Keen's daughter. She only pretended she was goin' to take that train when we dropped her off at the station. She knew as early as Saturday that sooner or later Mrs. Constable was goin' to challenge Pennik; she knew when it would happen; and she had it impressed on Pennik's gullible brain just when he should fire the next bolt of Teleforce. She walked quietly back to Fourways: she had all the time in the world. She knew Sanders was alone in the house; and if by any chance he caught her, she firmly believed in her somewhat conceited soul that she could persuade him to cover her up.

"She got into the house by way of that outside staircase leadin' up to Sam Constable's room. All she had to do was snaffle another of the omnipresent electric fires, from that unused top floor of the house, hide there, and wait for the proper time. It wasn't likely Sanders would sit up all night with Mrs. Constable; and he didn't.

"Mrs. Constable was only half drugged, and put up somethin' of a struggle. But Joe Keen's daughter knew how to deal with that: you saw what she was goin' to do with her stepmother. Everything went slick as goose-grease until just after the murder. She'd got her victim out of the tub; dried her and put on her nightgown; when all of a sudden she realized something. Up to then she hadn't made a sound to betray herself—but what about that water running out, in a downstairs pipe that somebody on the floor below was almost certain to hear?

"She had to know. She went down the main staircase, into the kitchen by the hall door without touching the dining-room, through the kitchen door to the conservatory, and looked into the dining-room as Pennik's astral projection. Never mind that astral bit now!" said H.M., raising his hand. "She didn't mean the picture of Pennik to be seen—not then.

"But it was seen. Sanders didn't pay much attention to

185

the runnin' water, but he did jump when he caught a flash
of Pennik's face. And she knew she had to act quick. She
was certain Sanders would go up straightaway to see whether
Mrs. Constable was all right. If he found Mrs. Constable
dead then, the whole game was up. It wasn't a question of
explaining her own presence in the house, for which she
might have found some coy excuse. But she'd left her
properties all over the place: the candles in the bathroom,
the *extra* electric fire hooked in to do the dirty; the tub
still damp and the fuse still blown. If the body were discovered before she could dispose of the evidence, the whole
myth of Teleforce would be exploded then and there.

"Well, she managed it. She made no sound: you've seen
how light on her feet she is, and it's ducats to an old
shoe she was in her stocking feet then. When Sanders saw
her through the conservatory door, she nipped across the
room, opened the conservatory window from the inside, got
out, and went back upstairs again by the outside balcony—
while he was searching the conservatory. She pushed Mina
Constable's body under the bed, put on the dressing-gown,
and crawled into bed with her head under a pillow in the
way Mina always slept.

"He couldn't have turned on the light if he'd wanted to, because the fuse was blown. In the very huge relief of findin'
woman alive, he wouldn't be likely to investigate close; and
he wouldn't be likely to look past the closed door of the bathroom. He didn't.

"The interval while he was on the stairs she spent quietly
playin' possum. She enjoyed all this, y'know: it was exciting,
it stimulated her excess of thyroid. When she heard him go
downstairs she put Mina Constable asprawl on the bed, and
repaired the lights with one of the extra fuses: a matter of
a couple of minutes. She opened the bathroom door,
which he'd locked on the inside, slipped into the bathroom, closed the door as though it were still locked, and
gathered up her properties.

"Afterwards was the real audacity of the business. I
didn't work this out for myself: you'll have gathered it from
the screamin' she did at us when we walked in on her at
her stepmother's—"

"Never mind," said Sanders quickly.

"Go on, sir," grunted Masters. "I think I know what you
mean."

"The wench actually stayed in that house all night. In the
general confusion after findin' Mrs. Constable dead, Sanders couldn't be everywhere at once. He was only one man.
He had to telephone. He had to get the police; and it was

186

unlikely the police would get there before morning. He even had to sleep at one time or another. So she repaired all her little omissions. At one point she nipped back into the now open room and locked the bathroom door again on the bedroom side. At another she returned the burnt-out heater to an unused room on the top floor. It was a game of hide-and-seek; and she liked it. At half-past five in the cool dawn she slipped out of the house carryin' her trim little suitcase, walked along the road, caught the early bus to Guildford and the early train to town; after which she appeared fresh-eyed and dignified at the office, a cat back from the tiles and a saint in its niche again. That's all.

"So that was my dawnin' conviction about her and her character on Tuesday. But Pennik was still in the background, elusive and perplexin'. Was she working with Pennik? There seemed to be evidence for it. And yet I couldn't believe it. Havin' seen Pennik on Monday night, I was gatherin' a few cloudy ideas about him while I sat at the Corinthian Grill-Room. There's such a thing as psychological truth, gents; and, burn me, I could *not* see him as anything but a feller who believed in what he said. You've felt that, Masters. So have you, son. I defy anybody to talk to Pennik for five minutes and still think he's party to any plot. I told you over and over he was the lone wolf. I told you that, within his limits, he was a perfectly honest man.

"Before I'd even met him, I'd got a bit of a notion about the African ancestry, from makin' an excuse to get a look at those little blue half-moons at the base of his finger-nails. Which was all the more reason for wantin' to find out what made him tick. I had to break him down. There was only one way to do that: Mrs. Constable suggested it to me on Sunday. If I could get him locked up for a month or two? Yes, And the only way to do that was to start such a roar of publicity that the plain Briton would arise in all his majesty, saying: 'To hell with common sense stick him in clink.' to the old wangler," explained H.M., suddenly rubbing his hands together with a ghoulish expression of pleasure, "started wanglin' again. I wasn't really loopy, Masters. Honest I wasn't.

"For the truth of everything shone out at that lunchtable on Tuesday, when we three sat there with Hilary Keen and Pennik. I'd just gone through a spiritual abyss of wantin' to know why. I was sure Joe Keen's daughter was up to games. I was sure Pennik wasn't up to games in the practical sense. But whether they worked together or whether they didn't, why, *why* should Joe Keen's daughter kill Mrs. Constable? Surely not just to bolster up a belief in Teleforce?

187

"You know the answer. Mrs. Constable could have exposed Pennik. What's more, she would have. Several times she'd already been within an ace of breakin' down and blurtin' out everything; you saw that. If it had happened again, if someone else died and Pennik claimed the credit for the second time, Mina Constable would have blown the whole sham higher than Boney's kite. So Hilary had to kill her before Pennik's triumphal progress could go on. The name of the real victim, the intended victim, Mrs. Cynthia Keen, was as plain as though somebody had said it aloud over the table. Do you remember how curtly and finally Hilary cut off the conversation when Masters started asking questions about the possible victim and Pennik, in an expansive mood, was within two steps and a whistle of telling him? I had got it. I had found Frau Frankenstein.

"And glorious was the thought, *We've got 'em both now.* D'ye see? Let Pennik go to Paris and give his speech. Let the gal try to make Teleforce work again; when she does we'll nail her flat with all the evidence we couldn't get otherwise. At the same time, keep Pennik away from that inquest; let the honest jury return a verdict against him; arrest him as soon as he makes his speech, break him down and make him admit the real truth; and with one double-barreled shot we bring 'em both down at once.

"Only—"

"I interfered," muttered Sanders. "And I challenged Pennik."

"Son, I could have murdered you myself," said H.M. "You made Hilary as sick as you made me. For it wouldn't be any good to her if Pennik reared up and said, 'Sanders dies.' And I told you, she was workin' her head off to keep him from turnin' on you. She was praying for that. The atmosphere at the lunch-table was impregnated with it.

"She had to stop it somehow, I only hoped she would. We might break the Teleforce bogy if Pennik said, 'Sanders dies,' and Sanders didn't die; but that wouldn't help us catch the real murderer. While my hopes shrank, I had to go after another line of attack. First, now I was convinced electric heaters had been used for the dirty work, to find some evidence of it. The heaters themselves were no good. I couldn't very well wave a burnt-out fire and say, 'Hoy! This heater won't work; and that proves it was used to kill people with.' The scrap-book was a better lead. I could 'a' sworn Mrs. Constable had hidden it, and that Joe Keen's daughter didn't know anything about it: she had pieced together the game, as you heard her say, by hearin' Mina Constable talk in her sleep. Thinkin' about electricity in general, it sud denly occurred to me what an uncommon fine place to hide a book a fuse-box would be. But in that case Hilary Keen would have known about the book. She did: and she left it behind because it was no betrayal of her—and, I groan to say, no good to us.

"That left my second line of attack: to get Pennik snaffled by the jury at the inquest. But to get the verdict in his absence, so he wouldn't be arrested until after he'd made his Paris speech.

"What we had to guard against was that Pennik might show up at the inquest, as he swore he would. He might try to do it in spite of knowin' he wouldn't be admitted. In that case we'd have to arrest him on the spot, and that would be bad. For the whole point of the secret inquest behind locked doors was that, in case we got the verdict we hoped for, no word should get back to Hilary Keen that Pennik had been arrested or was goin' to be arrested. We could keep it from the press; we could even detain the jury until it was too late to make any difference.

"Well, Pennik did attend the inquest. And we did get the verdict we hoped for. Pennik first went berserk and then broke down. Masters and I took him into that little room—"

"To which," Sanders interposed bitterly, "I was not admitted."

"No, son. You were too dangerous to be let in on it. You wouldn't believe anything about the gal until you saw her at her games. It was touch and go, but we got the truth out of Pennik. I told him I had wangled this; and, if he would tell me the truth, I'd wangle him out of clink again. He believed me. He gave us a case-history of himself, and his Teleforce was only the Bantu fetishism of his grandfather.

"Now here's the delicate point I want to ram into your head. Judged scientifically, even his mind-reading was a fake. It was based on information received beforehand, or obtained painlessly from the patient himself. He learned a whole lot about Masters, for instance, from the Superintendent at Grovetop, who knows Masters. *But* Pennik doesn't regard it as a fake. That's the whole point. He really has got a remarkable brain, a stunnin' penetration, an ability to read thoughts in the sense of reading people and judging (by their features, like the Muscle-Readers) exactly where their thoughts are likely to go. Whether they're thinking of serious things or trivialities. What sort of serious things or what sort of trivialities. He'll read you to an almost alarmin' extent in that respect; and give him a little infor-

189

mation to work on and he's got you. He told us he made you jump—yes, you, son—by correctly sayin' you were thinkin' about a bust of Lister at the Harris Institute. Yet you once told Chase, who passed it on, that when you wanted to make your mind a blank you always concentrated on that bust. You've probably forgotten all about it. Pennik's ability was this: he decided you were tryin' to make your mind a blank (one up to him); he took a shot at what he thought might be it; and he was right. Unsubtle persons he'll scare out of their trousers.

"The trouble is that he's gradually hypnotized himself into a different belief. He's hypnotized himself into thinkin' that this gift, which even children and idiots have sometimes had, is a great scientific power. He thinks that Bantu spells can be allied with it, and that they've got the same root. When he lost his head, reverted to type, and threw the Bantu spell which killed a man—well, that tore it. He thought the last barrier was surmounted.

"That was the feller I had to break down. That was the feller whose secret I had to get. I slowly and carefully explained to him exactly how Sam and Mina Constable had died. He didn't believe me, and for a while we were dealin' with a lunatic: particularly when I explained what Hilary Keen really was. Obviously, d'ye see, his native intelligence was no good as far as readin' *her* was concerned; he was blind gone on her; blind, deaf, dumb, and stymied. He admitted that he was goin' to try out his 'power' on Cynthia Keen that night. And, having got to the root of a secret which was about as dangerous as an insect spray, I was pleased like billy-o; for the game was ours.

"I said, 'Right-ho, then. You don't believe me. You don't think this wench is makin' a fool of you. You don't think she'll kill that woman with an ordinary dose of electricity. Very well: help us out and see for yourself. Go to Paris; make your speech. I'll arrange it so you can go. Then watch what happens.'

"He agreed to that. He went, with a plain-clothes officer along; and so no word ever leaked out that he'd been arrested, because there he was, pale and free, steppin' into the plane before all the cameras. That was all I wanted. I wanted him away, with no word to the gal. But I knew he'd never make that speech. He couldn't. The hide was off his pride, and he was cryin' like a child.

"We know what happened now. He went to Paris, but he couldn't stand not knowin' about Hilary. He dodged our officer and vanished. Before anybody knew where he was, he was flyin' back to London in an air-taxi. He was goin' to
190

be in at the death. He was goin' to break down his last doubt."

Chief Inspector Masters drew a deep breath.

"Oh, ah!" he said. "You predicted he might do that, sir. I'm bound to admit it didn't surprise me much when I saw him barge in on us just as we were all ready to snaffle the young lady—with," Masters added with a broad grin, "considerable help from her stepmother."

Dr. Sanders was bitter. "Well, it surprised me. When I looked round and saw him coming up the balcony stairs at me, I thought he was there for me. Did you know he had a knife?"

"I did," returned the chief inspector grimly. "I had tight hold of his arms every second we were outside those windows. That knife wasn't for you. It was for Miss Keen. He'd have settled matters, all right: blubbering like a baby and yet wanting to get at her all the time! I've not got much pity for *that* gentleman, Sir Henry, even though you seem to have."

"Now, now, son!"

"Not me. Trying to lord it over all of us, and yet still going back once in a while to his tribe and lording it over them in a native hut like he told us! Him and his rubber masks!"

"Rubber masks?" demanded Sanders.

H.M. scratched the back of his neck with an air of apology. "You heard Hilary mention them," he said. "A copy of his own face in dark painted rubber. The fetishman's mask, son. It's made a little larger than life, and of rubber so it can be sort of pulled about and made more hideous than it is. D'ye know what that kind of fetishism really is? It's too late at night or early in the mornin' to maunder on about comparative religions; but its principles in the African savages are exactly the same as the witchcraft heresies of the European Middle ages. Uh-huh. The Vaudois, the Poor Lombards, were an eleventh-century sect from which we get, resplendent and beamin', the word Voodoo. (Mina Constable did tell you, didn't she, that Pennik couldn't stand it when a professor aboard ship once called him M. Vaudois?) Pennik had a couple of those fetish-masks, and one with him. Little Hilary Keen, a nice gal, begged or stole it. It was always useful if she wanted to be Pennik's astral projection."

Outside the windows, the sky was growing gray. For some moments Chief Inspector Masters had been contemplating the corner of the desk with a growing twinkle in his eye. He picked up his almost untasted drink, stirred it, drained it. He chuckled. His chuckle deepened and became a guffaw.

"Lummy!" he said comprehensively, and slapped his thigh.

H.M. peered at him over his spectacles.

"So? What's so funny, Masters?"

"I was just thinking, sir, about the old gentleman on the train: the one who wanted to put Pennik in a zinc-lined box like a tube of radium. Teleforce! And a lot of people getting the wind up. And a death-ray that'd knock bombers out of the air. And—well, and all because an electric heater dropped into a bath."

"You think that's funny?"

"Don't you?"

"No," said H.M. "Why do you think all this fuss has been allowed?"

"How do you mean?"

"For the salutary moral lesson," said H.M., "when on this bright day the menace of Teleforce is turned into howlin' nonsense, and pseudo-scientific rubbish gets the kick in the pants it deserves. That's how the campaign has been planned. The long-threatened raspberry bursts forth. The Press tells what Teleforce is, and who had the managin' of it. And the next time alarmists go scurryin' from house to house, the next time they tell you about a super-bomb that'll drop from an enemy airplane and wipe out a whole county, the next time they picture London as one cloud of poison-gas from Hampstead to Lambeth, then you look at your back-garden and softly murmur, 'Teleforce' and be comforted.

"We know what we're doin', son." He swept his arm towards Whitehall. "Don't let the outside alarmers scare you. The trident's still on the coin. They don't speak Esperanto in Billingsgate yet. When you hear about these super-planes, these super-gases, these super-weaknesses on our side, think of Teleforce too. This tendency to believe anything puts a leerin' face on people. It's a face made a little larger than life; but it's still rubber that can be pulled about to look more hideous than it really is. Most of it's Voodoo, son; and, d'ye know, there never was much room for Voodoo here."

Pulling himself to his feet, he snorted once, lumbered over to the window, and, with the growing daylight on his bald head and square jaw, he stared out across the river and the mighty curve of London.

THE END